JEMMA7729

The civil unre
American citizer
only safe and he
told and believe
Countryside, and
the first time, she
And to challenge

On her Choos
what she will do
is a lie and a trap
arrest, remand w
tion in a rehab fa

Her spirit ca
Countryside and
criss-crossing th
Government of N
the labs that ma
control rebelliou
but skillful sab
Fedguard and b
Jemma is a heroi

She loves her
all changes whe
group working to
ballot or the bulle
a mentor, even lo

But her luck
rebellion, female aggression, failure to make choices, and
inappropriate behavior. If Jemma7729 is caught, she faces
immediate, permanent and uncontestable deletion.

Green Spirit Project

JEMMA7729

by
Phoebe Wray

EDGE SCIENCE FICTION AND FANTASY PUBLISHING
AN IMPRINT OF HADES PUBLICATIONS, INC.
CALGARY

Jemma7729
copyright © 2008 by Phoebe Wray

EDGE

Edge Science Fiction and Fantasy Publishing
An Imprint of Hades Publications Inc.
P.O. Box 1714, Calgary, Alberta, T2P 2L7, Canada

Editing by Richard Janzen
Interior design by Brian Hades
Cover Illustration by David Willicome

EDGE Science Fiction and Fantasy Publishing and Hades Publications, Inc.
acknowledges the ongoing support of the Canada Council for the Arts and the
Alberta Foundation for the Arts for our publishing programme.

Library and Archives Canada Cataloguing in Publication

Phoebe Wray
        Jemma7729 / Phoebe Wray.

ISBN-13: 978-1-894063-40-1
ISBN-10: 1-894063-40-6

        I. Title.

PS3623.R39J45 2008   813'.6   C2007-907561-4

FIRST EDITION
(i-20071221)
Printed in Canada
www.edgewebsite.com

Dedication

For my dear sister, Mary Gregory Wagner (1926-2004),
who always steered my boat with such a generous heart.

Thanks

Jemma stalked me for a long time, so her vagaries are well known to my good and patient friends whom here I thank as sincerely as words can convey.

Two splendid women especially helped this novel get written. The wonderful actress and my long-time friend, Cara Van Zandt, was the first to tell me my short story was a novel, and read a gazillion drafts without complaint and with good ideas. My best buddy and consort outlaw, the innovative thinker/writer, Francesca De Grandis, encouraged me persistently, liberally, with zany humor and immensely helpful editorial input. I owe them both a very great deal.

My life (and work) is greatly enriched by the love, laughter, and sweet but feisty wisdom of my dear friend Pamela Usrey. Dave and Loren Davidson have stuck with me and enjoyed the ride. It's been fun.

The grand cabal I hang out with in cyberspace — Carroll Bishop, Deborah Mattingly Connor, Mike Dickman, Alice O. Howell, and Suzanne Schecker — read various versions, were wise readers, and are great friends and fellow seekers of the paths of understanding.

Two gentlemen have been with me through thick and thin and have made my life nicer, for which I thank them: the kindest heart in the world and terrific actor Harry Hart-Browne, and the perspicacious Michael York, with whom it is always fabulous to tangle mind and soul. Don Congdon was an early encourager, and taught me a lot about the business of writing. He liked this story.

I've also been encouraged by the mission and the camaraderie of my fella broads at Broad Universe — all of us working together to support and celebrate women who write science fiction, fantasy, and horror.

I'm sorry that Lauretta V. Harris can't hold this book in her hands. She was a marvelous lady and wonderful teacher, who mentored me for twenty years.

At Edge, Justyn Perry is a constant delight to work with and has great ideas. My skillful editor, Richard Janzen, put up with my plethora of semicolons and whimsical capitalizations, had excellent suggestions, and asked hard questions with grace. And, of course, my sincere thanks to the genial Brian Hades, publisher, who here throws in his lot with Jemma and me.

JEMMA7729

Chapter 1

I survived my first encounter with State Security of the Administrative Government of North America. They didn't come after me and Mother wasn't punished. Someone at AGNA must have found the incident amusing. Years later I learned it *was* reported in my dossier with a brief note: possible discipline problem. Oh, yeah.

I had played with all the voicechips that were hidden in the plants and around the big paintings at my mother's party. I wasn't allowed to attend her charity art show because I was only five, and besides, Mother didn't like me hanging around her when she was working. Or any time, really. I seemed to embarrass her somehow, although I'm legal and was planned. "Working" for Mother was throwing parties like the one that day, where she invited people from our social class and chatted with them and then handed over the vid and voicechips to her boss at StateSec. She didn't know I knew what she did.

She let me watch the technicians set up, though, and I saw where they hid all the surveillance stuff. They let me follow them around and help them and they joked with me and were funny. Big guys. Alters, which surprised me. They had that blank stare that alters have when they talked to me. It's mostly women who are altered, so if these men were, it meant that they once did something horridly anti-social — like stealing or rape — and were convicted of inappropriate behavior. Of course, they're harmless now.

You can always tell the alters. It's something in the eyes, as if the pupils don't reflect the light. I learned in art class that in the eyes of all portraits there is a little white dot — a spark of life. In the great portraits, it's a double dot.

Well, alters don't have that. Their eyes are opaque. No fire inside. Smile at them and they smile back, like petting a dog to see its tail wag.

I had watched a concert earlier on the children's hour, on the vidscreen in my bedroom, and there was one song that I liked. I sang it into the voicechips, just like Halli4077 did on the vid. I had a pretty mean kind of croon. I had no idea it would get me into trouble, and Mother, too. But it did.

The next day, when I got back from school, Mother was waiting for me with her hands on her hips, standing in front of the big mirror in our entrance hallway. She looked pretty in a soft blue dress with white chrysanthemums splashed on it, but she wasn't smiling.

"Into the living room, Jemma."

She wouldn't tell me what was wrong when I asked, and — even worse — told me not to say a word until Daddy got home. It was big trouble if we had to wait for him.

So I sat for a couple of hours on a chair in our living room, looking out the French doors at the flowers blooming outside, watching the wind snaking through the trees, and our neighbor drinking coffee out of a shiny black mug on her patio. She's always friendly to me, and when no one's around she gives me coffee, even though children aren't supposed to have stimulants. She's a wife but doesn't have any children yet. I think she's getting too old now.

Our house was a big one because we're stable class. It's in L.A. but under the Santa Monica dome, which meant we got blue skies in our dome most of the time, and rain only when we needed it. L.A. has twenty domes, all interlocking to keep out the bad stuff from the Countryside, the toxins that kill people. Well, they kill women anyway. It is a marvel of technology that the climate is controlled under each of them. We studied about it in science class.

Where I lived was a sprawling house called a ranch-style, a replica of one that was popular in the olden days, in the mid-twentieth century, with much more space than we needed for just Mother and Daddy and me, but we're privileged, and besides, Mother has all those parties.

I loved our house. My bedroom looked over the back lawn with its swimming pool off the patio and what's called an English-style garden at the far end, with a birdbath and two statues by Cliff What's-his-number, who was very famous and went to college with Daddy. The whole yard was enclosed in a stockade fence made of real wood, with vines and flowers twining over it. They flowered most of the year, and the smell of night-blooming jasmine sneaked into my bedroom sometimes.

Mother had spy-parties out there, too, and I'd flop on my bed to watch them. I liked to see the patterns that people made and re-made, clustering around the food and the drinks and each other, especially around my mother. Weird how grown-ups got drunk and stupid. I usually picked out two or three people to follow throughout the party. I gave them goofy names that reflected how they looked, like Bowlegged Bignose or Fake-haired Fanny, and I kept a record in my comp unit of how much they ate and drank and what they did in the shrubbery. Mother didn't know that. She'd board up my windows if she did. (Just kidding.)

My official name is JE2MDRA77290FF400RT913. That's the DNA tag, regional files, blood type, class, all that stuff the government takes care of for us. But I'm called Jemma, except by my teachers at school, where they used the more formal Jemma7729.

In school we were divided into quads, with all the social classes represented in each quad. There was one other stable, like me, plus four each of the productive, useful and necessary classes, and two kids who were X-class because they're gifted. In mathematics, I think. Mixing up the classes was supposed to teach us to get along with each other and I guess it did. I didn't have problems with anyone except Thom7726.

Daddy was a muckety-muck in the government. He was the Regional Administrator for the Environment for the whole L.A. Basin, and that made him important because, of course, most of our food comes from the Near-Countryside around the L.A. Megadome. Beyond the farms and gardens, the land was ruined and pretty desolate. We'd all seen pictures of it.

Mother was important, too. She had chosen to be a woman who marries when she was young, which meant she got to have a child (me) and could also do other work. So she spied for AGNA and we all pretended she didn't. She looked for something called "malcontents." I didn't know what that was. It seemed silly to me but Daddy said I wasn't old enough to understand and I should just keep my mouth shut. So I did.

I thought about school while I waited for Daddy to come home. We'd started preparing for our first Choosing Day, when each of us, of our own free will, decided what we would do and be. That happened every January first and you have to be seven to do the first ceremony. For me, that would be in two years, and then we made the final choice at the official Final Choosing Day, after we're ten. My birthday is August 12, so I made my final choice on January 1, 2193. I thought about that, too, while I waited, and how I wished we stables had more choices.

I had homework, but Mother had said I wasn't allowed to do anything — no vids, no reading, no getting up and sitting down. She had gone somewhere else in the house so I tried to think what I'd done that was so bad.

I had spilled some yellow paint at school but the teacher wasn't upset and I had cleaned it up. I couldn't imagine that it got reported. The art teacher likes me. I'm not gifted, but I'm good.

Then Daddy came home. I heard his GAV whirr in. We had a private ground/air vehicle because he traveled a lot. We also had a hovercar, with a driver, which Mother used because she didn't like to fly. Daddy left his GAV in our circle driveway instead of putting it in the garage. That meant no rain was scheduled even though it seemed to me the flowers needed it.

Mother met him in the entrance hall. He gave her a kiss on the cheek but she didn't respond. She said something in a voice too low for me to hear and Daddy frowned and looked into the living room where I sat trying to keep my feet still, then back at her and smiled.

They looked wonderful together so I liked to watch them. He was tall and tanned. His hair and carefully groomed mustache were silver. His white shirt was without flaw and peeped correctly out from the sleeves of his summer light blue jacket. When he touched Mother's face, I saw the flash of a gold watch.

Mother was slim and pale beside him, her hair glistening purple-black. It swung slightly on the sides when she moved. She was very beautiful. Her eyes were a pale, icy blue. Daddy's eyes were blue. Not mine.

I have my mother's dark hair, cropped short with bangs, and my father's slightly upturned nose, but no mustache. I have nobody's eyes. Mine are like lumps of coal. I could have been deleted when they saw my eyes were the wrong color, but Daddy said they liked me anyway. Or *he* did, at least. He teased me and said I was a "keeper." My best school friend Lila said you couldn't tell what I was thinking from my eyes. I still don't know if that's good or bad.

They came into the living room and Daddy sat in a chair across from me.

"So, Jemma, what's the trouble?"

I grinned at him. "I don't know."

Mother paced between us. "The trouble is that I took the chips from yesterday's party to StateSec and they called me in today and told me that there was a child singing on all of them! They're contaminated."

"Singing?" Daddy frowned again but he didn't look angry, just puzzled.

Mother stopped and pursed her lips. "Jemma. Singing some stupid song on every single chip!"

Oh. I guess that had not been a smart thing to do. Daddy laughed and my mother wheeled around and gave him a nasty look.

"It isn't funny, Roger! I'm in trouble! They want to know why a child knew where all the surveillance devices were planted! And if a child knew, didn't everyone? What could I say?"

Daddy stopped laughing but his eyes were merry. "I'm sorry, Elane, it just struck me funny. You're right, of course." He turned to me. "How did you know where they were?"

"I helped plant them." I looked at Mother. She was shaking her head back and forth and flexing her fingers. "You said I could, Mother. You said I could watch them set up the party. The guys were nice to me and I helped them."

Mother sat down on the couch with a sigh. "Well, then, they're in more trouble than I am."

I didn't like the sound of that.

"Oh, Elane," and Daddy went to sit beside her, putting an arm around her shoulders, "it was just a childish prank. No harm done."

"Yes, harm done!" She snapped at him and he withdrew his arm and waited until she calmed down.

He leaned back on the couch. "Security has no sense of humor. What did you say to them?"

Mother made a worried face. "I told them the truth. I don't know if that was wise, but I didn't know what else to do. I said that it was probably my daughter who had done it, that she was a bit mischievous."

"Well, then."

"They don't want it to happen again!" Mother looked at me with those glacial eyes and it felt as if the room got chilly.

"And so it won't," Daddy said, sitting up and leaning towards me. "Will it, Jemma?"

"No. I'm sorry, Mother." I was. I didn't want her to be in trouble. "I was just imitating Halli4077."

Daddy grinned. "I'll get you a mike of your own if you want to practice singing. It's not a good idea to use your mother's."

Mother stood up. "Roger! That's rewarding her for bad behavior! She ought to be punished, not coddled. Honestly!" She shook her head and turned away from us. "You keep spoiling her and she'll wind up deleted after all!" She pushed the door open and walked out of the house.

I squirmed. Daddy played with his mustache like he always does when he's thinking. He looked tired. "What did she mean, Daddy? That I'll wind up deleted after all?" I thought, *after all what?*

"Nothing, baby. She's just upset. But she's right — I shouldn't reward you. You leave your mother's parties alone. Stay out of her way."

I studied my shoes. "Yes, sir."

"Jemma, look at me." I did. His eyes were kind and his mustache wiggled at the corners. "Promise me."

"I promise." I thought about my files on her guests and decided I should get rid of them before anyone found out I had them. I don't know why I never did that. I wonder if anyone ever found them.

"Okay. Now," and he patted the couch beside him, "tell me what happened at school today."

I went to sit with him and told him about spilling the paint and what we had learned in science and that I had done well in computer class. Mother returned inside but went into her study and Daddy and I talked until the cooking woman told us supper was ready.

# # #

I was jumping rope with Lila and some other girls on our recreation break. The boys were playing ball on the other side of the courtyard. Someone hit a long one and the ball came over to our side, so I picked it up and threw it back to them.

Thom7726 yelled at me, "Hey, Jemma! Who taught you to throw a ball?" I just waved at him, but his friends chimed in.

"Yeah! Hey, Jemma, you going to do a sex change on Choosing Day?"

The boys came over and interrupted our game. Thom grabbed the rope and started whipping it around. Lila wanted to stop playing but I didn't. Two of the other girls left us and went to play on the far side.

Thom was the other stable class in our quad and Teacher likes him. Some of the girls do too, but his ears stick out. He'd had an operation on them but it hadn't worked and someone told me he was going to have them fixed again over our vacation break. He was a year older than me and tall for his age. Aside from his ears, he was a handsome boy but not very nice.

"How can you see out of those eyes, Jemma?" he yelled, and the boys laughed. I hate it when people talk about my black eyes.

"How can you hear out of those ears, Thom?" I yelled back.

Lila grabbed my arm and tried to pull me away. "C'mon, Jemma, you'll get into trouble." She looked scared. I wasn't scared. I thought the boys should leave us alone.

Thom came right up to me, shoved Lila away, and poked his fist under my chin. He gave me a shove.

I stood my ground so he kept shoving me, pushing me backwards until I was against the wall that encloses the courtyard. The other boys were grinning and following him, egging him on. I couldn't move away because there was no place to go.

"You're a genetic mistake!" Thom made a terrible face at me and stuck out his tongue. His breath stank. I told him so and tried to push him away.

The other boys started chanting, "Shark's eyes! Shark's eyes!"

"You're not even your father's child!"

"Don't talk about my father!"

Thom hit me on the shoulder. It didn't hurt and I laughed. "You're a de-fect, Thom! You've got elephant ears!"

He hit me again. I slapped him in the face, but not hard. He staggered sideways and started to snivel and Teacher came from nowhere and grabbed me by the back of my tunic, literally lifting me off the ground. The schoolyard got quiet. Everyone just stared at us with their mouths hanging open.

"Thom7726, go to the quiet room," Teacher said in a low voice. "Jemma7729, you come with me." He didn't let go of the back of my shirt and pushed me ahead of him into the building, me walking on my toes because he was half-carrying me.

It was hushed inside the school. Teacher released me when we walked down the long hall to the master's office at the end. He knocked on the door, then opened it and pushed me in ahead of him when the master said we could enter.

The master's office was deeply carpeted and quiet and cool. There were six monitors built into the storage shelves on the walls, an outsize vidscreen, and two overstuffed chairs in a dark green floral pattern. There were flowering plants in the window, perfuming the air. I had only been in his office once or twice before, and never for anything like this.

The master sat behind his desk, reading on a small comp unit. He looked up at us, his eyebrows rising high on his forehead, absolutely symmetrical, like cartoon eyebrows. He was so blond his hair looked white in the sunlight slanting in the window behind him.

"Yes?"

"Jemma7729. She struck a boy."

"He hit me first," I said, and then wished I hadn't.

The master's expression didn't change but he got fine tense lines around his eyes. "Is this true? You hit a boy?" He had a wonderful voice, like a vid announcer on AGNA's News Network, syrupy and sweet, but he spoke very fast.

I looked at him straight in the eyes, the way Daddy said I should when I talked to adults. "Yes."

"Thank you, Lans." The master didn't even look at him but Teacher left us, closing the door carefully. It made a clicking sound when it shut.

The master put his comp unit carefully to one side, straightened it so that its edge was parallel with an envelope, and came around to the front of his desk. I hadn't noticed before that he was as tall as Daddy, except he had a round stomach that sagged over his belt, and big ugly hands. He towered over me and it made me feel little, but I stood still and waited. My guts were jiggling.

He asked me what had happened and I told him. He didn't interrupt me, he just kept nodding to keep me talking. I told him everything and then said I didn't think it was fair that Thom went to the quiet room. I said he should be there with me, since he started it.

"Fair? Fairness has nothing to do with it. This is about aggression. Aggression is not tolerated in females. You do know that?" I didn't say anything, so he repeated the question with his eyebrows moving up again and I nodded.

"I didn't aggress. I defended."

He leaned against his desk, his mouth puckered. He had the same squinty look Teacher gets when he asks me a question. "You're the regional administrator's daughter, aren't you?"

"Yes, sir. He's the regional administrator for the environment."

"Yes... well, that's neither here nor there. The boy shouldn't have hit you. Males should be gentle and kind to females, that's a given, but sometimes boys get rambunctious. However, *you* were absolutely wrong to hit him. Girls do not hit — ever. That is inappropriate behavior and a punishable offense. You realize that, don't you? And answer me, don't just nod."

"Yes, sir. But—"

He wasn't listening. He strode to a small wooden table below the flowers hanging in the window, opened the center drawer, and came back to me with a narrow leather strap in his hand.

"A punishable offense! Jemma7729, you've learned our history. It was the aggression of women — women challenging authority, fighting, practicing martial arts, behaving in ways inappropriate for the female — that started the wars that nearly destroyed North America in the past. That will not happen again. Turn around."

I did. He put one hand on my shoulder and held me firmly. "I want you to repeat what I say after me."

He hit me hard with the strap across my butt and I flinched. It made a cracking noise and it hurt. "I am a female. I do not fight. Repeat it!"

I did, and got nine more whacks, saying the words nine more times as clearly as I could, gritting my teeth. When he was done he let me go and tossed the strap on his desk. I had to blink fast to not show my tears.

"Women are precious vessels. We love them, we protect them, even from themselves. That's what I am doing right now. Millions of females have died, Jemma7729, for just the sort of behavior you have exhibited here today. You cannot win; you should not try. Is that understood?"

"Yes, sir."

"You know that it was women who caused the Countryside to be toxic, so that you can't even exist in it anymore. Right?"

"Yes, sir."

"You know that by fighting the Necessary Genocide, in the early days of our Republic, it was women who inspired the massacres, caused the famine, fought the reforms that finally saved the planet?"

"Yes, sir. That was a long time ago."

He pinched his lips together and stared hard at me. Then he sighed and shook his head, his eyes darting towards the desk and the strap. I was afraid he was going to pick it up again.

"I'm aware of your record. You're a good student. You seem to do best in music and art. Is that right?"

"Yes, sir. And communications. I do okay in that."

He grunted. I took a deep breath. It felt like the worst was past.

"I'm going to recommend that you have special classes in history. You obviously have not understood it. Tomorrow you will apologize publicly to the boys, and to the whole school. I'm going to send you home now, so you don't contaminate the others this day. I want you to think seriously on your crime, Jemma7729. Don't discuss this incident with anyone except your family. I'll send a report with you and will want to talk to your parents here in my office. Do you have a driver?"

I turned to look at him. My legs were shaking and I felt cold. "No, sir, I take regular transport when my mother is using our hovercar." Most people thought I had a regular chauffeur because of my social class, but Daddy usually dropped me off on his way to work, or Mother did, or one of our servants walked me to a designated stop so I could pick up a schoolcar. Thom7726 had private transportation just for himself.

"Well, one of our drivers will take you home. Go wait in reception. I'll want to see you again, after you've completed your special history studies."

"Yes, sir."

I left and waited for half an hour in the reception area while someone wrote up a report and the school's hovercar was called. It took a while because the driver was off on another errand. No one talked to me, not even the Secretary when she handed me the sealed envelope. She usually smiled at least. I felt like an outcast.

# # #

Our cooking woman's name was Resa7629 and I called her Reesie. She belonged to the useful class. She was a small woman with large breasts that stuck out and wiggled. Her hair was gray and short, and her eyes were brown with thick, straight eyebrows over them. She had a nice, rosy kind of complexion. She was cheerful and sociable to me and made me extra things — cookies sometimes, or pudding. And she let me sneak coffee now and then when I caught her in the kitchen drinking some herself, alone and not busy. I didn't tell on her and she didn't tell on me.

I was seven and the Choosing Day was looming, so I often went to talk to her after school, before Mother or Daddy got home. I was supposed to go right to my room and do my homework, but if nobody was around I went to talk to Reesie and drink coffee. This day I really needed some company.

"So," she said to me, pouring me a half a cup, loading it with cream and sugar, "have you decided? Are you ready to choose?"

"No."

"Jemma! What's the problem?"

"I don't know what to choose."

She sat down at the table with me and pulled her full mug closer to her. "If I had your choices, I wouldn't hesitate."

"What would you choose?"

"I'd be a wife. I would love to be able to just stay home and look after a house and do the shopping and all that."

"You have children, Reesie. It's like being a wife."

"Not quite, Jemma. A wife doesn't have to work at anything else. It would be heaven." She peered at me over the rim of the cup. "That doesn't interest you?" I shook my head. "Well, you must have *some* idea."

"I'd like to drive a hovercar or a GAV."

"You can't do that."

"I know. Or I'd like to be a park worker, but I can't do that, either. Reesie, I don't like the choices I have. They're boring."

She chuckled. "You should be like your mother — be a woman who marries."

"I suppose. But I don't like boys."

She laughed out loud then, a big whooping kind of laugh that made her eyes water and made me smile, too, although I didn't think what I'd said was funny, especially not this day when boys had made me so miserable.

"You will, darlin', you will." She glanced at the chrono over the sink. "You're home early. Why?"

I sighed and leaned my chin on my hand, "I'm in trouble." She stiffened her body and moved her feet under the table and her face screwed up and she pinched her nose.

"What kind of trouble?" I didn't think she really wanted to know because she had pulled her body back in the chair, like the snake in the bio lab recoiling when I stick my hand in its cage.

I shook my head. "I can't tell anyone but Mother and Daddy. Maybe tomorrow I can tell you, but they made me promise not to discuss it." She got up abruptly and started to take my cup. "I'm not finished!"

"Well, finish it and give me the cup. Go do your homework."

She turned away from me as if she were angry, though why she would be I didn't know. I guess it's because people don't want to get involved with other people's troubles. I asked her if that was the case and she agreed. I finished my coffee.

She took my cup to the sink to rinse it. "Jemma, you're a good kid and I like you, but there's something... different about you, and I don't mean your eyes, so don't get mad. I worry."

I grinned at her and stood up to give her a hug. I liked to hug her hard because those big breasts squished and she made an oofing kind of noise.

"Thanks for the coffee, Reesie. I'll be okay. I hope."

I ran upstairs and not only did my homework but cleaned my room and brushed my hair and my teeth, then watched the vid and waited for my parents to get home. I would have to give them the note the master had sent home with me.

I was going to do it when they first got home, but supper was ready so I put it off until after we had eaten.

Mother and Daddy were going to have coffee on the patio. I followed them out and waited until Reesie had brought the tray and left. They were surprised that I was hanging around. I didn't usually stay with them once we were finished with food.

Mother poured coffee out of the silvery pot into two elegant china cups. She did it so gracefully I always liked to watch. She had promised to show me how to do that some day, but she never got around to it. She glanced at me.

"Don't you have homework?"

"I did it already." I took a big breath. It made a noise, so Daddy looked over at me as he took his cup from Mother.

"Something on your mind, Jemma?"

"Yes." It was hard to do. I had stuck the letter in the pocket of my skirt and now I brought it out and handed it to him. It had crumpled around the edges. "I had a problem at school today."

Both of them set their cups down. Mother closed her eyes. So she couldn't see me, I guess. Daddy opened the envelope and read it. His face was neutral but he clenched his jaw.

"Oh, Jemma!" His voice was full of disappointment. I winced. "What happened?" He handed the note to my mother. She read it and threw it down on the table in disgust.

"It was Thom7726. He teases me all the time. He drives me crazy."

"Boys tease, Jemma. You know that." Mother fluffed out her hair in the back and stared at the swimming pool.

"But — he started pushing me. We were outside in the play yard, and he kept teasing me and pushing me into the wall and he hit me."

Daddy picked up the letter again and read it out loud. "Jemma7729 shows definite signs of aggression, which must be dealt with now before an irrevocable pattern is established." He looked up at me. "Do you know what that means? What 'irrevocable' means?"

"Yes. It means something that can't be changed."

Daddy put the letter in the inside pocket of his jacket. "What did you do when he pushed you?"

"Nothing at first, except to tease him back. And then, when he wouldn't stop and he hit me twice, I slapped him."

"Oh, God!" Mother shook her head and rubbed her eyes. "What did you hit him with?"

"Just my hand."

Mother got up and stared at me. "You deal with this Roger. I can't." She quickly went into the house and I was surprised to see tears in her eyes. *What did that mean?*

I turned to Daddy in a panic. "What's wrong with Mother? Why is she crying?"

"Sit down, Jem." I did. He thought a minute but didn't pull his mustache, just stared across the lawn. "So, you hit this boy. Then what happened?"

"Teacher came and pulled us apart. Thom cried, but I didn't hit him that hard. He hit me harder and he's bigger than me."

"Slow down... then what happened?"

"Teacher sent him to the quiet room and I had to go to the master. He was mad at me."

"Did the master punish you?"

I chewed on my lip. I had never been so uncomfortable in my life. I nodded. "With a strap."

"Did it hurt?"

"*Yes.* He hit me harder than Thom did. Ten times."

Daddy made a kind of grunty noise. "Did you cry?"

"No!" Of course I didn't cry. I couldn't let the master see me crying.

Daddy leaned back in his chair with a sigh that puffed out his cheeks. "Oh, baby..." He motioned for me to come nearer.

I stood in front of him and he put his arms around me. His eyes were so sad they made me hurt. "I want you to promise me something, okay?" I nodded my head. He thought a minute, but didn't let go of me. "I want you to promise, on your solemn oath, that should something like this happen again — and it damn well better not! — if the master, or anyone in authority, punishes you, I want you to cry. Do you understand? You must cry."

I didn't understand. "But..."

"Don't argue. Punishments are supposed to hurt. If you stand up to them, that's an act of defiance. You're not allowed to defy authority. You know that! You know the Woman's Creed." I nodded but he shook his head. "Say it!"

I sighed. It was boring. "'I am a female. I will not question nor defy authority. I will not be aggressive in thought or action. I will obey the request of any male unless what he asks is immoral or unlawful.'" I took a deep breath and spit the rest out. "'I will accomplish all that is required of me cheerfully and without complaint I will not discuss nor think about topics forbidden to my sex. I will graciously submit to my husband.' Daddy, I didn't mean to defy him. I just didn't want him to think I'm a baby."

"But you are, Jemma! You *are* a baby. You're seven years old! You're female. No defiance is allowed you. Period. Promise me!"

His hands were tight on my arms. The look in his eyes was so intense it scared me. "I promise that I'll cry." He let me go and picked up his coffee cup. "I'm sorry, Daddy."

"So am I, Baby." He sipped his coffee and didn't look at me.

Oh Daddy, darling, you have no idea how that solemn oath came back to haunt me. Actually, I'm glad you never knew. But it was you who taught me how to lie, and that came in handy.

# # #

That night I couldn't sleep. I worried about school and what would happen to me. I felt guilty for upsetting my parents. Choosing Day was coming up and I hated the things that were possible for my sex and class. I didn't have to choose absolutely until after I was ten, but it was the law that a person chose at seven and then concentrated on being prepared for the final choice.

Mostly, though, I thought about hitting Thom and what the master had said and done. I didn't like it. And I didn't know what had made me break the rules. I felt sorry for myself. It didn't seem fair that boys could hit girls but not vice versa.

There were diffuse lights on the skydome, a springtime gift from AGNA for the citizens of L.A., a monthly light show that would continue for several nights. It took the place of moonlight, which of course we never saw because our city had its miraculous roof, or at least that's what I was told. The domes on all the cities in North America kept the toxins of the Countryside out. They protected the females. I had studied about the light projections in science class. Night-time light exactly echoed the phases of the moon in the Countryside, where women cannot go, to make our environment more natural. Scientists said there was a connection between something called women's cycles and the real moon, so they lit up the sky for us. Except, of course, they never showed its image. It was just a satellite, anyway.

The projections also made my bedroom bright, so I got up and looked out at the back yard bathed in the soft light.

Mother sat by the pool, all by herself, drinking a glass of wine. She was wearing a white robe and she glowed bluish in the light, like a ghost. I glanced at my chrono. It was 03:27. Guess she couldn't sleep, either.

I crept downstairs and sneaked out onto the patio as quietly as I could. I didn't want to bother her, but she heard or saw me.

"Jemma?"

I walked slowly towards the pool. "I didn't mean to disturb you, Mother."

She shook her head. "You didn't. What's the matter? Can't sleep?"

"No."

"Come over here, please." She straightened in her chair. She was barefoot. I couldn't remember ever seeing her feet. They were long and delicate, like the rest of her.

I went to sit beside her. We didn't talk for a while, then she said, "The light is beautiful. And it's so quiet in the middle of the night. I guess it doesn't matter that there isn't a real moon."

"I'm sorry about today, Mother." I whispered because I didn't want to disrupt the peace.

"So am I." She sipped her wine. She wasn't looking at me. She didn't look at me much at any time, as if I were repugnant to her, even though people said there was a strong resemblance between us.

"I don't mean to make trouble." She didn't respond, or wasn't listening. I was so depressed by everything that I actually said, "I'm sorry that you don't like me."

She turned to me with her lips parted in surprise and carefully set her glass on the table. "Is that what you think? That I don't like you?"

I was afraid to answer.

"Oh, Jemma," she whispered in a husky tone and held out both arms to me. For a split second I didn't know what to do and then I was in her arms in a flash and she pulled me close. She smelled faintly of lilacs. I could hear her heart beating in my ear.

"I love you." She held me tightly. "I love you, my girl. But you frighten me to death." I squirmed but she didn't loosen her hold. "I'm so afraid you won't — that you won't be able to do what you need to do."

"I try to do everything right."

She smiled. "I know you do, but — it isn't what you do, Jemma, it's who you *are*. You have a stubborn streak, an independent turn of mind. Sit down." She let me go back to my chair. She picked up the glass while I basked in the glow from her embrace. "Do you know what? I'm going to tell you a secret."

"What?" My heart pumped right in my throat.

"I was a bit like you at your age."

"Were you?" I would never have guessed that.

"Not as troublesome, but I had some ideas of my own, too."

She took a sip of the wine and handed me the glass, as a kind of token, I guess. She chuckled when I tasted it and made a face. She was softer than I had ever seen her, there in the quiet of the night.

"Jemma, I have to keep a distance from you, because I couldn't bear it if you fail. You're dangerous, to yourself and to your father and to me."

That confused me. She brushed my hair back gently from my forehead and looked at me with a little smile. Her eyes were sad. "Get some sleep. You have a big day tomorrow."

I felt on safer ground discussing real things. "It'll be awful. I have to apologize to the whole school, and the boys. Probably have to apologize to Thom personally."

She leaned forward and touched my knee. "Yes, and you will do that graciously, simply, with humility. Keep your dignity. Be smart." She lowered her voice and I had to lean even closer to hear her. "You're a woman, Jemma, and we endure. We survive. I *want* you to survive. Remember that."

She sat back then and sipped her wine again and looked away from me. "Go to bed."

I got up and kissed her cheek, but she didn't respond. I went upstairs full of conflicting emotions. I'm dangerous? How? Why? We survive, we women? Is that what she'd said? Survive? Endure?

I looked down on her from my window, hovering back in the shadow. She stood up. She looked toward my window but didn't see me. She glanced around the yard, then she loosened her robe and let it drop from her body. She was naked. I was shocked. Women were not allowed to be naked outside of their houses. I glanced away for an instant, but she was so beautiful that I had to keep watching as she slipped soundlessly into the water.

Chapter 2

"I apologize to the master, and to the teachers, and to all of my fellow students for my inappropriate behavior yesterday. I'm very sorry. What I did was wrong and I'm ashamed."

I stood on the stage of our assembly hall. I tried to behave as Mother had counseled: dignified, simple, sincere. I was all of those things, and a little more. I remembered Daddy's lesson, too, and I cried — not so much that they couldn't understand what I said, or that my nose would get red the way it did when I broke my arm when I was four, just enough that it put a catch in my throat and they could see it, to convince them that I was unhappy and remorseful and repentant.

The master came to stand beside me at the end of it and said that I had paid for my crime and was forgiven, but that the incident could not be forgotten. He also talked for fifteen minutes, while everyone tried to look interested, about the lesson to be learned from my transgression.

To my surprise, I was suddenly a secret heroine among the girls for a couple of weeks. People who had never talked to me sought me out. Lila was jealous, since she was my best friend, and got downright snippy with some of them. I was embarrassed at first, but then it felt good. People listened when I said something.

Even the boys were more respectful. I heard that they teased Thom because he had cried when I hit him, and I — Jemma the Shark — had actually been whipped ten times with a leather strap. During the assembly, when the master had mentioned that, I had kept my eyes on the stage floor.

I don't think any of the boys in my quad had ever been disciplined. I was the pioneer.

But all that was left behind, although the admiration lingered for awhile among the girls at least, because The Big Day was approaching. Choosing Day.

Suddenly no one could talk of anything else and it seemed everyone but me had already made up their minds. Lila was excited about being a communications worker. I envied her. She had a lot more choices than I did.

We had special instruction on the rightness and the appropriateness of the class structure, and the reason for Choosing Day. I had wondered about that, and although we had been taught what the classes were and how they worked, and certainly each of us knew where we belonged, this time their value seemed clearer.

The class structure was old, going back to the founding of AGNA at the beginning of the twenty-second century, when the survivors of the wars and riots were divided into their natural classes by federal law. They were based on ethnicity, property holdings, loyalty to the government, and a need for balance in society. A strong class structure made jealousies, greed, ambition, and a lot of other bad things unnecessary. Everyone had a place and a contribution to make the greater good. The strict adherence to the structure ruled out dissatisfaction.

Teacher handed out chips to everyone and we put them in our comp units and pulled them up. He told us to study them and ask if we had any questions. Mine read:

> Choices for JE2MDRA77290FF400RT913
> Class: Stable
> Age: 7

All women of the stable class are permitted and encouraged to marry within their class and to produce children. Permits are required for childbearing.

Women of the stable class will choose one of the first two categories. They may also choose a further sub-category, with permission of the AGNA Regional Director for Women's Affairs, their husbands, and other permitting agencies as noted. All work is done without pay.

Notes: [A]   Often are or elect to become alters
[A25] Altered after 25th birthday (mandatory)
[L]   Lock-up jobs, quarantined after training
[AO] Available only to alters

STABLE CLASS

Woman who marries: Females choosing this category are expected to fully engage in charitable, educational, and cultural work, and, in some cases, assist AGNA on special projects. They must be willing to assume a leadership role for their sex and class. They are responsible for the well-being of their husbands and children, the smooth running of their homes, and the supervision of servants. They are permitted nearly unlimited movement within their city for their good works, and for shopping and entertainment.

Wife [A]: Females choosing to be a wife stay at home. They are permitted access to the markets and do their own shopping. They are permitted access to civic buildings and public entertainment. It is not practical for a wife to do any work outside of the home. They may elect to do their own cooking, gardening, and other household activities. They are expected to bear children.

SUBCATEGORIES:

Fiction Writer: Females choosing this category must have some talent for writing. They are permitted to write romances, historical romances and mysteries, and a few other types of entertainment fiction, with permission. They need not be gifted writers, but must be competent ones. Permission of AGNA Arts Council is required.

Facilities designer/Interior designer: Some talent is required for this work, especially a good sense of color. Females choosing this category assist in the decoration of private and public buildings under the supervision of a male designer licensed by the state. Permission of AGNA Arts Council is required.

Corporate assistant [A25]: Open only to those women who show special talents for methodology and an interest in financial and organizational problems. Permission of AGNA Department of Commerce required. Women choosing this category will be altered after their 25th birthday. Some positions with AGNA are available.

Listener [A]: Females who show a particular aptitude for sensitive understanding of others and a broad interest in human problems may choose this category. Strenuous training is required, which may result in late marriage or the absence of children. A listener works with all classes, providing guidance and sympathy about personal problems.

Museum worker: Females may volunteer to work as docents, guides, and in some cases, as catalogers and specimen handlers. Permission of the AGNA Museum Council is required, and training is mandatory.

PRODUCTIVE CLASS

Communications worker
Data handler [L]
Non-fiction writer (Public Relations/Vids)
Lab technician [L]
Medical Technician [L]
Tutoress (decorum/femininity/home-maker skills)
Teacher (some limits, subject to approval)

USEFUL CLASS

Cook/Brewer
Baby caretaker
Seamstress
Recreation director
Personal hygiene worker (hair/style/skin care/
    exercise/etc)
Consumer goods saleswoman

NECESSARY CLASS

Animal handler
Flower lady
Sex worker [A]
Parks worker
Farm worker [AO]
Cleaner
Punisher [A25]
GAV/hovercar driver
AGNA facilities guard [AO]
Service worker (waitress/dishwasher/server)
Messenger [AO]
Production worker

X-CLASS

Based solely on proven extraordinary ability and
    subject to reclassification.
Musician/Composer
Actress
Singer
Announcer
Entertainer [A] (vids/concerts/parties)
Painter/Decorator
Clothing designer
Mathematician [L]
Athlete [A]

All women must marry within their class and may
have children upon application to the proper AGNA
administrative office, with some restrictions. Political
and Medical clearance is required.

That didn't give me much to choose from, and certainly nothing I wanted. I couldn't see myself as a writer or working in a museum. I got high marks in art but wasn't interested in decorating and design. I liked to paint pictures, but I wasn't gifted enough to choose that. We had just begun to learn about marriage and so far the classes had bored me.

Teacher droned on about the timetable. Our choice now was preliminary, just an indication of where our interests lay. At the final choosing day, there were a few other options: confirmation; a different choice (not recommended, but possible with clearance); females could opt for a sex change and choose from the male list appropriate to their class; and, in a very few cases, "something else" could be done. He didn't explain what that last one was. He did explain that choosing was mandatory. Failure to make choices was a punishable offense under the AGNA Constitution.

I was only half-listening, staring at the green glow of the screen on my comp unit with my mother's words teasing through my mind, what she had said about my failing, about my being dangerous. I didn't want to choose but I had to, I did know that, and if my choosing made me less dangerous to Daddy and Mother, then I would do it.

Teacher stood right over me and his voice jolted me out of my daydreaming.

"So, Jemma7729, have you decided?"

I blurted it out. "Yes, I'll be a woman who marries." The moment I said it I felt as if I had swallowed a stone, a jagged stone that cut me as it went into my guts. I could see Lila out of the corner of my eye, her mouth open in surprise.

Teacher beamed and literally rubbed his hands together. "Excellent! Like your splendid mother! And your good grades in art and music will support that choice. Of course you must discuss it with your parents, but next week, on the big day, this school will recognize you as a female leader of your class within your quad."

There was smattering of polite applause. I stared around the room, desperately wanting to run, to scream, and — to my horror — I wanted to hit him in his stupid, grinning face, the unctuous bastard. The pit of my stomach boiled. Why was I thinking these forbidden thoughts?

I didn't do any of those things, although I clenched my fist so hard my fingernails scraped blood. When he walked away I sucked at it, finding solace in its salty sweetness.

I had done the right thing. Then why was I so desperately unhappy?

# # #

My life changed after that choosing day. They hadn't told me that my parents could opt to keep me at home, privately tutored, because of my choice and my class. Daddy was reluctant to do that, but Mother insisted.

"We'll all be safer if Jemma is here at home, where we can monitor her. Trust me on this, Roger."

He did. Obviously, she didn't trust me.

My quad broke up into different units, the boys going one place, the girls another. I wondered if I would ever see Lila again. I didn't care about anyone else.

Staying home could have been fun if I'd had someone to play with, to talk to. Parties and so-called play times were arranged with other girls, nobody I knew. All of us were learning to interact appropriately with strangers in a recreational situation.

Plus, the wife next door left, without even saying goodbye to me. I went over one afternoon to visit her, as I often did when I had my free time periods. A strange woman peeped through the curtains, then opened the door cautiously. She seemed alarmed to see me there and she didn't want to talk to me. She told me she was the wife. She wouldn't answer any questions about what had happened to the old one. That made me sad.

The next couple of years I went through a series of tutors and a couple of tutoresses. The music and art teachers were good but the rest of them were a bore. They said I knew enough about computers and wouldn't upgrade mine. I learned all the preliminary stuff I was supposed to know about decorating, style, and handling large groups of people of all classes. The lessons called "Conversation" could have been interesting, but the teacher was a woman who marries, one of my mother's friends, and none of the topics on her list excited me. Was I really supposed to care about appropriate toys for two-year-olds?

One tutor continued to teach me history. It was in my file that I was historically deficient. They didn't give up on me and I had to write research reports with titles like, "The Effect of the Satellite Mirrors on Agriculture," and "Murals and Mural-Making in the Over- and Underground Tunnels of North America." That last one was a bitch to research.

The last tutoress, whom I secretly called Poop — her name was Poppe7624 — was alarmed by my active lifestyle. She said it was unfeminine to swim as fast as I did and that I was entirely too physical and got too much sun. So I was allowed to go into the pool only when there were other swimmers, which wasn't often enough. She took away my chemistry set and my beautiful miniature GAV, which Daddy said was exactly like a real one except that it couldn't get off the ground. She substituted dolls. I hated them, but I dutifully played doctor with them, and when they all died I did autopsies.

Mother was furious. I had to stay in my bedroom and do nothing for two days for that one. Isolation became Poop's torture of choice thereafter. I guess she saw how much I hated it. Boredom was a terrible punishment at first, then I discovered that I could live in my head, could imagine and dream, could even have forbidden thoughts, and no one knew what I was thinking and doing, so I pretended to hate it more than I really did. But still, doing nothing bothered me.

I often felt guilty for what I thought, especially when it was about the women who had been incarcerated during the early days of the Necessary Genocide. When the race riots got out of control in 2059, what was then the United States Government cracked down on the rioters and the law was passed that made protests illegal. Lots of women took to the streets, illegally protesting the law against protests. It struck me as a terrible irony. The army and the police opposed them. This was, of course, long ago, before the police and the army were consolidated as the Fedguard. Many women were killed and many were arrested and held for a long time. They were the Bad Women.

I felt a connection to them, not just because I was incarcerated in my bedroom and had been told I was bad, but because I was trapped in the system. My skin itched and sometimes I thought I couldn't breathe. I wasn't allowed to open the windows. They might as well have put me in a dungeon in chains, like in the ancient histories. I could imagine dying of boredom.

I began to wonder what the Bad Women were like. My exploit at school had given me a taste of leadership, the kind that comes when people seek you out and look up to you as someone different from themselves and are interested in your opinions. I didn't understand it, and it only lasted a few months, but I had liked it. I found myself admiring those nameless women of the past centuries who had fought and died for an idea.

I decided I needed an idea that would be good enough to fight and die for. But I couldn't think of one. Not then, when the teachers and my parents were still trying to help me be a woman who marries.

As the time went by, and I got closer and closer to Final Choosing Day, I worried a lot but didn't dare discuss it with anyone. Who would understand? Just the imaginary women in my brain, and they couldn't help me.

Then everything changed again. Irrevocably.

# # #

It was your fault, Daddy. Silly to say. You made me what I am because you showed me possibilities. You opened a window and let me look outside. I couldn't close it after that.

I date my true rebellion from one night a few months before Final Choosing Day, when Mother announced that she would be gone for two weeks. She had to go to an

AGNA-training retreat. Daddy said that was too bad and inconvenient since he had to go to an important meeting, too, at the Sacto Justice Facility upstate. That would leave me alone for a long time with Poop and the thought made me desperately unhappy.

That morning I had got into serious trouble with the new wife next door. I missed the one I had liked, who had shared coffee with me. Daddy said she left because she couldn't have children. That made me angry and sad. It wasn't fair. I know she had loved her husband and her house and was a good wife, so I wasn't much inclined to like the new one.

And so I did another crime. I kicked the new wife's shins. She had been talking to the flower lady about me, and I overheard them. The wife said Daddy was not my real father. That's why my eyes were black, she said. That's a lie! All you have to do is check my DNA file. She was being mean-spirited and prejudiced. I squeezed through our picket fence, ran at her, and kicked her hard. She screamed and Poop came running and spanked me all the way home. The wife cried. I didn't — not that time.

Mother and Daddy talked about the incident that evening. I sat at the top of the stairs and listened to them. Mother wanted me to be altered. I knew that I would never be me again if it happened. They squeezed your brain, Lila had told me. She knew, because her mother was an alter.

"She *is* aggressive, Roger. And she will bring us down with her! If we don't make the decision, AGNA will make it for us."

Daddy was furious. It was the first time I ever heard him throw things. He broke a pretty crystal vase full of flowers. Mother yelled at him, too, louder. She said he was as inappropriate as I was and that he would lose his job if he didn't stop covering up for people. I heard his voice say her name and it sounded so different from the way he usually talks to her that I thought that there was someone else in the room.

She was quiet for awhile after that, then she said, "I'm sorry. Forgive me. I overstepped. But, you're not going to

be able to protect her forever. If you can't — if you want
me to do it, I will. We must do something."

"She still has four months before the final choosing,"
Daddy's voice sounded normal again. "She'll be all right.
She's a great kid, Elane. Think of her, not yourself."

Mother sighed so loud I heard it all the way upstairs.
"I am thinking about her — about her welfare. The way
she's going, she'll wind up deleted if not altered."

I heard a noise like something slamming then Daddy
said, "End of conversation. Do not repeat this to me, Elane."
I didn't hear Mother's voice for the rest of the evening, not
even when they were sitting by the pool together.

I cried myself to sleep that night for the first time ever
and vowed that I would be good for the rest of my life.

Mother went on her retreat. Daddy took me with him,
something he had never done before, all the way to Sacto
via the overground tunnel in a fedcar. I think he didn't trust
Mother. He took me to keep me safe.

The Sacto Overground has lovely paintings of flowers,
color coded to mark off counties: blue when we left L.A.
and brilliant oranges and golds as we neared the Sacto
dome. Since I had written the long report on them, I told
Daddy all about the tunnels as the fedcar sped along, and
he was impressed. This one was nicer than most, except,
perhaps, for the one between ClevErie and Chicago, which
is painted like a continuous forest. Some underground
tunnels have murals, too, but artists are still working on
most of them. Only the BosWash one is finished completely.
It shows vignettes from the history of AGNA and is said
to be beautiful and inspiring.

Then, there we were, father and daughter in the big fed
installation at Sacto with its high dome and hot artificial
weather. He had meetings, I got to wander through the
mall, and Daddy gave me a credit card. I had a bodyguard,
which was expected because of my class, but he was a good
sort who had been with Daddy from the old days, right
after the Third War of Inclusion, the one with Canada. He
found me amusing, I think. He didn't tell on me about what
I bought, or that I drank coffee.

I knew all about the War of Inclusion, too, from those special classes I took. It ended in 2169, thirteen years before I was born. I asked my bodyguard if he had fought in any battles, and he said just one, with a bunch of women. He said it as if it didn't count. I didn't ask him anything else.

After the two days of meetings I was bored with the mall and had seen all the vids and live performances. In the morning, very early, Daddy came into my room lugging a big carrybag and a smaller package. He woke me up.

"Come on, Jemma," he said, and smiled. "I have a surprise for you."

I sat up in bed. He was dressed in a light blue shirt and dark cotton trousers. I had never seen him without a tie, but he wasn't wearing one and he looked happy. He put the smaller parcel on the bottom of my bed.

"Wear these," he said and left.

I had laid out my skirt and blouse to put on for the trip home. What was in the package surprised me. Boy's clothes. A white teeshirt and a blue shirt like his, with a pair of dark blue cotton pants. The pants were baggy, but there was a belt and I snugged them up. And really great boots.

I smirked at myself in the mirror. I was gorgeous.

Then he came for me and we went up to the roof of the hotel and got into a private GAV. No bodyguards, no officials. Just us. The back was full of lumpy canvas bags. He fired us up and we were out of Sacto in a flash, zipping through a gate in the dome, heading towards the mountains in the open air. Daddy actually whistled a tune.

The earth beneath us was a thousand shades of green and brown, with warm tan and gray rocky outcrops. It didn't look like the pictures of the Countryside we saw at school, but maybe those were taken somewhere else, because in them, there weren't any trees and the earth was blackened and barren.

I had never seen clouds in my life except in pictures and they were sensational. They made me laugh. Daddy looked over at me. "What's funny?" When I told him, he laughed, too, and winked and flew right under them just to show me what they were.

We landed in a wide clearing beside a bright river, where it curved along a rocky beach. He made a good landing, despite the uneven terrain, and I helped him stow the GAV under the trees at the edge of the open space and unload all the bags. I had never been outside of a city before. I stood just looking at the sky with my heart pounding. It was so big. The air smelled new and wet.

"Jemma," Daddy said, taking off his jacket and rolling up his sleeves, "you and I are going to have some fun."

We did. I helped put up the two tents and stash the sleeping pouches in them. We dug a hole and built a fire in it. I got water from the river and tested it with a toxinchek strip — it was clean but tasted different from the water at home. We fished and ate what we caught — beautiful slimy little trout like tiny wet rainbows. I found some berries he said we could eat. He identified the birds that were singing and tested me on them. I did very well. It was like music and we all know I'm good at music.

We swam in the river in our underwear. It was very cold. I found special rocks: rose quartz and field jasper the color of blood, but Daddy said I couldn't keep them. After we had washed the supper dishes we sat on a big, flat reddish-gray rock.

"I could live up here, Jemma," he said. "But I can't." And he sighed. He laid back, arms behind his head. I copied him. The rock was still warm from the sun even though the air was getting nippy. The insects droned and the light got dimmer and dimmer and then, slowly, the miracle began to occur.

It was so scary that I couldn't talk. My words were stuck in my throat. Finally I managed to whisper, "What is it?"

"Stars. Stars, Jemma. There is the universe."

It was The Real Thing.

I glanced at him and there were tears glistening at the corners of his eyes.

"But, everything we learned in AGNA history says that we don't need the stars, that the stars disappeared after the wars, when the helpful satellite mirrors went up. When North America brought peace to planet Earth."

He didn't answer me. I had tears in my eyes, too, and didn't know why.

He was quiet for what seemed a long time. "Just don't be afraid of the stars."

"Are they always there?"

"Always. You can't see them in the city. Be still and listen to them sing."

I can't put into words what seeing those first stars was like, the canyons and towers and swirls of glistering bright lights in the blue-black sky. And then the moon, the real moon, came up so bright we could read by it, and I thought my heart would burst. It still hurts to remember.

We lay under the sky and watched the moon glide past the stars and fell asleep, crawling to our tents only when we were chilled by the heavy dew.

My life changed utterly when the stars touched me. I knew then that there were possibilities, that life held things other than what I was told. And I knew, too, that there were realities hidden or lied about that I would have to discover for myself. I believed I could find something big enough to fight and die for.

I needed to know why I had been told the stars weren't important, that we didn't need to see them, and that the moon was just another satellite. Why did women have to stay in the cities or in lock-up jobs? In AGNA history, the Bad Women's opposition to the wars and the Necessary Genocide and the ethnic cleansing was called our original sin. So many women had died back then that we were precious and protected. There was an old story that there were still feral women in the Countryside. Original sin had happened a long time ago. What did it have to do with stars?

I had been taught that the Countryside was toxic to the female. But that couldn't be true, could it? I was female and I was there. Daddy would not have brought me if it would kill me.

I was certain that the stars had changed me profoundly, had filled me with awe and terror and happiness. They had squeezed my brain. And I was still me.

The next morning I asked, "Daddy, is there a way that I can choose that will let me watch the stars every night?"

He thought about it as he stirred up the fire to make breakfast. "No. Women can't be in the Countryside, you know. And I don't think you want to change sex. Or do you?" He looked at me in an adult way.

"No. But I'd like to be in a place like this forever."

He emptied a food pack into a pot, added water and set it on the fire. "There are choices in astronomy — but it's a lock-up job for women, and I think you have to exhibit X-class mathematical gifts. There's probably some data entry. Boring, and limited to productives."

"Could I choose to be a farmer person? or a wildlife engineer?"

"No. Wrong class, wrong sex. Farm women are all alters." He stirred the pot and didn't look at me.

"Is my being in the Countryside going to kill me?"

"No." He stood up and rummaged in a sack for more food, muttering. Then he came to where I was sitting and hunkered down in front of me.

"Jemma, you must stop asking questions now. You must never tell anyone about our coming here. You must give me your oath."

"Why?"

"I shouldn't have done this to you." He touched my face gently, pushing my wind-scattered hair back in place. "I have dreamed of sharing the stars with you. But..." He stared at the river and made a huffing kind of sound, as if it hurt to breathe. He looked back at me, and his teeth were clenched. "Remember that this exists, Jemma. But you must forget this trip. Coming here was wrong and illegal. Females are not allowed here. I could be arrested and you would be altered if anyone ever found out. I wouldn't be able to stop them."

I believed him. I promised.

He smiled and ruffled my hair. "Good girl."

That was the end of it. After the sun was high, we put the gear in the GAV and flew to Sacto. I changed back into girl's clothes, and we took a fedcar back through the overground tunnel to L.A.

I must tell you that I never loved my father so much as I did that day we swore an oath and he touched my face with his eyes so warm they bubbled. I learned to be proud of him when I heard of the times he had helped people, made sure they weren't deleted for silly things. He didn't fight the system, as I came to do, but he didn't fight the fighters, either.

I never told anyone about our trip. It wouldn't matter now. Both of my parents were butchered in the L.A. Terror in 2208. AGNA blames that insurrection on me, but I didn't do it. I swear that on the stars.

Chapter 3

There was no going back after that. No going forward, either.

I couldn't imagine spending my next six years learning how to please my husband, how to arrange flowers, how to do household accounting. I didn't want to be a spy like my mother, constantly monitoring her friends. My head was full of the rising of the moon.

I dreamed a lot, worried a lot. My future was impossible to contemplate. Daddy sometimes gave me odd looks at the dinner table — odd, as in questioning, sometimes coldly withdrawn, sometimes mischievous — wondering, I guessed, if I had told anyone about our adventure. Mother remarked that I was quieter than usual and grilled me often, trying to discover my secret. I know she knew I had one.

Final Choosing Day was a ceremony held at the People's Hall in Santa Monica Sector, bringing my quad back together for one last time. Parents accompanied their children, everyone dressed in their big day finery, everyone presumably eager to begin their real life's work. AGNA Network News covered it.

Mother had taken me shopping for new clothes and we had settled on a brushed linen mouse-gray suit with a blouse the color of bachelor's buttons. This was meant to show off my new pale complexion, complement my black hair. The saleswoman told me that I looked stunning and exactly like my mother, and Mother took me to lunch at a fancy restaurant. People stared at us admiringly and she was pleased with me, for once. A seamstress tailored the suit to fit. I had begun to get hips but my breasts were slow to develop, and I was going to be tall, like Mother. The tailoring helped to make me look less gangly. I wanted to look good for my quad. After three years, I feared that all my peers might be more advanced than I.

Daddy gave me a gold ring for my index finger that was a delicate twisting of vine leaves.

I wept in the shower. I thought of running away.

When Mother called upstairs that it was time to go I vomited.

When I got in the GAV to go downtown, Daddy frowned at me. "Are you all right? You look pale."

I tried to smile. "I haven't been in the sun much. Working on my complexion."

"Ahh," he said, and grinned, "well, you look beautiful, Jemma. Any man would be proud to have you on his arm."

I accepted the compliment properly and gave him a demure smile, the way I was taught, with my chin lowered slightly, so I seemed to be looking up at him. "Thank you, Daddy."

Mother got in the front seat, glanced at me and then stared out the window. "It's normal to be nervous." She didn't say anything else for the whole trip.

People's Hall is a glass and plasticrete two-storey edifice, designed as a multi-use building. We walked in, me between my parents, just like all the other young people. The hall was decorated with flowers, so many that the air felt close and too sweet, like a drug.

I think everyone was happy but me. Daddy smiled at me from time to time. Mother's heels clicked crisply on the tile floors and she didn't touch me.

I knew my father was important but I hadn't really thought about it until we were with strangers. People got out of our way because of him; attendants kowtowed and catered to us. They smiled at him the way people do, with their bottom teeth showing. They bowed slightly to Mother, acknowledging her place, and even once to me.

Then we were in a big room with a stage. There were too many flowers in there, too. I looked around for Lila and almost didn't recognize her. She had long hair and was plump. It may have been baby fat, but if not, she'd have to lose weight to be a communications worker. She waved and grinned and I waved back. I hoped we could talk afterwards, but now we had seating assigned by class.

Thom7726 had filled out and his looks had improved. His ears didn't stick out any more. Mother noticed him and leaned toward me as we sat down. "Who is that devilishly handsome young man over there?"

I made a sour face. "That's Thom. My nemesis."

She and Daddy chuckled. Daddy took my hand and his expression changed. "My God, Jemma, you're cold as ice."

Mother touched my forehead lightly, as if checking for a fever. I trembled. I was about to die and I knew it.

"What's the matter?" Mother whispered, her face close to mine. The familiar faint lilac perfume of her body brought tears to my eyes. "Are you sick?"

Daddy moved closer, too, his eyes full of concern. He put his arm around me.

"I can't. I can't do this." I turned to my father. "It's all a lie. You know it is! Help me!"

Both of them stiffened. Daddy's eyes squinted and glittered; Mother took a deep breath. We had about fifteen minutes before the whole thing started, and we stables were first on the list.

"I can't help you!" He talked with his jaw clenched. "Don't make trouble, Jemma. Just go through with this. You've made the right choice! It's the most freedom you can have."

"But I want to *do* something!"

Mother snapped at me. "I do things!"

I turned to her. I didn't mean to hurt her feelings. "Yes, I know you're busy, but you're not happy. I want—"

"Happy!" Sarcasm dripped from her words. "The child wants to be happy! The only way to be truly happy is to be altered!"

Daddy's eyes opened wide. "Elane! Have you gone out of your mind?"

Mother glared at me. "There are no choices now, Jemma. It's over."

"It can't be! I want to do something with my life!" I grabbed Daddy's hand. "Please!"

Daddy stared at me for a moment. I had tears in my eyes, real ones, not the kind I'd learned to turn on and off. He looked around to see if anyone was listening. No one was. They had given us a private sort of space, and besides, not everyone had sat down yet.

"You're breaking our hearts, Baby. Just do this. It will work out fine."

I let go of him and stared at the floor. Out of the corner of my eye, I saw him catch my mother's eyes and hold them a moment. She shook her head.

I mumbled at them. "Teacher said there was one other thing, some other choice, but he didn't say what it was."

Daddy sighed. "Rehab."

"Roger, no!" Mother laid her hand on my arm.

"What is that?" I whispered because people were sitting down two rows away.

"It's a prison, Jemma." He was grim.

"And having to choose woman who marries isn't?" I didn't mean to be snippy, but Daddy visibly ground his teeth and Mother made an exasperated noise.

We sat not talking for a few agonizing minutes while Daddy pulled at his mustache and Mother unbuttoned and buttoned the cuff of her blouse. I was miserable.

"We could say she's ill. I'll speak to the Director," Daddy said, getting up. He was going to lie.

"They won't accept it. She *has* to choose today."

"We'll work this out privately."

Mother and I watched him walk away, catch the eye of the Director and move to the side of the room. The Director nodded, adjusted his tie and followed him immediately. They put their heads close together to talk.

Mother leaned closer, her hair touching my cheek. "Jemma, stop this. Women do what they must to survive."

I closed my eyes. She had said something like that before. We do what we must. We endure.

"Then I must choose to not choose," I said.

"Do that and you won't survive to your sixteenth birth-day, at least not intact." She turned so she was facing me directly. She didn't raise her voice. "We can't change the system. You choose; you change sex; you're altered; you're deleted; or you go to rehab, where they will break your will and assign you to something. You'll come out years later, if they don't delete you for a petty offense, with the same choices you have today, but you won't be the same person. You're smart — figure it out."

Across the room, Daddy argued with the Director. He had a fierce look on his face and shook his head vehe-mently; the Director was as placid as a mud pond. He kept opening his mouth and then closing it, unable or unwilling to interrupt Daddy. His coat sleeves were too short and a bony wrist showed when he held up his hands to stop my father's words.

They disappeared through a door, and a few moments later an usher came to take us there. We followed him into a private room as spare as a jail cell.

Daddy's face was so strange and twisted that I thought he might cry. He couldn't bear to look at me. Mother went to him, slipping her arm through his.

"Roger? What's wrong?" He shook his head and turned away from her.

The Director stared at me, then he smiled a sickly kind of smile.

"Jemma7729, sit down. Madame, will you sit?" He held a chair for my mother. "I'm sorry. We already had a flag on your daughter's dossier. There are notes about a dis-cipline problem — going back to when she was five, in fact — and a directive that, should there be any trouble at all today, she was to go to rehab or be altered."

Daddy stepped near my chair. "She's not a problem, Director. Just... intelligent and... spirited."

The Director gave my father a stony look. "Spirited? She's aggressive! There's nothing I can do. Which is it to be?"

"I'll go to rehab," I said, sitting as straight as I could and trying to look ladylike.

The Director wheeled around and pointed at me, his wrist bone showing again. He had long fingernails. "My point exactly! *I was not talking to you, Jemma7729.* The choice is out of your hands. You're wrong to express an opinion."

"It's *my* life!" There it was again! The feeling that rises up in me burning like flame — this was not fair, not fair to any of us.

Mother stood up and went to Daddy. He slipped his arm around her waist.

"We'll choose rehab." His voice was pinched and cold and it shut me up.

Mother held my eyes in her own for a moment. Her lovely face was as blank as an alter's, except for the tension around her mouth. She left the room without a word.

The Director nodded. "I'll give you a few moments alone with your daughter, Regional Director, then, as is the custom, you must leave as well. Jemma7729 belongs to the State now."

My mouth fell open. The State? I belonged to the State? I looked at Daddy in panic as the Director walked out. I ran into his arms. "What did he mean?"

"I'm sorry, Jemma. I shouldn't have said anything. The moment I mentioned your name he said you were already suspect. There are two complaints of aggression in your file, Thom7726 and the wife next door. Plus other things. Stupid, silly things!"

"But, Daddy—"

"There's nothing I can do." His eyes were glistening. "This is my fault. I shouldn't have encouraged you, showed you..." He took a deep breath and clamped his mouth shut, his eyes darting around the corners of the room. Doubtless there was surveillance. "You must obey, Jemma. Be cooperative, friendly, smart, all the things you are. Play their game, don't give them any reason to hurt you. I'll try to get you out."

I held him so tightly I rumpled my suit. "I'm scared, Daddy. Will I see you again?"

"I hope so, darling." He laughed then, and I tried to smile. It was all phony. "Of course you will! We'll see you on your first visiting day at least." He looked scared, too, but he added, "If not before."

There was a knock on the door. We went back into the big room. Mother was gone, to the GAV, I guess. Daddy pressed my hand, whispered "I love you," and left.

An usher led me to a seat in the front row. One sallow-faced, overweight boy was sitting there. Everyone stared at me and I could hear the sound of whispering like a kind of white noise.

The boy and I had to sit through the entire ceremony, even the necessary class, and had to wait until everyone had left the building. No one was allowed to speak to us, nor could we talk to each other.

I was too numbed by guilt to be frightened. I sat in utter despair in my beautiful new gray suit until a man in a black uniform came to lead us to the fedcar that took us to Rehabilitation Facility 23.

# # #

"There it is, you two losers." The Fedguard driver stopped the car. "Take a look around — it's the last freedom you'll see for awhile."

He inched the vehicle forward, and I did, indeed, look around. We were in a run-down neighborhood, something I had never seen before. There was trash on the streets and men and women sitting together on the front steps of their houses. We hadn't gone through any tunnels, so we had to still be in L. A. The area reminded me of pictures I had seen from the race riots in 2059.

He didn't let us look long. The boy only glanced out the window then went back to looking at his fingers. His hands were dirty.

I leaned forward and the driver gave me a cold stare. "Where are we?"

He grinned. His teeth were crooked. Why hadn't he had them fixed? I'd seen that before in necessarys and wondered. It was a free service from AGNA. "Welcome to the rest of your life," he said as two Fedguards moved forward, one on each side of the car, to look in at us, ducking to peer in the windows. I tried to disappear into the back of my seat.

Rehab 23 had a twelve-foot-high wall around it made of plasticrete in the form of old-fashioned red bricks. Vines, some of them flowering, clung to the walls. There was a gated entrance, with iron doors, beyond which lay another wall, metal, and another gate, an invisible electronic one — just lasers, or something like it, across the roadway.

The Fedguards at these portals were armed. I didn't know anything about weaponry but the guns looked dangerous and formidable. All the guards wore black uniforms with a triangular shoulder patch on their tight jackets, and tall black boots. Rank was indicated by the slash marks on their jacket sleeves, I guessed, since not many soldiers had them.

The fat boy and I were driven to the front of the one-storey stucco admin building, the first structure of the maze of low, square buildings, most of them windowless, that were contained within the walls. The reception area looked inviting enough, with double glass doors under a small overhang, flowers in planters splashing color around the outside, and a lovely old acacia tree shading the flagstone steps to the entrance.

A Fedguard opened the car door and another one said something to our driver then motioned for us to follow. I wondered if I looked as scared as my companion did.

"Jemma7729 and Erol7734, come with me."

A guard opened the heavy glass door to the building but it looked dark inside. I stopped. He turned around to glare at me. I panicked and bolted.

"Hey! Stop! Stop her!"

Guards were shouting all around me. I don't know what I thought I could do — escape? Not likely. But I ran anyway, clomping and awkward in my unfamiliar heels, until a guard jumped in front of me and reached for my arm. I turned back but there was a guard there, too.

They laughed and made a big circle around me. No weapons were out, just big men with their arms extended at their sides. They moved in on me, and shooed me into the center of their circle as if I were a chicken. I felt I was about to be slaughtered.

I stopped trying. It was wasted effort and I couldn't breathe. I was cold. I wanted to go to sleep.

"That's better," one of the guards said in a soothing voice. "Come on now, Jemma7729."

Another guard took my arm and escorted me inside.

We walked down a short, wide hallway to a room at the end of it. It was a bright, pleasant place with overstuffed chairs and sofas, small round tables scattered about, a view of the patio, pictures on the walls of sunny landscapes, and half-dozen vidscreens. None of them were on.

"Wait here. No talking."

I perched on the edge of a sofa, feet touching the floor, as I'd been taught, catching my breath. That had been a silly thing to do — there was no escape and I knew it. I must play the game, as Daddy said.

Erol7734 settled in one of the overstuffed chairs and leaned back into it as if he needed to rest. I hoped, but didn't believe, that maybe rehab wasn't so bad. This room was nice, anyway.

Fifteen minutes later we were still waiting and Erol was grumpy. He heaved himself up, walked to the windows to look at the patio. "I'm hungry," he said. I didn't know if it was to me or to himself, but he looked at me and I shook my head and refused to answer.

"Nobody's listening.... That was stupid, to try to run away." He turned around to stare at me. "You're pretty."

His broad face was covered with sweat beads and he puffed as if he had been doing hard exercise. I shook my head at him again. Doubtless there were vids and mikes everywhere in the room. Didn't he know that?

His face had an unpleasant expression. He was a couple of years older than I. His greenish eyes were red-rimmed. From crying? From lack of sleep? His hair was either too fine or too dirty to do anything but clump and hang. He kept moving his fat lips and swallowing, as if he had too much saliva.

He swaggered across the room and stopped with his leg touching my knee. "Don't be stuck up! I saw you at the choosing. You may be stable class on the outside, but in here you're just a Bad Woman."

I tried to move away from him but he had me cornered. *Don't give them any reason to hurt you*, I thought, so I smiled at Erol, but didn't intend to talk, no matter what.

He moved closer and I slid sideways to get away from him. He smelled rank and hot and slightly sour.

"You afraid of me? Everyone else is." He smiled and I could see why he kept swallowing, he was missing teeth in the front.

He reached out to touch me but a hand came from nowhere and grabbed his arm and twisted it behind his back. Erol yelled in pain. Where had the Fedguard been? I hadn't seen him come in. I looked past him to see another guard standing in the doorway. They must have been watching us.

I jumped up and got out of their way. Of course, I was right. The whole place would be loaded with surveillance equipment, and probably other stuff as well — zappers or containment doors. We were, after all, bad. I kept my head, breathing slowly, trying to stay cool and poised the way Mother would have done. I wasn't going to make another mistake.

Erol7734 bawled loudly as the guard pushed him into a chair opposite me. "We said no talking! Now sit down and shut up. You've been here less than half an hour and you're already on report with a demerit."

Erol sniffed and sank back in the chair as the guard turned around to me. I met his eyes and tried to smile. I had done nothing wrong and I was playing the game.

"Come with me, Jemma7729."

I followed him through a door into an empty, long hallway that had dead white walls and ceilings, with blue floors and a darker blue stripe halfway up the wall. His boots clicked on the tile, my heels echoing his. We sounded loud in the barren space. The hallway was more like a tunnel — there were no doors on the sides until we got to the end. It was spooky, like being underground. I had the feeling I was being led to an abyss. The guard stopped at the end of the corridor, opened the door there, and nodded to me to enter.

I stepped across the threshold and stopped dead. I was on a small raised platform at the end of a narrow conference room, with bright lights shining on me. It took a moment for my eyes to adjust to the sudden brilliance.

One man in a black tunic and gray trousers was in the center of the platform, sitting in a high-backed chair. He looked to be old, in his fifties maybe, with dramatic silver streaks through black hair, piercing blue eyes, and a pencil-thin mustache above full lips. He was wearing shiny black boots that almost reached his knees.

I bobbed my head to him, as the obvious person in charge, and looked into the audience. Six Fedguards ringed the seats, leaning against the walls, two of them women and one of those with many slashes of gold on her sleeve. There were at least two dozen adults sitting with their attention fixed on me.

I couldn't see their faces clearly with the lights glaring in my eyes, but I got the feeling they were older, too. They were all men, except for the two female Fedguards. Some of them were in uniform, others wore casual clothes.

I was suffocating with fear — of them, of AGNA, of myself. I wanted desperately to go home, to choose, to be a woman who marries, to be out of there. I was afraid I would pee my pants. I remembered what Mother said about how to stay calm in crowds, relaxing my jaw, parting my lips slightly, breathing through my nose and letting it out through my mouth so it looked as if I were smiling slightly.

Black boots stood up. He was only slightly taller than me, even with the heels, but imposing nonetheless.

"This is Jemma7729, stable class," he said to the audience. "Don't let this good appearance fool you, people. She is aggressive and clever. Despite the fact that she has had every advantage," and he turned to me, his voice dripping with venom, "she has been a disciplinary problem since she was five years old."

He came to stand beside me. Tears stung behind my eyes. "She's a disgrace to her sex! *Two* incidents of hitting already." The audience responded with gasps and whispers, and the tension in the room went up a notch. I glanced at him then looked at my feet. He addressed the crowd again, "She wouldn't confirm her first choosing. She obviously feels she is superior to other girls of her class."

"No! I don't. It's just that — I want to do something else with my life."

The room suddenly crackled with tension. He turned his head slowly, like some sort of reptile. "And what would that be, Jemma7729?"

Trapped! "I — I don't know."

There was a brief silence, then he laughed and the audience did, too.

A whisper from beyond the lights made my skin crawl. "Delete her," said a voice at the edge of my hearing.

Out of the corner of my eye I could see heads nodding. Fedguards sat up straighter and others shifted in their seats, whispering to each other. I believed they were going to execute me on the spot. It was a nightmare and I couldn't wake up.

"Would you believe?" He tsk-tsked at the audience. "She just tried to escape." He looked at me coldly. "But — she's bright, and attractive, has good genes and, importantly, good connections. And, Jemma7729, you will cooperate? You do want us to help you, don't you?" He had assumed a benevolent tone as he appraised me again.

"Yes, sir." My voice squeaked.

"Good. That's the right attitude. I am the Director, and these are your teachers and mentors. We're all going to work hard to teach you how to behave, as a good citizen and as a female."

He gave a sharp nod to one of the Fedguards, a pretty redheaded alter, who came up on the platform, took my arm, and led me out of the room. At least I wasn't dead.

More passageways, different colored stripes in each corridor — yellow and red and gray and black; doors that clunked shut behind us. Obvious color coding, I realized, trying to focus on what I could see and feel to keep myself from screaming or scrambling away from my escort.

The gray stripe led us to a room where two other female guards waited behind a counter. Beyond them were shelves full of clothes in various hues. More color coding.

There was a minuscule curtained area in a corner where I was told to undress. The redhead watched. It was embarrassing, but the expression on her face never changed. I took off the gray suit and folded it lovingly before the guard snatched it away. I was sorry to part with it. Wearing that beautiful suit, for one brief moment, had made me feel pretty for the first time, and nearly the last, in my life. But I had no further use for it. By the time I could wear civilian clothes again, if that ever happened, I would have outgrown it.

The guard led me across the room and I showered. That, at least, relaxed some of the tension that pressed like a hot band around my heart.

I stood naked, trying not to shiver, to look indifferent, while another female guard got my new clothes: two sets of underwear and socks, two red jumpsuits, a pair of clogs. I put on one set while they watched.

"We'll take the ring, too," the redhead said.

"But — my father gave it to me. I want to keep it." She just stood holding her hand out. "Please, it may be the last thing I'll ever have from..." I started to cry. "I mean, it's really really important to me."

It wasn't fair. I needed *something* to keep me sane, remind me that I was Jemma, that I didn't belong to the State. But they were unmoved and unmovable. The redhead grabbed my hand and twisted the ring off.

The tall guard behind the counter said, "You've just earned one demerit, Jemma7729. Arguing about the rules is open defiance."

I pleaded with her. "I won't wear it. I'll just keep it." She shook her head. "Will I get it back?"

They were silent for a moment and then the redhead smiled that empty smile that alters have. She handed the ring to the tall woman. "Of course you will."

But I knew the ring was lost forever. I wiped away my tears and watched as it was put in an envelope and marked with my name.

"Follow me, Jemma7729." The redhead led me from gray to blue. To keep my sanity, I tried to memorize the colors and guess what they meant. Gray was supplies. I had started at blue, so it must be admin.

The alter walked beside me. "I'm taking you to the Major, your mentor and our commander. She'll explain the rules." She knocked on a door, and I was ushered into the presence of the Major.

I had seen her before, of course. She was the Fedguard with all the gold on her sleeve at my presentation. She was in her forties, busty and tightly packed, with broad features and curly gray hair, a flat nose and beautiful brown eyes. She was business-like, neither cold nor friendly.

I noticed her eyes because she had a kind of amused expression as I sat down in front of her desk. I frowned. She wasn't an alter. But that couldn't be — altering was mandatory after the twenty-fifth birthday for Fedguards. Before I could stop myself, my mouth was open and I was about to ask.

"Don't question, Jemma7729. It will get you into trouble." Definitely not an alter. Her eyes got as icy as ever my mother's could and she leaned back in her chair.

Play the game, I remembered, so I ducked my head and looked at my knees. "Yes, ma'am."

"Here are the rules. You will do what you're told to do, *everything* you're told to do. You will not question; you will not complain. Is that understood?"

"Yes, ma'am."

"We try to be fair. We work on a system of demerits. Defiance, lack of cooperation, grumbling, shoddy work, inappropriateness — all of those will get you demerits. If you accumulate ten demerits, punishment will follow. And for you, especially, *any* sign of aggression will be dealt with immediately and severely. If you so much as frown at anyone. If you make too much noise when you walk. Anything. Understood?"

I stared at her, at the pleasant face and full, red lips saying these things to me. She was like a snake, hypnotizing me.

"Understood?"

I shook off my stupor. "Sorry. Yes, ma'am."

"Pay attention, Jemma7729!"

"I'm sorry, I—"

"Speaking without permission will get you a demerit. I'll overlook the one you just did."

"Thank you, ma'am."

"And *that* one." She chuckled and sucked her teeth. "You'll learn. Speaking without permission means anything and everything you say. Be smart. Keep your mouth shut."

My impulse was to agree, of course, but I didn't.

"Good, you learn quickly. You'll report to me every morning, after you've done your work." She glanced at the comp unit on her desk and scrolled on it, and I realized it was my dossier glowing on the screen. "You're scheduled for a series of assessments. And you will be cleaning the hallways in your building. A guard will show you, if you don't know how to do manual labor." She looked across the expanse of desk and smiled. "Sometimes you stable girls have your head up your ass."

My mouth dropped open and I sat up straighter, shocked. She laughed and punched a button on her desk. The redhead opened the door and held it open for me. I started to rise and thought better of it, waited for her.

"You're excused, Jemma7729." She had a nasty smirk.

# # #

I was assigned a windowless room painted dark red that was fifteen steps by fifteen and hot, with a three-inch mattress on the floor and one hook on the wall. There wasn't any other furniture. Not that it mattered — I didn't have any things to store.

The next two weeks were terrible. Every day I was tested and re-tested on everything from my virginity to AGNA history to physical skills and stamina to my psychological well-being, which they found wanting, although I answered nearly every question honestly. They seemed to believe me more when I lied.

Having only one change of clothes meant that I had to wash whatever I wore every night in order to stay clean. They wouldn't give me a teeth cleaner, so I had to scrub everything with my one towel, and then wash that, too. At least my basic wardrobe dried quickly in my hot room.

Besides all the testing and interviews, I mopped and scoured the hallways of the wing of my building every morning. I actually welcomed that work. It was mindless, but at least I accomplished something. The downside was that I used up both jumpsuits every day.

On the fifteenth day, after I had mopped and taken my morning shower in a bath the size of a closet, I changed into my clean red togs and reported, as usual, to the Major's office.

I rapped on the door and waited to be admitted. She looked up from her desk when I came in and lifted her chin, inviting me to sit. She finished reading a window on her comp unit, put it down, and leaned back in her chair.

"Well, Jemma7729, so far so good. One demerit after two weeks. And that one," she glanced at the unit again, "I think was understandable. You see now that you wouldn't want to wear jewelry here, right?" She tilted her head and stuck out her bottom lip, which I took as a signal to answer.

"No, ma'am. I mean, yes, I see."

"You're assigned to cleaning the hallway of your building. Is that right?"

"Yes, ma'am."

"The first round of your testing is done for the moment. I have your new assignments here. I guess you won't mind cleaning the toilets and washing dishes, helping in the kitchen."

"No, ma'am."

Her eyes narrowed as she looked at me. "Yes, ma'am. No, ma'am. So polite, so cooperative. What sets you off?"

"I don't know what you mean, ma'am."

She chuckled. "Oh, yes, you do. Never mind, we'll find it."

She was right. I did know what she meant. They wanted me to misbehave. Not me — I'd promised.

She picked up a red plastic chip — a building pass — and held it out to me. "Report to P-17. Their toilets have a problem."

I'd been there before. That was where the physical training took place. I took the chip. I had a question but had learned to be careful about asking anything. When I hesitated, she asked me, pulling on her earlobe.

"Something else, Jemma7729?"

"May I ask a question, Major?"

"Yes."

"Will I be taking academic classes?"

She thought about it. "Yes, eventually." I didn't mean to, but I must have made a face or blinked or something because she folded her hands in front of her and her eyes bored into mine. "You have no right to them, after what you've done. They'll be a gift, if you're a good girl. Get out of here."

I was always glad to leave her presence. Classes were a gift? Rehab obviously was not to teach me to take my place in society, it was to break my spirit and my will so that I would do whatever they wanted me to do. Mother was right, it would alter me.

That day was the first time I thought about escaping.

# # #

I spent six months living in that airless dark box, cleaning toilets, mopping floors, serving dinners, washing dishes. They reversed my class and had me doing everything the necessary people do.

Companionship was not allowed me. I ate alone and slept alone and sat alone in the dark. In all those months I never saw a vid or heard music, unless the sound came from a room somewhere near where I worked. I missed music. I missed reading.

I lost weight and believed I had grown an inch, though that's probably not possible. Only once during that time did I see myself in a mirror and I was appalled. They wouldn't let me cut my hair and it had become a shapeless mop. I was ghostly pale because I wasn't allowed outside, and my face looked small from the shed pounds and the abundant hair. I felt ugly.

I pretended to be a bit sullen, but not so much that they could give me a demerit for lack of cooperation. I didn't want them to know I didn't mind the chores. I was afraid they would find something worse. Actually, the physical labor was good for me. I'd never thought about how hard the servers had to work, the long hours it took to get and keep things clean. That experience toughened my hands and softened my heart.

I thought a great deal about the Bad Women. If I had identified with them before, isolated in my comfortable bedroom, now I felt I was their kin. A kind of madness made me think I could commune with their spirits. They must have been as lonely and as discouraged as I became when the days rolled into months and only my supervisors and the guards talked to me, and then only to give orders or insult me.

I questioned everything, sitting in the dark, dreaming of the stars. Why did the Bad Women think protest was good? In the Countryside with my father, I had realized that not everything AGNA said was true. Then perhaps the Bad Women were not so bad, after all.

After six months, I had only four demerits. They were for petty things and one of them was an accident. I was playing their game in top form. They were disappointed. And tightened the screws.

Two days before my six month anniversary, the Director himself sent for me and I was ushered into his inner sanctum — a huge, lavishly decorated office, lush with maroon velvet curtains and glowing mahogany furniture. It was exotic and seemed incongruous for the dapper little man. He sat behind an acre of desk, and I guessed his chair was elevated because he seemed taller sitting there.

"Jemma7729, sit down, please." I sat in an upholstered straight chair in front of the desk. He had my dossier and was scrolling through it. He looked up at me and smiled. "Four demerits in six months. You've been a reasonably good girl.

"The first one we dismiss. You didn't know the rules that first day, and we're inclined to overlook it." He glanced up and I properly smiled my gratitude. "The others..." and he played with his bottom lip as he studied the screen.

"Two demerits are for speaking without permission. The most serious offense appears to be that you threw water on a boy's shoes. Would you care to explain that?"

"It was an accident. I had just dumped water on the hallway floor to clean it and the boy came out of a room before I could warn him."

"Hmmm. Well. Accidents happen." He closed the file. "Your anniversary is coming up. Your first visiting day. Have your parents been notified?"

My mouth dropped open and I stared at him with disbelief and horror. I was supposed to notify them? How the hell could I? It was cruel of them to expect such a thing. I wasn't allowed near a comm unit. I bit my lip. "I don't know, sir. How *would* I know?"

His eyes narrowed. "You would do well to learn to suppress your emotions, Jemma7729! I want never to hear that tone in your voice again. Well, doubtless your father is aware of the date." He leaned forward, resting his chin on his hand. A flash of gold band caught the light.

I couldn't stop myself. I took a big breath and held it. My ring was on his little finger!

He tilted his head back, still smiling. "Yes? Something wrong?"

I shook my head, not trusting myself to speak. He had my gold ring, with the vines twining, that Daddy had put on my finger the last time I saw him. The sonofabitch! He stole it! Could they do that? Just take everything that's mine?

"Speak up, Jemma7729! And wipe that nasty look off your face!"

"That's my ring!" I half rose out of my chair. His expression changed and his lips twisted into a smile.

"This ring?" And he held his hand out to me, taunting. "I don't think so. This is *my* ring. Are you accusing me of stealing?"

"That's the ring my daddy gave me. It's mine. You have no right to it."

He smirked. "Your *daddy*, little girl?" He stood up. He must have had a platform behind his desk, too. That struck me as pitiful. "Daddy's spoiled rich girl."

"I'm not rich—" But it was too late. I looked into his sneering face and saw envy and malice. He was what none of us were supposed to be — jealous — of my class, of what I was, of my father, probably. How could he be envious of me, standing there in my ragged jumpsuit? I saw the trap yawning before me but couldn't make myself stop trembling with anger.

He sat back down and folded his hands on the desk. "This time you've crossed the line, Jemma7729. We've tried to give you leeway, to be kind, because of your background and your *daddy's* importance, but — accusing me of stealing, shouting at me, debating me without invitation..."

He touched a button on the top of his desk.

I swallowed the spit that wanted to fly at him, swallowed my pride, too, and sat back down. "No, sir. I'm sorry. I must be mistaken." *Play the game, play the game, play the game, you sadistic bastard.* I want my ring.

I attempted to avoid watching his hands, but he fluttered them around. I stared at the edge of his desk. He went back to my dossier.

There was a sharp rap on the door then two Fedguards entered, one of them the Major.

"Ahh, Major. I'm so sorry to take you away from your duties, but Jemma7729 has caused trouble, I'm afraid. Can you imagine? She has accused me of stealing this ring."

I couldn't sit still and listen to their lies. I jumped up. "It isn't fair! They said I'd get it back." Tears of frustration started in my eyes.

The Major sighed loudly, her face a study in mock horror. Her eyes were twinkling. She whirled around to me, putting on a mask of anger. "Sit down, Jemma7729! Your tears are wasted. You're a wicked, violent girl!"

They disgusted me. All the play-acting was ridiculous and insulting. A punishment was coming, so I decided it might as well be for something real.

"That *is* my ring! You're both liars! It's you who have committed a punishable offense under the AGNA Constitution!"

The Major smacked me on the side of my head so hard that it sent me reeling against the desk and made my ears ring. The male guard twisted my arms behind my back and hustled me out of the room, where another guard joined us.

They forced me down the hall and into an open courtyard, headed for another building. I could hear the Director and the Major laughing before the door slammed shut on them.

# # #

The building was stucco painted black. The inside was black, as well — everything, floor, ceiling, doors, doorknobs. *Symbolic of death and destruction*, I thought, as they shoved me down a narrow, hot passageway and into a small black room.

The guards were young and handsome, but their hands hurt me and their fingernails scratched when they stripped my clothes off. They managed to touch me all over, even though I squirmed and fought them.

They laughed and made jokes about how I "wasn't much to look at" and that I was no good because I "only had peach fuzz" and one of them twisted a nipple on my flat chest until I cried. They said they would report me and I'd get a demerit for fighting them. I didn't care. I was scared and humiliated and my head ached.

I wept out of pain and humiliation. But it was wasted effort. It only seemed to encourage them and make me feel rotten.

When I was naked and they were tired of their touchy-feely game, they shoved me into an upright black box, like a coffin, against the wall, slammed it shut and locked it. I heard them leave and close and lock the door to the room.

I couldn't move. The box seemed to have been designed specifically for my body, since it fit me so closely, except there was just enough tantalizing space that I thought I might be able to relax. When I did, I felt suffocated, my body crumpling into itself. I had to stand upright to breathe properly.

I endured it. I tried to imagine my bedroom in Santa Monica. I hummed songs. I remembered that Mother had said she wanted me to survive. I went over the scene in the Director's office a thousand times. Of course he had set me up. They had stolen my ring, lied, conspired, and I had fallen right into their trap.

The big puzzle was how the Major could be so old and not be an alter. I had been thinking about that ever since my first interview with her. The inescapable conclusion was that the categories in choosing were a lie, too, like the other lies about the moon and the stars. But why? How did she get away with it? Was it possible that there were gaps in what AGNA *could* know?

To make matters worse, the night I spent in the coffin I got my first menses. I wept some more, for myself and all the girls of the world. Mother had told me about it, had said I should not be ashamed, that it was a rite of passage and that after it happened, I would be a woman. She had told me we would celebrate.

I didn't feel like a woman. I felt like a baby, hot and stinking and aching. I could feel the blood trickling down the inside of my thigh, sticky, red blood. I squirmed and reached for it and dared to taste the bitter wound. I cried and wanted my mother.

I finally slept, and when I woke up I felt... different. I was no longer a child, I told myself. I knew absolutely that I was a rebel like my dead heroines. There were no more children's games for me to play, and it was time to engage in the biggest game of all. I would not accept AGNA's plans for my life. And I would endure.

For the first time, my confusion lifted and I saw the way AGNA treated women as wrong. The government had no right to dictate what we thought and did. If there had been evils done by women, that was long, long ago. This was now. Things had to change.

Why didn't women object? I wondered. *Fight back?* But then, how could we? Fight what? Complain to whom?

Make what choices that would change our lives? No, there didn't seem to be a way. But I knew in my heart there was something else. I had seen the stars; I had swum in a mountain stream and it hadn't killed me. Daddy had corrupted me utterly by making me feel intelligent and important. Mother, in her own way, had contributed to my rebellion by telling me the strength to survive was inside myself.

I no longer believed that AGNA was infallible. I would bide my time, take whatever came, and get the hell out of that place. It was clear there was no real alternative for me. Escape. Be altered. Or be dead.

They left me in the box overnight. In the morning, guards came with a new red jumpsuit and watched me put it on, smirking and holding their noses and making cracks, and occasionally a feint at me, as if they would grab me. They saw the blood. They said now I was a "stupid woman who dirties her panties every month." I didn't listen; I knew I was more than that.

I stumbled back to the other building. My legs wouldn't stop shaking, and I was uncomfortably dirty. I had sweated and peed on myself. Nonetheless, we marched back into the admin building.

I reported to the Major and told her about my coming of age. She clucked and frowned but did arrange for equipment.

The Major said, "You've had a taste of discipline now, Jemma7729. Believe me when I say that what happened to you was mild. Given the nature of your crime, I think the Director showed considerable restraint.

"Tomorrow is your six month anniversary. The Director has graciously decided to allow you to attend the visitor's day, even though you have gained his displeasure. You have tomorrow free. And then, because it's your time of the month, you will stay in your room until you're no longer unclean."

Unclean? That wasn't right. That was another lie, to humiliate me. I tried to remember what one tutoress had said about menses, but I hadn't been paying attention.

I went back to my own dark box, at last with something to look forward to. Six months. My anniversary. I had survived six months. I was proud of myself.

#

The next day I sat for six hours in the reception hall waiting for Mother and Daddy. At two in the afternoon, a Fedguard came with a message from the Director that my parents were busy and could not be reached. He was sorry. Perhaps they would make it to my next sixth month anniversary.

#

Without blinking an eye, without explanation, they changed my routine. I was allowed to interact with other 'habs, as we called ourselves, of both sexes, but primarily with the boys, hoping, I think, that their teasing would anger me. Daddy's importance had to be protecting me. They couldn't just kill me or alter me without a very good reason.

They issued nice clothes — skirts and tunics, blouses, all striped blue and white, a not unbecoming uniform. I got comfortable shoes. I no longer worked at the cleaning and serving. I moved into a spacious, well-appointed room with roommates — sometimes two, sometimes three, and one or more of them was probably a spy, always asking me what I was thinking. None of them stayed longer than a month, and I didn't make friends with any of them.

I asked for a hair cut and they shaved my head. I was ridiculed, of course, but that was easy to endure. I felt cleaner and, strange as it may seem, prettier.

My eleventh birthday passed without notice.

I spent another night in the coffin for asking when I would get another choosing day.

I took a class in biology, where I learned that the female is inferior to the male throughout nature, with many vids and charts and persuasive data to prove the point.

I took a seminar in women's history, the only woman in a class of rowdy boys. They teased me, saying things like, "See that stupid rebel? She looks just like Jemma7729," telling me that females like me had caused the deaths of millions and had stopped the progress of science. "We would have colonies on the moon now," Teacher said, "if the women had not rebelled and set back all technology, destroyed the laboratories and research facilities." The males gave me a hard time. The class gave me pause.

We saw a lot of vids in this class. Hours of warfare and public unrest. Men and women dying in the streets; awesome fire-fights on open terrain and in woodlands and deserts; wholesale devastation of the Countryside; explosions and bombs; cities and towns crumbling; GAV fights; sometimes hand-to-hand combat between men and women. The women were impressive warriors, but they always died horribly.

Teacher explained, and his voice was actually sad, that sometime in the twentieth century, women had begun to study martial arts, something totally inappropriate to the female. It was thought that diet also had something to do with their aggression, but most of the primary research had been destroyed in the wars, so we would never know the cause.

He said, and he got a fierce look on his face, "Back then, many women were raped and abused. It is thought perhaps some of them took up karate and other martial arts to protect themselves. Of course, that can't happen now," and he looked straight at me and raised one eyebrow, "because antisocial people are altered or deleted for the good of society."

Mostly, though, we studied the wars. My group really liked that; I did, too, but pretended not to. We used a big map — North America spread out on a table, in relief. Teacher showed us a holo map of what North America looked like before the wars, for comparison. There had been thousands of small towns and villages, cities along all the waterways, megacities on the coasts. Teacher swept his hand across the interior of the country. "All wasteland now," he said. He was standing right beside me and he put his hand on my shoulder. "Women did this."

The faces of the rebels came to haunt my dreams. They were full of fury and fear. The boys kept saying how ugly they were. The pictures were ugly, yes, but I was fascinated.

Sometimes one face would pop out from the crowd — a pretty woman without fear or death on her face, but determination, strength. One old woman's face etched itself in my memory. She was smiling as a Fedguard raised his gun over her, about to shoot or club her. Her expression was inexplicably sweet. She wasn't afraid to die. How could that be?

There were pictures of women who still lived in the scattered settlements in the Countryside, too, and they nearly made me sick. I had thought the stories were fairy tales. We saw vids and photos of feral women with deformed limbs, out-sized heads, misshapen bodies — the heritage of the Bad Women who had stayed in the Countryside when the domes and tunnels were built. There were sickly children, too, or kids with noses missing, or with only one eye. Generations of mutants, and more recent females showing the degenerative effects of living in the open air, beyond the protection of the cities. We were told these women were primitive, barbaric, dangerous.

I wondered if Daddy had lied to me about the Countryside. It hadn't made me sick, of course, but we were only there overnight.

We learned, too, about a group of outlaws who called themselves the Movers. They continued to defy AGNA, but had mostly been eradicated. The Movers were, Teacher said, small bands of feral women, effeminate men, malcontent minorities and the offspring of escaped criminals. We saw a vid of a Mover, a young man, being executed for rebellion. It was awful.

Teacher made an example of me to the boys, to illustrate what happens when women defy authority. While I sat squirming in my chair, he told them about my various crimes and punishments, including being isolated in my bedroom. Aha! So Poop had been a spy. Probably all of the

other tutors were, too. All of those silly childish misdemeanors must be in my dossier. And Poop must have
mentioned that I didn't like being confined. Now I knew
why the coffin was their torture-of-choice for me. I sent
a curse to Poop that she lose control of her bowels.

Adults don't figure it out. Teacher was wrong in what
he did, at least from AGNA's point of view. When the boys
learned that I had been whipped when I was seven, and
added to that my overnights in the coffin and the other
discomforts, some of them regarded me with envy and
admiration, the sort of strange respect I had earned in my
quad. Those who felt this way actually helped me, talked
to me after class, joked with me.

Laughing was the best. I loved Kurt7745 for his silly
sense of humor. Life in rehab was so grim and tedious, he
was a bright star in my darkness.

I was in the coffin for three days for stupidly arguing
with a stupid boy about the fact that female hawks are
larger than male hawks. I hadn't actually *said* that the
females were stronger, but he inferred it and so did everyone else. Kurt, at least, thought about it afterwards and
told me privately he thought I was right, because females
had so much to overcome, they needed to be strong.

I don't know what Erol the Fat Boy's problems were.
He was brilliant at something called anti-compression
theory, which presumably would one day mean we, or as
they put it — Man — would be able to create and manipu-
late atmospheres in a big way. Not just under domes, but
in general, to put colonies of people on the moon with an
atmospheric cloud, that sort of thing.

They stuck me in an advanced theories class with the
likes of Erol, even though I didn't belong there and couldn't
follow it half the time, proving, of course, that women were
unsuited to theoretical studies. When the topic of the moon
came up I acted dumb and wanted to see a vid of it. Teacher
threw me out of class for the day for asking an inappropriate question.

There was a patio where I liked to read. Except for one
gap in the greenery, it was totally enclosed by a thick wall
of spiky bushes. Most people didn't like it because the

plants were sharp and raised a stinging welt if you brushed
them. That meant that this poison place provided the most
privacy one could have at Rehab 23.

After the moon question, I went there. Erol tracked me
down and made a pass, which I properly rejected. Both
actions were allowed and considered normal, so long as
I did not respond in an aggressive way. He was quite
disgusting, really, with his slobber and his red-rimmed eyes.

"C'mon, Erol. Leave me alone. I'm not interested." I tried
to push past him, but he grabbed my arm.

"Jem-ma. Jem-ma. Just give me a little. Nobody's watching."

"Somebody is *always* watching. Haven't you got that
through your thick skull yet?"

He took a swipe at me, which missed. "Don't insult me!
I'll beat you up and then report you. You'll be in the coffin
for a week."

"Buzz off!" I moved towards the exit and he threw his
big stinky arms around me and we fell on the flagstones.
He weighed almost double what I did. The stench of him
was overwhelming. I brought my knee up in his crotch and
he howled and I was able to roll away from him.

I started for the gap again but he grabbed my ankle.
Really, there was nothing else to do. He was on his knees
in front of me, slobbering, and I made a fist and slammed
it into his nose.

He screamed. Blood flew. Fedguards rushed at us and
I was taken off in cuffs. Erol went the other way, leaning
on a guard's arm.

The Director made an example of me. An assembly of
teachers and Fedguards and my fellow 'habs was quickly
called in the big courtyard with a platform in the center,
where the public humiliations were performed.

The guards led me up on the stage, off to the side. Maybe
this was it. Maybe now they would alter or delete me. I
stood with a sorrowful heart. I didn't want to die, and either
way would be a death.

The Director and the Major were at the foot of the steps,
conferring with a Fedguard and looking at a small comp
unit. Running the vids of what had just happened, I

assumed. The Director nodded and came up on the platform, feigning his usual air of deep concern.

"Sadly, sadly," he began, with a catch in his voice, "we are here to once again chastise Jemma7729 for inappropriate behavior and female aggression. She has struck and injured Erol7734. He is being treated at the infirmary. This woman," and he turned and pointed a finger at me, "led Erol on, promising sexual favors if he would help her in her theories class."

I was so dumbfounded my mouth dropped open and then I laughed out loud. I knew instantly that was a mistake and caught my breath. But it was just too much of a fabrication. Most of the people in the audience bowed their heads or looked at their shoes or the sky. There were snickers, quickly stifled. The Director was unperturbed; he could lie without recrimination.

"You may laugh, Jemma7729, but it is a classic example of the way women prey on men. When he came to collect what was due him, you hit him."

"Due him? He was going to rape me!" I spoke quickly and flinched, expecting a blow from somewhere, but none came.

The Director's eyes widened in innocent disbelief. He looked to his audience for confirmation, agreement. "Rape you? Do you believe Erol7734 is capable of that?"

"Probably not. But he was going to try." Then I did get a cuff on the head. I understood. They weren't going to alter or delete me, they were having too much fun.

"That's enough! Hold your tongue, Jemma7729."

"I'm telling the truth! I should be allowed to defend myself. He grabbed me—"

The Director gestured to the two Fedguards who held me between them. They brought me to him, undid the cuffs, and pushed me to my knees. He turned to an associate standing at the edge of the crowd, held out his hand and was handed a shiny metal rod. He showed it to us all, lastly to me. When it was poking in my face, he flicked a button and within seconds it glowed white-hot.

The guards pulled up my left sleeve and held me. The Director burned a hash mark across my forearm just below the elbow. I was now a "marked woman," to warn men for the rest of my life, he said. It hurt so terrifically that I saw nothing but reddish-blackness for a couple of seconds. I screamed. Then I vomited. But I did not cry, did not acknowledge his authority over me. I think Daddy would have approved.

Chapter 4

My second six month anniversary came and went and Daddy and Mother did not come. I only waited an hour this time, then asked if I could go to the library.

I believed that a lie had been told to my parents about me. For all I knew, they thought I had been altered or deleted. It was possible, however, that they had abandoned me to protect themselves. Mother was still young enough to have another child.

My time in the library was well spent. I had an assignment to memorize the famous Executive Order of 2150, the "Proclamation for the Protection of Women" by President McColl — they were still cramming history down my throat — the one where he says, "Through education and counseling, women will come to realize that the cities provide their only safety, and that the regulations which appear to be restrictive are, in fact, for their own well-being. With this executive order I speak for all mankind. Women are precious and must be protected, even from themselves."

I got into the AGNA archives easily, but entered a link number wrong, couldn't correct it, and started bouncing all over the rehab files. I spent half an hour trying to figure it out, tried to find someone to help me but couldn't, and struggled alone, attempting to get out of the program I'd blundered into.

Then there they were in front of me on the screen — the security codes for Rehab 23. My finger was already on the key to delete but I stopped printed instead.

That night I memorized the string of numbers and then ate the paper. It was a very tasty meal.

#

I didn't need to hurry. For one brief, foolish moment, I considered taking Kurt with me but decided against it. I knew my way around the facility from my servant days, knew which doors and corridors were the least used, and had a reasonable idea of where most people were during the evening.

One night in the library I hacked into the security file again and unlocked the door to the supply area. There was not much traffic there, even at the busiest of times, and none at night. I stole a pair of trousers and a boy's tunic and hid them in a closet I had used when I had been a necessary.

The next evening, after dinner and during my usual study time, I opened the electronic gate in the rear wall of rehab, where the hovertrucks came with provisions. To accommodate the over-sized vehicles, there was no second gate at that location. I changed clothes in the closet, glad that they made me wear my hair short enough to look like a boy.

I walked through the corridors unnoticed. I knew how to get in and out of the buildings with the least possible fuss. Cleaning people aren't supposed to be seen.

There was a sticky moment at the gate itself. Two Fedguards were on duty. The "gate" was invisible, of course, and there was no way for them to tell that it was unlocked unless they checked the keypad, and they were loitering far from it.

I stood in a doorway, flattened against it, watching them, near enough to the outside to taste it. My heart beat so loudly in my ears I was afraid they could hear it.

One of the guards got a call on his comm unit. He grinned and walked away, with the other guard teasing him and following. They weren't watching.

I exploded out of the doorway, bolted right through the gate, past their astonished faces, and kept on running. I heard shouts. Shots. Sirens. The whirr of a GAV firing up.

I ran down the entrance passageway toward a corner and whirled around it just as the wall beside me blew up.

They were shooting at me! I could hear pounding feet and ran faster, crouching now and making zigzags because everything around me kept exploding.

The sound of the GAV got louder and a volley of shots rang out, smashing into the steps of a building as I ran past it, shattering the stone and raining it down on me. The noise was horrible.

No matter. I sprinted into the seedy, unfamiliar neighborhood around the facility, ran until I couldn't breathe and staggered to a stop. All that hard physical work they had forced upon me had served me well. By the time I was out of breath I was a good five blocks from Rehab 23 and in a maze of alleys and old streets, many of them too narrow for a hovercar to enter.

I could still hear gunfire and explosions behind me and wondered what they were shooting at.

The lighting in this part of town was dim. Many of the street lamps were broken or at half power. I stopped for several minutes, desperately needing to catch my breath and empty my bladder, then I crouched in the shadow of a dilapidated building to get a sense of where I was. I could hear the patrols going by, but they were staying on the wider avenues. The sirens from rehab continued, and they were loud, waking up the world. Windows and doors opened as people came out, or looked out, of their houses. Clearly, I was not safe here.

For the first time, I considered where I should go, what I should do. All I had thought about was getting out; what came next had not been a part of my plan. I cursed myself that I had not checked a map. I had no idea where I was in the city. My impulse was to find the Santa Monica Sector, of course, but that would probably be the first place they'd look for me.

I needed to get off the streets, but first I wanted more distance from Rehab 23. Only then did it occur to me that although I was dressed as a boy, it was still a uniform. I'd have to find different clothing.

I had a panic attack, overwhelmed with what I'd done. If they caught me, I was sure to be altered at least, probably after they'd had their sadistic fun. My chances of success were slim. Every Fedguard in the city would be looking for me.

I moved carefully for the next several hours. It was night, and in this section of town there were few people on the street. GAVs and Fedguard patrols were still prowling, but I could hear them coming in the silence and hide long before they passed. Their brilliant search beacons swept across the buildings like fingers reaching out for me. I had to rest again. I was using up too much energy in anxiety.

I was thirsty. I hadn't thought about that, either. Food and drink. Where was I to find them? I had no credit card, no ID.

As the first pale light before dawn began to glow on the L.A. Dome, I was aware of two things: the direction of east, and that I was being followed.

# # #

"Are you lost, son?"

The man stepped from behind a broken sanitary disposal unit, indistinct in the faint light of a half-powered street lamp. Medium height, burly, abundant hair on his face and head. He looked shaggy, like a feral animal.

"Yes, sir." I had been sitting but I got up to face him, to run again.

"Running?"

I stared at him hard. I knew I couldn't trust anyone, but he didn't look like the spy type. AGNA likes its representatives cleaner. His eyebrows were so bushy and his beard was so full that he almost had no face to study. I took the high ground. "Yes, I've been running. I needed to rest."

He stepped nearer and I backed up a step. His voice was soft, husky, warm around the edges. "Don't run, boy. They have motion-detectors on those cars. They'll be looking for anything moving fast. Especially this time of night."

I hadn't thought of that. "Thank you." He didn't come any closer but he was examining me with his head tilted down, looking at me out of the tops of his eyes. It was vaguely menacing.

"Do you know where you are?" I shook my head. "This is the Santiago Sector. Where are you from?"

I hesitated, but what was the point of lying? Besides, I needed to know where I was in relation to something I knew. "Santa Monica."

"Mmmm. Well, you're south-southeast of that. I'd say go west if you intend to stay in the city. Along the water-front you'll find vacant warehouses, storage sheds. The water still works in some of them and the Fedguards don't go there much. That is," and he brought his head up and I think he smiled, "if you intend to stay in the city."

I started to back away. "Much obliged." I assumed he was telling the truth.

"Remember, don't run. And better get different clothes."

"Yes, I will."

"Good luck."

I turned and scurried around the corner, trying to keep a normal pace, still hugging the buildings. Why should he help me? He clearly knew I was a runaway. He was probably already looking for a Fedguard to report my whereabouts. I glanced at the rising concentration of light we called the sun and walked away from it, heading west, as the man had suggested, despite my suspicions of his motives. West was toward the ocean, and I could follow the shoreline instead of a jumble of streets.

I moved like a shadow along the crumbling buildings but no Fedguards came close to me. Maybe I was wrong about the hairy man. At least he had immediately assumed I was a boy. That was good. I suspected so much of what I had been taught, but I knew boys had more freedom than girls. A boy could be on the streets unaccompanied, for instance; could carry a private credit card; could talk to people.

What had he said? If I "intended to stay in the city." I stopped dead in my tracks. I hadn't even dreamed of it — the alternative place. A place under the real sky. I took a deep breath and let it out slowly, thinking of that, of the possibility of seeing the stars again. A woman's voice calling someone's name floated from the inside of a house and brought me back to reality. I moved on.

A couple of blocks further west I ducked into a doorway to avoid a man coming out of his building. Obviously, I was in a neighborhood used by the necessary people. It had never occurred to me to wonder where they lived. I thought with regret that I had never even asked Reesie about her home and what she thought of it.

It wasn't in the lessons, the vids, or the news, that there was a place like this — a poor place, a place where the streetlights didn't work and the garbage wasn't collected every day; where sidewalks were broken and there was a pervasive smell of rot and dirt. Another AGNA lie. Why hadn't I been told about this? And why was it here at all? Wasn't there enough of everything to go around?

I thought of my beautiful, spacious house in Santa Monica. I'd taken it for granted, not because I was a snob, but because I didn't know there was anything else.

In the next block, another worker emerged into the early dawn. It was a boy, older than me and slightly taller, but not yet grown. AGNA is right about one thing, I'm a Bad Woman in my heart. I went renegade immediately. I searched around and found a piece of metal, a chair-leg I think, tracked him, accosted him, and hit him on the head hard enough to knock him out. I checked to make sure he wasn't dead. I didn't mean to hurt him.

I dragged him into an alley and stripped him, with embarrassment and, I must admit, curiosity. He wasn't wearing underwear. I left him there, naked to the world, and fled westward until I found an empty building where I could change into his clothes. I stuffed the rehab uniform into a storm drain. Lucky for me, the boy had been wearing a cap. It shaded my eyes from the glare and completed the disguise.

I started my life of crime in the Santiago Sector of Los Angeles in February of the year 2194. I was eleven years old.

# # #

My plan was simple. I would stay alive by providing the first two of the big three necessary things in life— sustenance, shelter, and sex. Escape from the city would come later.

Shelter was easy. There were many abandoned buildings and vacant apartments. They were simple to spot
because they stood open and were empty to the bare
floors. Sometimes those were missing, too. I often saw
smoke and bonfires on the streets, so I think people
burned them.

Getting food was harder. I knew there were open-air
markets where produce from the Countryside was sold,
because my quad had been taken to one on a field trip,
and Daddy had talked about them. Wives went there to
shop. I figured I could at least steal fruit off the displays
if I could find a market. In the meantime I checked in
the alleys for garbage. It was distasteful, I punned to
myself, but necessary. I drank at public fountains and
filled a plastic container to carry water with me.

I wasn't interested in the sex part.

I avoided the parks, major intersections, and commu-
nication centers, where public vidscreens broadcast
AGNA Network programs. The first one I came upon
showed a picture of me — an old one when I had long
hair — and told the story of my escape, with considerable
embellishment. A reward was offered. In AGNA's version, I had killed two Fedguards and a young woman
necessary, destroyed part of the computer network, and
was armed and dangerous. The part about the killings
made me wince. The guards had doubtless been deleted
because they had let me escape. I felt bad about the
woman. She was probably the target of that gunfire I'd
heard far behind me when I escaped, and they killed her
because she was a woman on the street at night and might
have been me. Or maybe they just needed to shoot somebody.

It took a month for me to work my way through the
miles of L. A. cityscape. I mugged people, anyone who
looked vulnerable, stole and used their credit cards and
then ditched them before the Fedguard could track the
incident. I was a shameless thief. I changed clothes so
many times I stopped counting. My stolen carrybag grew
with an assemblage of stolen tools — fire-starter,

toxinchek strips, scissors so I could keep my hair short, extra socks, boots, an extra shirt, and a beautiful antique pocket knife I had found in a garbage heap. I was thinking Countryside and looking over my shoulder the whole time.

The reward for my capture was substantial and grew as I continued to elude the Fedguard. It started at 1,000 govcredits in March and was 5,000 gc's in early April. Obviously, they wanted me back badly. Their inability to find me was an embarrassment. I was delighted by the thought that the Director and the Major could lose their jobs, or worse. I hoped it was the "or worse".

I sat on a bench one late morning, thinking about lunch and watching the wives at the farmer's market. This one had a medieval theme, with turrets on the booths and sellers dressed in period costumes. The wives looked beautiful, and serene, even happy, as they gossiped and shopped and propelled their motorized carry-alls from stall to stall, buying fresh things for their husbands' dinners.

There was a big vid screen at the market, but it only showed pleasant things, topics AGNA assumed would interest a stay-at-home wife. There were cooking and fashion shows, comedy turns, gardening tips, heavily edited news, nothing that would disturb the women or interfere with their pleasurable shopping. There was an easygoing, even festive climate in the market. No vehicles were allowed inside the squares, which meant that I was fairly safe, except for the Fedguards who circled around the outside. They were easy to avoid and they didn't pay much attention to what went on inside.

The wives made me sad. Many were alters and those who weren't might as well have been. They were people in a bubble who had no connection with the reality I had experienced from the first moment of my escape. I wondered if they were really happy. I guessed some of them might be, thinking of what Reesie had said to me, that looking after a house like a wife would be heaven. I wondered what the hell happiness was and if I had any business trying to find it.

"Daydreaming?" The voice was right beside me. I literally jumped and turned quickly.

A young man had sat down on the bench beside me. He was deeply suntanned, blond, longish hair falling over his forehead, eyes a brilliant blue. He wore short beach clothes. He looked like a vid star. The expression on his face was questioning but pleasant. I laughed, not knowing what else to do.

"You've been sitting here for a long time, frowning, watching the wives."

"Have I? I'm just waiting for my mother."

He nodded and looked out over the busy square with its gaily decorated fake medieval motif. I stood up. I didn't want to talk.

He didn't raise his voice at all, but there was an urgency in it. "The Fedguards are going to do a sweep of this sector in an hour or so. You might want to be somewhere else."

My heart stopped and my knees turned to water. I sat back down on the bench with a thud. He didn't seem to notice, just kept talking and smiling in a nonchalant way, not looking at me.

"You're running out of time, and luck. You should get out of the city."

"I don't know what you're talking about. I'm waiting—"

"Forget that. I don't know your story, but I don't believe what AGNA tells us."

"Who are you?"

"That's not important. *You are*, Jemma. Go north and east now. It's the nearest way. There's a gate at Santa Clarita used by the farmers that connects directly with the Countryside. It's your best bet. If you need help when you're out, find the Movers."

He stood up and punched me gently on the shoulder, the way boys do. "Good luck. You've done well so far. Just be careful."

I watched him walk away. My brain felt like mush. He knew who I was and had said things to help me. A trick, maybe, but I didn't think so.

For the first time, I was meeting people who didn't accept the official statements and weren't dead and weren't running, the hairy man who helped me first, and now this surfer. *Aha!* I thought. They were *malcontents*. I suddenly understood my mother's job and it made me laugh out loud, then I was ashamed that she would do such a thing. And then I nearly cried because I missed her so much.

I went north. I found the farmer's gate on a Friday morning. That was easy. It was marked with signs. I observed for a while to see how it worked, sneaking close enough to hear, hanging around like the other boys I saw gathering in groups.

"What's going on?" The boy I asked was a handsome kid, a necessary by his clothes. Well, so was I at that moment.

"They need bean pickers outside. They're paying ten credits for a weekend's work. And they'll feed us." He smiled at me. He had nice eyes. "You looking for a job, too?"

"Yeah. Can anyone join?"

"I think they're desperate. Didn't you see the announcement on the vid?"

"Oh, yeah," said I, pulling my cap down lower.

The Fedguards were overwhelmed by the number of people, but two of them walked around, guns cradled in their arms, looking at the gaggle of boys. One looked right at me. I did what all the others did, just stood expressionless, my mouth hanging open and my hands stuffed in my pockets. In the end, they only checked the bosses' passes. Like the other kids, I jumped into the back of a hovertruck, and was chauffeured out of L. A. to freedom.

#

Out under the stars, all of my perceptions changed. I looked back at my life in L. A., and the lives of everyone I knew, including Mother and Daddy, and was filled with rage. Rage at the waste of my mother's intellect, at the arrogance that limited us with deceptive choices, at the cruelty of AGNA and all its officers for upholding a brutal system that was just *wrong*. In the Countryside, I didn't monitor myself for subjects forbidden to females.

There was plenty of time to think. Talking while we worked was forbidden, although a lot of jokes were passed around anyway and no one got into trouble. The fields were laid out in one-acre squares, with low wooden fences around them. Hal, the boy I was paired with, said it was to keep the animals out, but that didn't make sense to me. I figured they had some sort of monitoring on them.

Besides, what animals was he talking about? I'd learned at rehab how the animals were killed by the bad women for food and clothes. And AGNA admitted that some of their own biological weapons had destroyed a lot of wildlife. Not to mention the toxins that were supposedly still in the air and soil — those poisons that would kill women who ventured outside the domes.

But that couldn't be true. Lies. They made my stomach hurt.

After dinner, in the barn where we slept, the boys played cards and other games. There was a smuggled comp unit with porno that we all watched. I found it fascinating but couldn't think of any jokes like the others. I imitated Hal so they wouldn't get suspicious.

Hal and I had made a sort of bed of straw and put down the sleeping pouches they gave us. I was tired from the bean picking, and sleepy from the hot food, but Hal was excited and wanted to talk.

"Jimmie?" He rolled over to face me.

I stayed where I was. "Yeah?"

"Ever done this before?"

"No."

"It's fun! I like it. I think it would be good to be a farmer."

"It's hard."

He made a raspberry at me. "What's your dad do?"

My heart stopped. Not because I couldn't think of a lie — that was easy — but because I was suddenly cold with fear and loneliness.

"You have a dad, doncha?"

"Yeah. He's a lifter."

"Ah. Mine's a welder." He sniffed. "That's what they say I should do, but I'd like to be a farmer."

"So choose it."

"You think I could?"

"Why not?" Actually, I wasn't sure he could do that. I just assumed boys could do what they wanted.

Hal sighed. "Dad wants me to be like him."

"Yeah," and now I sighed, too, "so does mine."

That was true, in a way. Why else would he have shown me the stars? I had to bite my lip to keep from shouting out loud. He set me up! I saw it suddenly, so clearly. *That* was why he was so odd at the choosing day. I was what he had made me, and it wasn't fair. I loved him and he had betrayed me.

Hal was droning on about his dad and his quad and I wasn't listening because all I could think of was Daddy and how much I loved and missed him and what a shit he had made of my life. I was furious with him. And hurt.

Mother had often threatened to have me altered. I feared it, but I had never thought about the *idea* of altering. How could someone allow such a thing to happen, to themselves or anyone? It turned ordinary women into unthinking persons — baby-makers, things, or efficient and uncomplaining assistants. Alters did exactly as they were told. Altering took away all the bumpiness of life, reduced all textures to smooth, bypassed disappointments. Joys, too, I guess, although alters were even-tempered and seemed content. *They were benign zombies*, I thought, remembering research I had done on exotic female beliefs for my women's history class, thinking of the shoppers in the Medieval Mall.

Here in this dusty barn, I realized Mother was probably right. For me to be a good credit-carrying AGNA woman who marries, I should have been altered. She had made something of her choice. I could see that now. And for only the second time in my life, I thought she probably loved me.

I squeezed my eyes shut, not wanting the memory of Santa Monica and my mother's naked body, lithe and beautiful, diving into our pool.

"Doncha think?" Hal's voice saved me from tears.

"Yeah. I'm tired. Gotta sleep."

Hal sighed again and settled himself. "Right. More beans tomorrow! G'night, Jimmie."

# # #

I stayed with the bean pickers for the weekend, relishing the regular meals and the camaraderie of the boys. They were a good lot, easygoing, amusing, hard-working. I slaved as much as they did, joined the race for the most boxes picked, and no one questioned my gender.

Early in the morning of the third day, the day we were to go back to the city, before the sun was up I stole the sleeping pouch they had provided for me, and sneaked out of the barn where the boys continued snoring. No one was around. The big farmhouse where the Fedguards lived was still, the dark windows gaping like empty eye sockets.

I shouldered my pouch and walked up the road, away from the house and into the woods. Half an hour later I emerged from the trees at the edge of a rolling meadow. I froze to listen for sounds of pursuit, but there were none, so I set off into a sunrise that gilded the tops of the mesquite bushes, that made the shadows of rocks a purple blur.

I was free.

I had stashed hard rolls and cheese from our dinner the night before and filled my water bottle. These, added to my city equipment, completed my survival gear, and thus outfitted I began my life in the Countryside. I walked north and west, remembering that there were deserts and toxic dumps to the east of L.A.

I can skip the next three months except to say that it was damnably hard to make a living in the wild. I stoned fish, occasionally, when I could chase them into riffles in the streams. I roasted their battered bodies and ate them gratefully, recalling the beautiful fish Daddy and I had caught cleanly and eaten so long before. I ate berries and any fruit I could find, including one that made me sick once; I also preyed upon lizards, frogs, and pretty birds and their eggs. I sighed at yet another AGVA lie. Wildlife was abundant after all the years without people, and they were tolerant enough to be easy to catch once I was hungry enough to kill them.

The Countryside was more beautiful than I could have imagined and totally different from AGNA's propaganda. More lies upon lies. It was not a wasteland but a wild garden. Hot, cold, or wet, I didn't complain. The air was fresh and the water sweet. The sunsets were extravagant, reminding me of the colors in my crayon box. The animals that crossed my path were more curious than menacing. I slept under the moon or in makeshift shelters, sometimes staying a day or two in an especially pretty site. I was skinny and suntanned and stronger by the day.

Once in a while I saw people and avoided them. I didn't want to run into the barbarians, or the mutants, or the outlaws. Or the Fedguards, of course. Even though the surfer had said I should find the Movers if I needed help, I still had visions of the horrible vids from women's history and dismissed the idea.

I was lonely. It was a deep kind of gut loneliness. I couldn't think of anyone with whom I could share the breathtaking scenery and the moonrise. I tried not to think about that. I talked to myself, and sang, and thought.

# # #

One afternoon in late July, I was astonished when I stumbled into a real settlement. I had been on a kind of overgrown track for half a day because it was easier walking, thinking it was probably an old road from before the wars. It wasn't paved and didn't seem used, but was fairly easy to follow through the forest.

Up a hill and a hill and around a bend, the road suddenly widened and beyond it was a small, verdant valley with gently sloping sides, cleared to a tree line at the top. A hundred feet away from me was a wooden house and I could see a dozen other houses beside the road and arranged around an open space below me, like the village greens of colonial times in Old America. Smoke drifted up from chimneys, lazy in the still afternoon. The houses were tidy, each with a vegetable garden in the back. Some of them even encouraged flowers to grow along their fences. A smooth dirt road ran through it all, circled the square, and led off towards a meadow on the far side of town.

The sun dipped low on the horizon, burnishing the scene with a golden light. It was as lovely as a romantic painting of the hills of Tuscany I had once made an indifferent copy of for my art teacher. I paused on the California hill, warmed by the beauty of it.

Dogs barked from near and far and one big black dog came running straight at me. I stood stock-still and it slowed down and then sniffed at me, its tail wagging slowly like a flag.

"Stop where you are! Who are you?" A woman's voice. I couldn't see where she was.

My impulse was to bolt, but I didn't trust the dog. I heard myself speaking. "Hello. I'm a friend."

I set my carrybag down on the ground but within easy reach, in case I had to run for it, and searched the landscape. My heart was in my mouth. Was she going to be one of those mutants, with no nose or festering sores all over her body?

The woman stepped out from behind a shed attached to the nearest house. She was in her late twenties perhaps, a tallish woman, with dark hair pulled into a cascade down her back and tied with a bright red ribbon. Her face was long and narrow, with thin, high-arching eyebrows, like pictures I'd seen of the French aristocracy from olden times. She was pretty in a pinched sort of way, and she was certainly not deformed.

The dog sensed her tension and stopped wagging its tail but it didn't leave me. I smiled. It felt strange to be talking to a person after months of talking to myself.

"I found you by accident, following the old road. What is this place?"

"What are you doing here?" There was hostility in her voice. She came one step nearer, squinting, as if she needed her eyes fixed. I backed up a step, but the dog moved closer to me.

"I'm lost. I'm sorry." I didn't know why she was so unfriendly. I picked up my bag.

"Set the bag down and step away from it."

The deep voice came from behind me. I whirled around to confront a tall, redheaded man, in his forties. He had an axe in his hand. I did what he asked. The dog growled.

"Who are you?"

"Jimmie7795." I spoke quickly and swallowed my fear. "I'm sorry, I didn't mean to intrude."

The man sized me up then looked past me to the woman. "It's all right, Felice. It's just a boy. A runaway, I'd guess." He came nearer, the axe held loosely at his side. "All right, all right, Turnup. Back off." The dog backed away a step and began to wave his tail-flag again.

"Turnip?" I giggled, prompted partly by my tension.

The man smiled but his eyes were still coldly scrutinizing me. "That's what we named him, because no matter where we go, he turns up. Jimmie, you said? We don't use the numbers."

"Yes, sir."

"Running away?" I hesitated. And didn't meet his eyes. "That's not a crime up here, Jimmie. Where are you running away from?"

"Sacto." I didn't blink as I lied.

His eyebrows went up and the woman said "My, my," behind me. They seemed impressed. "You've been walking quite a while then."

"Yes. I'd be grateful if you'd tell me where I am."

He laughed, picked up my carrybag and tossed it to me, put an arm around my shoulder and we walked together towards his house.

"Felice — we'll have another plate for supper." The woman smiled at me finally and went into the house. The man kept his arm on me, which made me uncomfortable but I didn't know how to get away from him. "Come with me, Jimmie. I'll show you where you can wash up. I'd say you need to do that."

It was a pleasure to use a real bathroom, to get clean. I took a long, hot bath with the door locked. I slipped a piece of the pine-smelling soap into my carrybag for later. I changed into the cleaner of my two sets of clothes, then went into the kitchen where the woman was stirring a big pot of stew that filled the room with the tang of garlic. I hadn't had a real meal since the bean picking. She pointed at a chair and I sat with my mouth watering.

The kitchen was rustic and small and surprisingly well equipped. The stove she cooked on used wood, but I noticed a couple of gadgets that clearly ran on power of some kind — solar, maybe. She didn't talk to me, or look at me, just kept alternately stirring the pot and fixing a big green salad.

Without turning around, she said, "Why don't you go into the garden and bring in two tomatoes. There are still a few good ones at the end of the row."

"Yes, ma'am." I was happy to help. She handed me a bowl, I went out the back door and stopped on the porch. I could hear the whirr of a GAV. I couldn't see it, though. I stayed where I was, hoping I couldn't be spotted from the air. I hadn't seen any fedcars for the last week and had begun to think they didn't fly over this area. I didn't really think they were still looking for me — I hoped they thought I was dead — but the presence of the GAV made me uncomfortable. The noise stopped and I got the tomatoes.

At supper, the man told me I was in the Santa Lucia Mountains, south of San Francisco. He said there were a number of what he called frontier settlements in these hills. They didn't ask me any questions, and the man said I should spend the night at least. The thought of a real bed was tempting and I said yes, but from the moment we sat down at table I knew I was going to leave as soon as I could.

Felice was an alter. She sat opposite me at the table, friendly, sweetly smiling, but her eyes were flat, like those of my dead dolls. That meant they were lying when they said they had both lived in the settlement for two generations. I had never heard of frontier settlements, and my guess was that they belonged to AGNA.

But I cooperated, went to bed, and after the house was quiet, I explored quickly. One room was locked. I looked into it from outside, standing on a shaky bench, peering in a window. As I guessed, expected, and feared, there was surveillance equipment and comp units in it. A sophisticated set-up. I was sure the man had reported me, or would do so.

That night marked a step up in my adventures in crime.

I glided ghost-like through the pretty village, walking slowly in the shadows. One dog barked but when a man yelled at it, it shut up. On the outskirts, I found the large grassy field I had seen from the top of the hill, and sitting in the corner of it was an unmarked GAV.

The moon was high and nearly full, flooding the scene with blue light. The night thrummed with insect voices and a few night birds. Any other time I would have been reveling in it, would have flung myself down in the tall grass and watched the parade of dazzling lights across the sky. This night, I figured the brightness was a sign to me, a sort of gift or approbation. I needed to get out of there fast, and the Countryside was cooperating. I had the moon's blessing.

I climbed inside the GAV and examined the controls. It was exactly like the miniature one I'd had in Santa Monica, the one Daddy had given me for my eighth birthday. Ignition was made with a code on the keypad, and of course I didn't know the password. I laughed out loud when I saw I didn't have to. Someone had scratched ABCDE on the dashboard. Five digits, that had to be the key.

I stowed my carrybag behind the seat, took a deep breath, and punched in the letters. The GAV coughed, sputtered, caught, whirred, and started to move before I had a good grip on the T-bar. I grabbed it and accelerated, handling it just like my beloved mini. The controls were wobbly and overly responsive. I would have to be careful, and lucky.

I lifted skyward, tilting and yawing a bit, and laughed all the way into the deep blue night, above the trees, pointing the GAV's nose at a row of three bright stars flying ahead of the moon.

I was free again! And this time, I could go far and fast.

Chapter 5

I went fast, but not very far. I smashed that first stolen GAV into a hillside trying to land north of San Francisco. I crash-landed two more over the next six months before I had the hang of it. GAV's are sturdy. I walked away from my mistakes but had to keep finding new transportation.

All those days of thinking and dreaming had finally given me what I had been seeking. I had decided what I wanted to do with my life, had found an idea worth fighting for.

I wanted to stop the altering of women.

I intended to live in the Countryside and find and destroy every AGNA facility that had anything to do with altering. If that eventually turned me into a mutant, I didn't care. Doing something positive was worth more to me than staying safe. And besides, there wasn't anyplace safe for me.

My plan was risky. It meant I would have to go into San Francisco, would have to learn a number of things before I could actually begin the work.

Everything I needed I knew could be found in the AGNA archives and scientific repositories by using computers in public access libraries and hacking into files. Since I was passing as a boy, no one would pay much attention to me. The security code I had used to escape Rehab 23 had contained one AGNA encryption that I thought would allow me access to areas forbidden to the general public, and from there I could find others. I was not all that surprised that the files were not better secured, simply because so many people used them. AGNA was, after all, the largest employer in North America, probably in the world.

I had a check-list. I intended to celebrate my twelfth
birthday by completing the list:

- Learn where alteration facilities are located
- Learn how to make explosives
- Get materials for explosives
- Learn how to bypass a GAV keypad
- Get a vehicle

I sat on a hill in Marin County, gazing across the
choppy waters of the bay at the dome over San Francisco,
planning my next move. Unless I could hitch a ride by
water, I would have to go all the way around, and that
could take weeks. I shifted my weight, because the sharp,
hot dirt was digging into my bony butt. I was at a cross-
roads. I was ready to act.

S.F. had a high dome, accommodating the hills and
the remaining span of the ruined Golden Gate Bridge,
recently declared a national monument.

It was a pretty day, smelling of eucalyptus and sorrel.
Insects whined — a sharp, chipping sound. Boats of all
sizes moved in erratic patterns across the greenish-blue
water. A half-dozen big ships flying foreign flags were
docked at the nearside, in wharves such as I had seen
in L. A. AGNA still carried out commerce with other parts
of the world, about which I knew little. I fervently hoped
that somewhere in the world there were other people and
that they were free.

From what I had heard at rehab, S. F. was a strange
place. Nearly the entire population had been destroyed
during the first stage of the establishment of AGNA
because they had rebelled against the moderates. I shook
my head, wondering how to sort through the lies.

I knew the tale of the battle called the Siege of San
Francisco. Well, part of it was probably true. The city had
refused to accept the new constitution, declared its in-
dependence, and fortified its perimeter. They were
isolated, starved, bombarded, and destroyed. I couldn't
remember what happened after that, except that it was
now a prison, and that the surrounding area was sparsely

populated. That made me smile. Who would expect me to voluntarily enter a prison? It might be the safest place in North America for me at that moment.

Or not.

I stashed my gear, now augmented with the medkit from the GAV, in a hole dug under a bush, and made my way to a place called Tiburon, down on the water. It was a picturesque settlement, with a big boat basin, and colorful, trendy restaurants and shops. It was crawling with Fedguards, dressed in the black garb of prison personnel, apparently doing nothing but eating and drinking. R&R?

I hung out around the waterfront, watching the fishing fleet. There were many boys my age working there, scraping hulls, sorting fish, running errands, or painting boats. I didn't like so many soldiers around, but they didn't interact with the fishermen and paid no attention to me.

I slipped back into my city-self, following a drunk down a street and into a vacant lot. When he unzipped to pee, I bashed him and took his credit card. It didn't have much on it, but I figured it might be enough for a passage.

"You wanna go into S. F.?" The woman wrinkled her nose as if I smelled bad. Maybe I did. I hadn't bathed in days.

"Yes, ma'am. My dad's over there. There's a visiting day." I wasn't actually sure that could be true, but apparently it was.

She nodded her head and blew her nose and pushed her tangled reddish hair away from her face. She had a cold, and her nose was red and swollen. I commiserated with her and that made her like me more.

"Well, my man's going over tomorrow morning with the catch. I suppose—" She appraised me, a tiny smile tipping up the corners of her mouth. She was wearing scarlet lipstick, which made her look older and harsher than she seemed to be.

"I can pay, a little." I tried to look sorrowful, and remembered to let my mouth hang open, as boys do. I stood,
hat in hand, shuffling in embarrassment.

"Naw, naw, keep your credits, child. You can help him
unload and that'll cover your passage."

I nodded. "Then, could you tell me where I might find
a mall to get a clean shirt? I'd like to, you know, look nice."

She smiled at that. "A mall? Well, naw malls here, but
shops." She gave me directions to a store and told me how
I was to meet her husband's boat the next morning. She
was pleasant, except for the cold, and an alter. The kind
I wanted to help.

I walked away from her knowing it was a risk. I hoped
she wouldn't report me as a stray. I hoped the drunk
wouldn't recognize me if I changed my shirt.

Tiburon was expensive and I paid too much for a beige
tunic. I guess being the pleasure spot for the prison guards
allowed them to jack up prices. I stopped by a woman's
store, pretended awkwardness, and enjoyed the scents and
soft colors of the merchandise. I bought a perfumed bar
of soap to give to the woman in the morning as a thanks
for her kindness.

I slept in a boat, snuggled under a canvas tarp. It was
uncomfortable and damp when the fog rolled in, but I'd
slept in worse places. I was awake early and very hungry.

I had no more credits, and there were few people stirring
at the early hour, so I went hungry. I retraced my steps to
the woman's house. Her husband, a tall, angular man who
was missing his front teeth, nodded his agreement that I
get on board. I handed the woman my little gift and she
hugged me. I felt her ample breasts against my own flat
ones, and tears sprang into my eyes.

"Why, you love!" she said, not knowing I was thinking of Reesie and Santa Monica and all that I had forfeited.
She pressed a paper bag into my hand — my lunch. She
was the love, and deserved better than to be denied her
full life. I regret that I never learned her name.

# # #

San Francisco. Getting in was easy.

We docked. I helped unload the catch. There were Fedguards with weapons prowling around, but most people ignored them. My fisherman touched my shoulder when we were finished.

"I come every third day. To this wharf. If you want a ride back."

I nodded and he turned away from me and strode down the pier towards the Fedguard custom's building. I went the opposite direction.

The waterfront was built up with ramshackle wooden boathouses and piers. Behind that was a strip of open land, circling the dome of the city proper. Access to the perimeter road was through one wide gate where a couple of Fedguards lounged, guns held loosely.

I hesitated until I saw a few people walk through without being stopped. I followed them. One of the Fedguards looked at me then his eyes flicked away, dismissing me.

Inside was what was left of San Francisco: a broad avenue fringed by wood and plasticrete buildings, with two edifices that looked to be real stone. Looming over everything was a black, two-storey plasticrete wall. It reminded me of cultural studies in my quad, pictures of the Great Wall of China. The fog was lifting but still curled around the top of the prison enclosure. I couldn't see the end of it in either direction.

Who was in there? Why? How many?

"Are you lost, son?"

I stiffened and whirled around to encounter a squat, blond Fedguard, rifle cradled across his arm, smiling at me. He wore mufti, so he wasn't connected to the prison.

"Yes, sir. I want the library."

"Straight down Market Street. It's about a ten-minute walk. You'll see the big gray building on your left."

"Thank you."

"And don't tarry along the way. You're too young." He chuckled and so did I, not knowing why.

I moved away quickly.

There was no city here. Just the wall to my right, glowering over the broad street. All else was flat, open, empty.

Where did the people live? The buildings along this avenue were places for sex workers, vids, drinking houses. All of them painted in gaudy colors, with shamelessly explicit signs for the pleasures inside.

I was uncomfortable, not because of the sex stuff, but by the desolation and the horror the black wall exuded like a fog. Except for the music leaking out of the R&R places, there were no normal city sounds. No traffic, no people talking, nothing that could link this ruin with its history.

My heart was thumping; my mind was spinning; and there was bitterness in my soul when I checked into the library and set myself to my task. All of those negative things became a positive energy to ferret out all I needed to know to find and destroy the alteration facilities of AGNA, the acronym which I had just realized sounds like gagging.

I learned. I studied supply depots, maps of AGNA installations, maps of North America. I stole chemicals from warehouses at the docks. I learned some more. I ran back and forth from Tiburon with my loot, happy to have my hug every third day. I mugged people on both sides of the bay for credits and a pretty brooch for the lady. I found a small restaurant on the waterfront where no one bothered me and I ate well for a change. I worked hard and I was ready to begin.

I was glad to abandon San Francisco. I took to the hills, away from the coastal settlements, and practiced making bombs.

All that remained was to steal another GAV, and I knew where to get that. I had discovered that bypassing the keypad was easy. Apparently people often forgot their codes, so they just entered reset, picked another one and reconfigured the pad. I hadn't known how to do that because my mini GAV had had a permanent ignition code.

There was a Fedguard station at the base of Mount Tamulpias, a few miles away from the abandoned utility shack where I lived after leaving the city. I sat screened by the mesquite bushes on the hillside above the facility and watched the post for hours to become familiar with their routine.

There were a dozen Fedguards, with the highest rank a mere sergeant. They had three GAVs and didn't take good care of them. They only put them into shelter when it rained, so they were rusty from the fog. There was one large house where the men lived and worked. The communications room was in the front and had big windows, brightly lit at all times, so there must have been surveillance monitors of the area around the quarters, but I rarely saw anyone working in there. Security was lax. The men were bored and often went into San Francisco or Tiburon, leaving the post undermanned.

I waited for such a time. It came four nights after I had decided I was ready to begin my life's work.

This night, two of the GAVs left around 18:00, heading toward the city. I watched the guards load up and leave, seven of them in dress uniforms, obviously heading for R&R, for the pleasure strip on Market Street or the pricier delights of Tiburon. It didn't matter; they were gone. When everything settled down, I left my perch on the side of the hill, lugged my two carrybags, one now full of chemicals and demolition equipment, and stashed them in the remaining GAV.

I crawled into the pilot's seat, keeping as low a profile as I could, and punched in the reset code. I waited while the screen ran a series of numbers that seemed to take forever.

The door on the building opened and a guard stepped out. I ducked and held my breath — and covered up the screen because it was glowing with its plethora of digits.

"Are you going to play?" I heard a voice from inside the house.

"Yeah. Thought I heard something." There was a pause and I could hear the guard walking, his boots crunching on gravel and desiccated grass. "Guess not," he said, then I heard him pee. It sounded as if he was right beside me.

He went back in the building. The keypad had stopped scrolling so I punched in a new five-digit code: JEMMA.

The GAV caught instantly, I grabbed the T-bar and lifted off sweetly. Below me, quickly diminishing in size, I could see the Fedguards rushing out into the yard, waving their arms and readying weapons. Shots pinged off the side of the car but didn't hurt anything. I smiled. They were stuck — the other GAVs were in the city.

I flipped on the navigation system and went north-northwest as fast as I dared, heading toward the ocean. Between San Francisco and SeatVan, the Fedguard presence was insignificant, the Countryside was nearly vacant from what I had learned from spy files, and there was a laboratory outside of old Seattle where AGNA manufactured the drugs they used to alter women. I wanted it dead.

# # #

"Goodnight, Talli!"

"'Night. See you tomorrow. Bring that picture!"

"I will. 'Night."

I watched the last of the workers leave the facility, walking in the twilight toward the small cluster of AGNA-built houses about a quarter of a mile away. I had already checked out the settlement. It was a neat grid of one-family dwellings, all alike, equally spaced. I saw no evidence of individuality — no toys in the yards, no unkempt lawns. We were twenty miles from the Seattle dome, so I assumed the few women inside the modest houses, moving past identical windows in similar rooms, were alters.

I had also found their transportation depot. Four GAVs, two hovertrucks, and a couple of fedcars were parked on the opposite side of the precinct from the facility. I was going to need one of them to escape after I'd done my work. I reconfigured only one with JEMMA, reset the codes and then disconnected everything I could on the others. That would slow them down if they tried to chase me.

I crouched in the bushes and waited to see if anyone else was hanging around the lab. It was a drab, square one-storey building, hunkering in the middle of a clearing, surrounded by magnificent, towering cedars. It looked benign, as if it could manufacture toys or clothing. Nothing distinguished it as a chemical factory except the shiny storage tanks in the back.

My munitions were crude, but I was sure they would work. I was going to set a chemical fire and trust the other compounds in the building to respond and blow up. The structure itself was the standard plasticrete, so it was fire-proof. I didn't care about that — I wanted to destroy what was inside.

The only windows were in a narrow strip just under the eaves. I assumed they were unbreakable; but the entrance door, which opened onto a small reception area, was glass and wood — the only claim to architectural decoration. It would blow, and I could toss my fire bombs inside.

It was my initiation and I was anxious. I was an amateur using amateur equipment, ingredients used by welders, construction people, fishermen, the police. I had packaged highly flammable materials into small boxes and called them bombs. Presumably, if I'd done my homework correctly, the separate breakable packages inside each box would burst open and mix and explode when I threw the bomb, then I would toss additional packets to fuel the flames.

I moved cautiously around the perimeter to the rear of the building. The open area around it was only half-lit because some of the lightstrips were missing. I was delighted with their shoddy maintenance but felt there must be surveillance of some kind — motion-detectors at the very least.

I set a bomb under each of the storage tanks, hurriedly, trembling in my nervousness, thinking that at any moment a siren would go off, or emergency lights would come on. The lack of movement made me uneasy, but nothing happened.

That done, I crept around the side of the lab. It felt strange and the hairs on the back of my neck were bristling, but the coast seemed clear, so I walked boldly to the front entrance, lit the fuse sticking out of my special starter bomb and pulled back my arm to throw it.

"Hey! Who's there?"

The voice came from the far side of the building. A Fedguard stepped out into the dim light, leveling his gun, peering at me. For a second I didn't know what to do, then I threw the bomb and ran.

It exploded bigger, hotter, quicker, greener than I expected. I had added barium compounds to make a green fire as an experiment. It knocked me down and the Fedguard, too. Glass and wood shattered and flew at me. Sirens went off. Bright auxiliary lights pierced the gloom.

I had another bomb in my hands — it had to go through the now-open entrance. I scrambled to my feet, staggered towards the lab and threw it. The ground exploded around my feet as the guard shot at me. I fell down again.

Flames from the first bomb were still curling around the reception area, and the second one did its job. There was another explosion. This time it was so bright it dazzled me. I couldn't see which way to run.

Fire inside the building raced past the strip of windows and then the storage tanks went up like rockets. The roof of the lab blew off, dragging a column of fire and smoke upward taller than the trees. Huge chunks of burning debris rained down on the area. The guard stopped shooting.

I ran, stumbling and falling over pieces of roof and tangled metal and bits of furniture, back to the carrybag I had left on the periphery, grabbed it and ran on, going to my right through the forest, meaning to circle to the other side of the settlement towards the GAVs.

Ten minutes later I stopped. It took a few minutes to be able to hear. My ears felt stuffed with cotton from the explosions. I was out of breath and my heart pounded so loudly it would have deafened me if the blast hadn't done so already.

I couldn't stay where I was. I was too close to the scene. There were still explosions, and the forest around the lab had caught on fire, lighting up the evening sky. Now there were more sirens, wailing ones. From the settlement, I guessed. Good, they would keep me in the right direction as I worked my way through the darkness of the forest. I picked up my carrybag and yelped as a shooting pain went through my arm. It was too dark to see what was wrong with it, but I could feel it. Half of my right little finger was gone. Just gone.

Oh, hell! I would have to find a better way to do this. But I *had* done it. I had killed the lab. Probably that Fedguard, too, I thought. I hoped not. I didn't mean to kill people, just things.

I dug in my carrybag with my good hand, found a reasonably clean sock and wrapped it around my fingers. I hiked on at a steady pace, putting distance between myself and the fire, knowing now that AGNA could be reached, touched, hurt. Knowing, too, that I had been lucky, not competent. It was a start.

# # #

I did get better, lots better. Proficient, in fact. I'm not sure which was my real calling: demolition or thievery.

I stole fedcars, private GAVs, even a hovertruck once because nothing else was available. I always used the ignition code JEMMA. AGNA discovered that when they ran a check on the keypads of my abandoned vehicles and I got a little reputation. Well, actually, a big reputation.

I guess we could call it ego. I didn't feel important, but I did want people to know someone out there cared.

In the cities, still passing as a boy, I saw reports about my criminal activities on the big screens in public places. I was infamous on AGNA Network News. Every crime that hadn't been solved in the last two years was blamed on me. I was amazed at how many unsolved crimes there were in that uh... how shall we say?... perfect, well-ordered society?

My sabotage was surprisingly easy in a way. The monolith that was AGNA didn't work well. Mechanisms bogged down, biological systems decayed, broken things were not repaired, and routine maintenance got skipped. It was obvious that nobody in AGNA gave a damn. The administration lied about everything, maintaining control by keeping people in their niches, by keeping them busy with useless programs, by catering to their presumed or invented needs, and, if all else failed, by cruelties and fear.

It rewarded ignorance and boredom and punished any deviation from the status quo, blundering through people's lives like a blind bear. I hated it.

I blew up six labs as I made my way from SeatVan to Denver, to Houston, to St Louis, to TwinCities, to Chicago. The seventh was in Cinci and that's where I ran into trouble.

I had discovered something called "demolition dirt," which was a nifty chemical compound in powder form that could be transformed into putty and thrown like a softball, packaged into a bomb, or sprinkled and set off with a spark. It was safer to handle than my previous bombs, so I kept the rest of my fingers. If I needed to work at a distance, I could spread it around, throw a flame at it and BOOM! I pilfered the ingredients, of course, but all of them were readily available at Fedguard outposts and garden supply stores.

In Cinci, a relatively modest dome as AGNA megacities go, it was raining and chilly for early August. The small lab was on the north side, outside the city proper, in an industrial suburb. I should have been more careful, knowing Cinci was so close to my last job, but I did my usual explorations: a stake-out to watch the workers and get their routine; a day prowling the neighborhood; a night watching in the dark.

It seemed fairly easy, and I meant to simply toss a half dozen of my dirtballs at it. I had a private GAV stashed within running distance.

I worked, as usual, during the dark of the moon, not that it mattered this night. The clouds were heavy and low and the wind smelled like rain. I watched for several hours as the last workers went home. Nothing moved around the facility except one Fedguard who checked all of the doors once then left. The rain was steady but light.

When I stepped into the clearing around the building, all hell broke loose! Sirens! Lights! Men jumping out of the shadows!

I crouched and tried to get back to the dark periphery, but bullets splashed around me. I ran, zigzagging my way, reaching into the satchel slung around my neck. I tossed off a dirt ball like a grenade, throwing it as far as I could while running, setting off a brilliant green-red explosion that flattened everyone and everything around it, including me.

I got up and ran again. A man was right in front of me, a Fedguard. Gun pointed at my guts. I didn't stop. Just plowed right into him and he fell with me on top of him. I couldn't possibly win hand-to-hand, so I spent my energy ripping his helmet off.

I hit him with it, and it hurt him. I grabbed his gun and smashed it into his head. He lay still then. I put his helmet on, stripped him of his jacket and gun, and got up shooting, struggling into his coat.

I shot the hell out of the building, yelling and running. The other Fedguards followed me, doing as I did. I tore around the corner of the lab, tossed another of my grenades, doubled back, still shooting and running. I caused a lot of confusion and no one realized who I was. The light was bad; the explosions were fierce; nobody wanted to die.

The third bomb I pitched at the building blew a hole in it, we all were thrown to the ground and it started a fire inside. I crawled forward to reach the darkness beyond the fire and the surveillance lights. I dumped the helmet and jacket but this time I kept the gun, and ran like a rabbit for my GAV.

I circled in the air, looked down on the dead lab illuminated by the fire, and saw bodies sprawled here and there. I never meant to kill anyone. Not then or anytime, except once — much later. I felt ashamed that it had happened.

After that, I had to stop for awhile.

I had found hundreds of ordinary people in the Countryside, living reasonably normal, if somewhat primitive, lives. They were not mutants, not barbarians, and not, I was surprised to find, rebels.

AGNA was easy to map. The concentration of government was in the megacities of varying sizes, under domes, and connected to each other, so far as possible, by over- and underground tunnels. Most of those tunnels were still in process of construction and had been for years, and the access roads to them were patrolled. The Countryside (and AGNA always styled it with a capital C) was said by AGNA to be uninhabitable, loaded with toxic dumps, evidence of the cruelty of the gender wars that maimed and killed with poison gas, hot nuke radiation, and so-called "practical" nuke small weapons.

That was a lie, of course. Yes, there were some hot spots, but those could be avoided. Much of the nation was unpeopled, and nature had recovered, with its amazing resilience, given half a chance.

I had stopped being a predator. I took too much pleasure from watching a hawk riding the thermals, or a quail teaching its young, to ever again prey upon them. They survived in pockets, which could get bigger and better if we were smart. If we could be kind. I didn't hold out much hope for us, but I had learned to value wildness.

The vastness of the country amazed me; the beauty of it thrilled me. If only people knew, I kept thinking — if they knew how wonderful it is, and all the space there is, they would bolt for the Countryside. But they didn't because AGNA wouldn't let them, had convinced them, as I had once been convinced, that only the cities were safe.

Females lived in the cities. On the outskirts of all the cities was a buffer zone where some agriculture and most industry was pursued. The women there were alters. The next outside ring around the cities was a series of frontier settlements and Fedguard outposts, and beyond them and scattered everywhere was open Countryside and isolated villages. Sometimes I would encounter a family or two traveling together. They disappeared when they saw me, with the same curious, hesitant look displayed by foxes and deer.

The frontier settlements were established by the government to buffer against the so-called "wilderness." to catch and return escapees from the cities, to pick up stray country people, and to retire government officials when they were no longer active. I avoided them after the first one because they would capture me if they could. They were depressing places. When freedom and a good life was there, why couldn't they take it?

The other settlements were inhabited by small groups of people, anywhere from thirty to fifty souls, living in a community. Most of these were many miles from the cities and presumably beyond AGNA's reach, even though some of them had tunnels close to them. If I had found them, I assumed the Fedguards also knew about them, and I wondered why they were allowed to remain. I blamed it on AGNA's usual incompetence. People told me that the Fedguards occasionally raided and plundered these settlements, taking the citizens prisoner or killing them. They altered the women, of course, and took them to the frontier towns or the cities. We were precious and had to be protected. Uh-huh.

There were variations on this, especially in the more remote parts of North America, those far from megacities. But some settlements were relatively near Fedguard outposts. I had stopped at one of them to get first aid supplies. A village man got what I needed from the Fedguards without any trouble. When I questioned this, I learned that some of the soldiers had married village girls and settled down. They protected each other and didn't make trouble.

AGNA had no idea, I thought, *what was really going on in the Countryside*. Or, if they did, they were powerless to stop it. Another example of AGNA's lack of control over the continent and its people.

I began to have trouble passing as a boy. I was nearly fifteen, and although my breasts were nothing to look at, I was curvy, with hips and a tucked-in waist. I had stopped growing at about 5'9", two inches over the maximum "perfect" height for women, according to AGNA. I looked older than I was, and not so boyish. I had to be more careful.

AGNA offered a tempting reward for my head, so, after Cinci, I found a deserted farmhouse in the Ozarks and holed up for a while. I was restless, though. I was tired and lonely, and after weeks of isolation, I put the GAV back in the air and headed east.

Even though it might be chancy, I needed to be around people, talk to someone, maybe even laugh now and then. I liked the independent settlements. The people were generally friendly, until, of course, someone recognized me. But they didn't turn me in, just asked me to please move on, and I did.

Most of the communities I had visited had vidscreens, so they knew who I was. They watched the AGNA news. They watched the Movers, whose intermittent broadcasts scrambled and replaced AGNA's lies for minutes or sometimes hours — until the administration's technicians were able to bump them off. I didn't have a chance to see many of the programs, but people in general looked forward to Mover news, or so they told me, to hear the other side of the story.

My reputation made them nervous, but they said they admired what I did. I became a kind of folk heroine. Someone told me that a song had been written about my exploits, although I never heard it.

This time, after Cinci, I reconnoitered in the splendid mountains of eastern Kentucky near the Virginia border, following a narrow stream that glinted with riffles I could see through the trees as it meandered southward. On the valley floor, flanking the river, there was a small settlement.

I landed several miles away and hid my GAV under a pile of brush. I left the demolition equipment with it, but took my weapons. They were too hard to get to risk losing them if someone found the vehicle, and walked in the warm, dusty air down a dirt road to the settlement.

It was a true Countryside village, and the largest I had seen. The nearest Fedguard installation was over a hundred miles away to the north, the nearest city was Cinci to the northwest, and the mother of all megacities, BosWash, was further to the east. This settlement in Kentucky even had an old, weathered sign on the outskirts. "Welcome to Athena," it read. I hoped so.

I walked in slowly, hands showing, my carrybag slung over my back, as I had learned to do. People in the Countryside towns monitored the roads, wanted to know who had found them, and some of them had weapons. I saw no one, although I could hear children shouting from

somewhere and the sound of wood being chopped, so
I kept on, past wooden houses with small yards and vegetable and flower gardens in front of them; a couple of
vacant lots full of late-blooming wildflowers, a smear
of yellow and blue; a stone house in process of construction; until I came to the ubiquitous town green in the
center of the settlement.

Athena's green actually had a dozen sheep grazing
on it, like in olden times. There was a bench and I sat
down, set my carrybag on the ground beside me, and
waited for the welcoming committee. The sheep looked
me over and one came nearer, reeking of urine, its eyes
reminding me of alters.

It was early afternoon and the sun was hot and
golden, sifting through the bronze and red of the maple
leaves, making a shifting checkered pattern on the short
grass. I leaned back and sighed. It was beautiful, quiet,
peaceful. I nearly fell asleep listening to the birds chirp-
ing, the breeze above me, the children's laughing voices,
and a steady chop chop chop from far away. I was achy
from my period and bone tired from traveling.

Then they came, four men and a woman, walking side
by side across the green. The men were wearing farmer's
clothes, the woman was in pants, with a pretty metal belt
and her bright yellow blouse tucked in. The sheep skit-
tered out of their way. I held my arms straight out from
my shoulders to show I wasn't concealing a weapon.

They stopped a few yards in front of me. They were
armed, if you could call it that, with long, straight staffs.
I hadn't seen that before and it interested me. I could
imagine what a whack from one of those sturdy sticks
could do.

"You've been in country towns before, we see." The
man lowered his weapon slightly, and he didn't look
threatening.

"Yes, sir, many. I've been traveling. I'm looking for
a place to rest. I'm armed but not dangerous. I have a
.620 Winner, Fedguard issue, in my carrybag. A machete
in there, too. And I carry a pocket knife that's quite sharp.
These weapons are not aimed at you."

"Are you a Mover?"

"No, sir." I'd been asked that before and found it odd I had never yet met any Movers. I had grown curious about them. I no longer believed what I had learned at rehab.

The woman took a couple of steps towards me, leaned on her staff, frowning, tilting her head as if she could see me better that way. "I know you." Her voice was a low whisper. She was a pretty woman in her forties, I guessed, with long, curly dark hair, glistening with silver at her temples. Her nose was sharp, but her lips were like an angel's, pink and finely drawn and curling upward at the corners in a smile.

The men looked at her, then at me, eyebrows raised.

"No, ma'am," said I, sitting up straighter, "though you may know *of* me." My heart sank. If they recognized me so quickly it could mean I might have to keep walking. I had learned it was best, with the true country people, to just tell the truth and take the consequences, so I smiled. "My name is Jemma."

"Jemma!" The youngest of the men stepped forward eagerly. He made a kind of hissing sound through his teeth. He was tall and lanky, a squarish face, with a shock of brown hair falling over his forehead, only a couple of years older than I. He looked idiotic, grinning at me.

"Yes," the woman said. "Yes, Jemma, a criminal." I shrugged. "The Fedguards are looking for you. What do you want with us?" She stopped leaning on her pole and hefted it.

I wanted to cry. I was suddenly so tired I didn't think I could actually leave if they asked me.

"Nothing, ma'am. I'm tired. I need to stop and think and rest. I hoped I could do that here in Athena. I won't make trouble. I'll work for my keep."

The oldest man in the group, with white hair sweeping his shoulders, now took up the interrogation. His staff, however, was at his side, held loosely. "Well, you don't look quite like the dangerous critter you're supposed to be."

I smiled at him. "I steal things. And I blow up alteration labs. That's all I do. The rest is AGNA lies."

His blue eyes squinted slightly. "We heard what happened in Cinci. It was on AGNA Network News."

I looked at the ground and shook my head. "I didn't mean to hurt anyone. I regret that. They ambushed me and I fought my way out." I looked up and met his eyes, willing him to believe me.

I heard the chopping again in the silence that followed, then he handed his staff to a companion, stooped and opened my carrybag, removed the gun and the machete and passed them over, too. "Let's see the knife," he said. I reached in my pocket — the staffs were leveled at me quickly — and handed it to him. He opened it and examined it, closed it up and handed it back to me.

His gaze was level and told me nothing. "I have a soft place in my heart for rebels," he said at last. The young man laughed softly.

He turned to the others. "This town, of all towns, should give this young woman refuge. I say we let her rest. She'll move on quick enough," and he turned back to me, "because she won't wear out that welcome. Right?"

I let out a groan of appreciation that made them all smile. "Absolutely! I just need to sleep in a bed, get clean; rest a short time, and then I'll be gone. You'll never see me again and I'll forget I was ever here."

The woman was standing with her head tilted to one side again, chewing on her bottom lip. "I'll take her. I have an extra bed since Grace got married. And I could use help with the apples."

"Good," the old man said. He picked up my carrybag, but threw it to the young man. "We'll put your weapons away until you leave. Here, Hank, you carry her gear." He turned to me and held out a sunburned, callused hand. "I'm Harris. Welcome to Athena, Jemma."

"I'm Lucy," the woman said, smiling at last. Her face softened and was pretty when she smiled.

"I'm Hank," said the young man, growing suddenly shy.

I shook Harris's hand and nodded to the rest. I felt unaccountably safe, and I had learned to trust my gut. It didn't matter that they kept my weapons. I was sure they would be returned.

We walked across the green to a white house with a vegetable garden that sprawled onto both sides of the fieldstone path to the door. Hank walked with us to the porch, while the other men went off in different directions.

"Thank you, Hank," I said, taking my carrybag. I couldn't stop myself from tucking my chin and looking up at him, a smile on my lips. He was handsome in a boyish sort of way. He backed off the porch awkwardly; I followed Lucy into her house.

It was a nice house: simple, clean, and comfortable. We entered into a hallway with the kitchen to the right and a parlor on the left with a fireplace, a few upholstered chairs, a round table by the window, and a polished wooden bench with bright red pillows on it. There were pictures on the plastered walls and a braided rug on the floor. A fat black cat sprawled in the sun slanting through the window. It looked up and yawned, sharp teeth showing, then tucked its head under an extended leg.

"Up here, Jemma." Lucy led the way up a narrow, steep stairway to the second floor and into a tidy room with two windows commanding a vista of the backyard garden and a woodlot beyond it. A double bed was in one corner, an oak dresser in another, and a small mirrored vanity table flanked the door.

"This was my daughter's room. She got married last spring and moved to the other side of town. It's a little dusty, I'm afraid, but you're welcome to it... for a short time."

"Thank you, ma'am."

"Call me Lucy, please. We're not formal here in Athena. But for the record, my full name is Lucy Battinger."

I stared at her with my mouth open. They had *last* names here? No one had used last names for over a hundred years. AGNA said it fostered divisiveness, confusion, and pride, that numbers contained more information.

She chuckled. "A bit old-fashioned, we are."

"That's a lot easier than JE2MDRA77290FF400RT913!" What was this place, so different from other villages I'd visited? "What did the man mean, this town of all towns should—"

"This is an original town, Jemma, founded by the rebels back at the end of the twenty-first century. Over a third of us, including myself, are direct descendants of those original people, the ones AGNA calls the Bad Women."

I sat on the bed because my legs wouldn't hold me up. Then some of them *did* survive! My heroines. And I was looking at a great-great-god-knows-how-many-greats granddaughter of one of them.

Lucy looked at me curiously. "Surely you've heard of them?"

"Heard of them? They haunt my dreams!"

She chuckled. "Well, you're like them, I suppose, bothering AGNA the way you do." She ran her hand across the top of the dresser, dusting it perfunctorily. "We don't make trouble here, Jemma. We have nothing to do with AGNA and we want to keep it that way. We're law-abiding citizens. We live normal, peaceful lives."

My mind was racing. "Some of them survived! How? How did they do it?"

Lucy chuckled. "In good time. There are lots of stories."

"I want to hear them!"

"And so you will. Get cleaned up now. The bath is down the hall, second door, and I'll leave a towel for you." She pursed her lips and tilted her head. "Do you need clean clothes?"

I stood up, still thinking about her ancestors. "No, I have a change, thank you."

Her look was dubious. "Well, we'll find something for you." She closed the door softly behind her.

I sat back down on the bed and kicked my boots off. I had not been so excited for years — not this kind of good excitement, at any rate. Now I would hear the truth from people who actually knew it. The feeling that I had in the presence of the stars came over me — a kind of awe and expectation. I had no doubt that Lucy's stories would squeeze my brain and I would still be me. I thought suddenly that my old quad friend Lila would never know the truth. That made me sad.

I lay back on the bed and closed my eyes, happy for the first time in years. When I woke up, it was nearly dark and Lucy was standing in the doorway, calling me to supper.

Chapter 6

"My many-times-removed Grandmother got involved with the rebellion early on, after what AGNA's history calls the Prison Incident," Lucy said, handing me a cup of coffee. "Do you know about that?"

"I only know a bit from AGNA's version. Wasn't it part of the Necessary Genocide?"

"Not really."

We went outside, the screen door banging behind us. She sat down on the back steps. The twilight chill was coming on, but I had eaten a big dinner and felt fat and warm, and the coffee tasted like ambrosia. The cicadas were strumming, the stars were winking on. "Although I guess you could call it the beginning of that horror...." She sipped and swatted at a mosquito.

I settled beside her on the top step. "This is good, Lucy. I miss coffee."

"You're too young to be addicted to coffee." She meant it as a joke.

It had been months since I'd had caffeine, and I had an instant buzz. "Please — just tell me anything. Everything."

She smiled. "Well, there's a lot to it, Jemma. In a nutshell, when the race riots got out of hand, the violence escalated, at all levels. Cities were just anarchies. The police, the army, the National Guard were all battling people in the streets. Real firefights. There were lots of guns in the cities then. People were angry and frustrated because they felt powerless and scared. There was a predictable backlash against the bloodshed and the ultra-conservatives came into power. I think most people just wanted the fighting to stop and figured a clampdown was the only way."

Hank walked around the side of Lucy's house. He had changed his clothes and his hair was still wet from a shower. "Mind if I join you?" He hesitated, but clearly wanted to sit down.

Lucy moved over slightly in invitation, but Hank sat on the bottom step, near me.

"If you want coffee, get yourself a cup in the kitchen," Lucy said. Hank shook his head, and Lucy continued, "So, Jemma, what happened was that these conservatives passed ferocious laws. The first big one was to do away with the prison system."

"I don't understand how they could do that."

She shrugged. "They had the votes, and they thought the climate in the country favored it. The prisons were overcrowded and over-flowing with protestors, rioters, and political disruptives of all kinds, besides the regular prison population. Many people thought prisons were a waste of taxpayers' money. Most didn't want to have to struggle with the real social issues. But," she frowned and sipped her coffee, "they didn't let the prisoners go, mind you — they executed them. All of them. No matter what their crimes."

It made me shiver. Hank rubbed his chin, as if he had a beard that itched. We sat a moment. AGNA didn't have anything officially called "prisons" except San Francisco, and no one knew who was held there. There was rehab, which of course was a prison of sorts, and there were so-called justice facilities. It was the same thing, I realized. Just another lie.

Lucy took a big breath and stretched her back. It seemed to be bothering her. "Well, you can imagine, many, many people did not agree with that — had not given a mandate for such a thing, — and saw it as a brutal, tyrannical murder. My ancestor — and Hank's — was one of them. She was a teacher — taught marine biology at a college in Rhode Island."

"Marine biology? However did she wind up in Kentucky?" It seemed an odd choice.

"We have a river," Hank chimed in, and then was immediately, acutely, embarrassed and took a shoe off to rub his toes. Lucy and I ignored him.

"That's part of another story. Be patient. That horror, those murders, are what finally brought women into the streets and bonded them together — all women, across classes and ethnic and economic backgrounds. The mothers, daughters, grandmothers, wives, lovers, friends of the men and women who were slaughtered took to the streets."

"And fought the government?"

"Fought everybody they had to. It was a bloodbath at first. In order to survive, to try to turn things around, they began to organize. They banded together, natural leaders stood up in the ranks, and by the time of the so-called Necessary Genocide, about ten years later, the women were a rebel army. Many men joined them, too, of course. They were good, but outgunned, outnumbered, and finally overwhelmed. Eventually, they all went to earth, as the hunters say. The Movers, and people like yourself, are what's left."

"Then it was a civil war, really," I thought aloud. I hadn't seen it that way before.

"Yes. The history books don't call it that, but that's what it was. And it went on for decades.

"Somewhere about 2094, some of the women dropped out. They were tired, discouraged, hurt, or simply needed to stop for a while." I could relate to that. Lucy looked at me in that instant and understood me, because she said, "I'm sure you know how that feels."

Hank moved up a step, closer to me, to stretch out his long legs.

"Anyway, it wasn't just that. I don't know how many women were killed in the first ten years. I'm not sure anyone knows. The Movers say, overall, nearly half the female population perished or disappeared. AGNA was forming, establishing the new constitution, and they said they regretted the "Woman Question," of course. Once they started altering women, it became a desperate situation for the rebels.

"It wasn't just the deaths, but the fact that women weren't having babies under those perilous conditions. So some of the rebels, including the founders of Athena, dropped out of the fight and set up isolated communities all over North America — in Canada and Mexico, too — where they could settle down and raise children to be free and, it was hoped, safe from whatever was to come. We say that they planted a garden, Jemma."

She finished her coffee and sighed. "And that's enough for one night."

"But—"

Lucy laughed. "All right, one question."

"I have so many. Okay, the big one: AGNA must know about the settlements. About Athena and the others."

"Yes."

"And they don't destroy them?"

"Sometimes they do. It depends on who's in power. This town was leveled once about eighty years ago. The people escaped and came back to rebuild it."

"But..." It didn't make sense to me.

Lucy put a hand on my shoulder gently. "Jemma, AGNA is a terrible, evil government; but not all of the people in it are bad. And, finally, there is a line of decency, of con-science, of historical necessity, that even AGNA cannot cross."

No, not all are bad, I thought. Daddy works for AGNA, and he wouldn't destroy Athena. And Mother spied for it; she's not bad, just cowardly. Or was she? I would have to rethink that. And the fisherwoman; and the surfer in L. A.; and... "Yes, I know that's true."

Lucy's eyes reflected the rising of the moon. "We harm none here."

Irrevocable change, again, squeezed my chest. I had to take a deep breath to ease the pain. They harm none. I harmed people; this town did not; the legacy of the Bad Women did not. Did I have another Choosing Day?

Hank stood up. "I'd better be getting home. Are you picking apples tomorrow, Jemma?"

I wasn't listening, although I heard what he said. Lucy answered for me. "If she's rested, yes, we need to get them in. Why?"

I roused myself and smiled at her. "Yes, I think I understand." They were staring at me, Lucy with an amused expression. I laughed at myself. "And, yes, I think I'd like to pick apples. If I actually manage to get up in the morning."

"We can work together," Hank said.

I looked to Lucy and she nodded. He waved and vanished around the corner of the house.

Lucy chuckled. "I believe you've made a conquest, Jemma."

"A what?" I stared at her blankly, thinking about fighting and decency and choosing and babies.

# # #

My bedroom was over the kitchen, and the muffled voices woke me. I stiffened, then remembered where I was. Athena. Under the protection of the ancient goddess of justice, wisdom, and warfare. Was I really? And wasn't that a contradiction in terms? I let myself relax slowly into the lumpy mattress, deliberately, like a balloon deflating. God, I was tired.

Sunlight filtered through a blazing maple tree outside the window and the ripply old glass glowed red. Sparrows were arguing; a crow called several times, sharply. I felt peaceful, happy even. I caught a snatch of their conversation.

Lucy and Hank, were talking. "She's not up yet, Hank. I'll send her out to the orchard when she's ready. The girl is tired. Let her sleep."

He mumbled something I couldn't hear, and Lucy laughed. Then the screen door banged and the sweet country sounds began again. A cow lowed in the distance, the sparrows still babbled, and then a loud, deep bell rang out, reverberating. I counted, but it rang too many times to be the time. An alarm?

I was on my feet before I thought to get up, tugging on my clothes, reeling around the bedroom looking for my carrybag. I stopped short. I had no weapons to draw.

The bell stopped. I sat on the edge of the bed to get my bearings, to still my heart. Lucy was right: I was exhausted. And paranoid. I almost fell back to sleep sitting in the quiet, but then I got a faint whiff of coffee. That brought me to my feet and propelled me down the stairs to the kitchen.

It was empty. A place setting was laid out, and there was a pot of coffee on a keepswarm. I poured myself a cup, got milk from the coldbox, sat down and added sugar from the bowl on the table. I helped myself to biscuits and butter and jam, all the time wondering where Lucy was.

"Ah, good, you're up! Sleep well?" Lucy entered carrying a wicker basket of pears. The screen door banged behind her. I started to rise to help, but she walked past me. "Sit still. Have your breakfast. You want eggs?" She deposited the basket on the side of the sink and turned to me, smiling.

"Sorry I got up so late." Her pleasant busy-ness allayed my fears that something might be wrong.

"Jemma, please. You're under no pressure at all to work today."

"I want to. As soon as I can get myself awake."

She sat opposite me and poured herself a cup of coffee. "I've already eaten, but I'll make you breakfast."

"This is fine. Good biscuits. Great jam. Did you make it?"

She nodded. "Going to make more today. Pear jam. The whole town likes it. I trade in condiments. My part of the economy."

"What was the bell?" I had to ask.

She leaned forward, elbows on the table. "Some folks have called a town meeting. About you."

My stomach churned and I set my cup down with a clunk. "Oh. What does that mean?"

Her face was still pleasant. I wasn't getting any negative feelings from her. "People just want to know what's happening."

"Will you throw me out?"

She laughed, "I don't think so. We're proud of our heritage here. People want to meet you. You're famous, you know."

"Or infamous, as the case may be."

She leaned back, suddenly serious. "Understand, Jemma, that most of us here have relatives that did what you do — fought AGNA, fought the tyranny, fought the rotten laws and the murders. We're proud of them. And maybe a little guilty because we don't take a stand any more."

"So I'll go to this meeting then?"

"Yes. People will ask a lot of questions. We like to know what's really going on, even if we don't do anything about it."

I nodded and drank my coffee. I didn't want them to do anything about it, didn't want Athena to ever be attacked. I needed to think that there was at least one place in North America where sanity and friendship and peace could exist.

Lucy studied me, her eyes narrowed. Then she got up abruptly and put her coffee cup in the sink. "Well, good. Meeting's tonight, after supper."

I took my cup to the sink, turned to her. "What can I do in the meantime?" Then I scoffed at myself. "Oh, yes: the apples."

Lucy shook her head. "That might be too strenuous. You can help me with the pears. There's another couple of bushels of them on the porch. Clean them and core them for me. Leave the apple picking for tomorrow."

She cleared the table quickly then began setting out big pots and little pots and bowls and various knives and spoons. "When that's done, you should go in the parlor and look at the stuff on the table. I pulled out a lot of old photographs, real antiques, and some scrapbooks and vids and other things about our ancestors. I thought you'd want to see them."

I couldn't wait.

But I did. When I rolled up my sleeves to attack the pears, Lucy's smile turned into a frown. "What's that scar on your arm? Looks like a bad burn. Is that from blowing things up?"

I couldn't possibly explain the circumstances around my "mark" from rehab and didn't want to. "No, that's a gift from AGNA. It reminds me to be a good girl... Do you want these cut in half or what?"

Lucy shook her head, still frowning, but she understood I wasn't going to tell the story. She opened a drawer by the sink and tossed an apron to me. "Put this on. You'll need it." Then she gave me a quick lesson in the art of pear slicing.

Until noon I was sticky with fruit juice to my elbows, happy from laughing. I was proficient at coring and slicing, but nicked a finger and bled into the pears. Lucy said it "sweetened the pot" and we'd forget about it. Such a simple thing — two women cooking together. She was astonished that it was my first time.

"Enough! Let's stop and have lunch." Lucy wiped her hands on her apron, I cleaned off my knife and arms. "I'll fix it, Jemma. Go meet my ancestors."

I had to move the cat off the table to get at a stack of scrapbooks — crumbling, blue, thick paperbound, outsized treasures. I took a deep breath before I opened the first one. It was another rising of the moon. A truth.

The eyes in the picture stared back at me, noncommittal. A pretty young woman in a striped turtleneck sweater, she posed on the porch of a white wooden house, beyond her lay a shoreline defined by breakers. It was Lucy. But couldn't be. I squinted at the faded legend: "Carolyn Amanda Battinger, PhD. Killed at the Battle of Pittsburgh, 3 June 2106."

A movement in my peripheral vision made my head snap up. Lucy leaned against the door jamb, a coffee mug in her hand. It was the same face as that in front of me.

"One of my grandmothers, Jemma. The marine biologist."

"I thought you said she quit. Founded Athena."

"She did." Lucy brought the coffee to me. "Lunch in about ten minutes.... She did quit; she did come here. She and my grandfather, Tim Arnold, helped to found the town. They had two kids before Carrie got called back. She was apparently a gifted tactician and the movement needed her. She died of wounds after the Pittsburgh battle."

"There's an amazing resemblance." I sipped my coffee, leaning away from the precious papers on the table. "Does your daughter look like — Dr. Battinger?" I couldn't insult her memory with over-familiarity, but that made Lucy smile.

"No. She looks like my lover, George." I must have made an inadvertent start because Lucy smiled even more broadly. "We don't marry in Athena, although lovers often live together, sometimes forever. Does that shock you?"

I felt my face heat up and I blushed for the first time in my life. "I guess it does. I guess I've never thought about... well, marriage or not."

"Jemma, I can't believe you're a prude! Not with your reputation. But then, I guess you're a warrior, not a lover." Lucy laughed all the way back to the kitchen.

I stared at Carrie Battinger. "Died of wounds" was not pleasant. I turned the page, and then another and another. Pictures of people doing things — playing games, swimming, posing in silly costumes, working in the fields, very few with weapons. I finished the first scrapbook and opened a second one full of printouts, yellowing pages I recognized as old newspapers from my history days at rehab. I left them for later and went to lunch and back to pears, my head full of questions.

I didn't get answers that night, because the good people of Athena were asking, not answering. We all met after supper in what Lucy called "Town Hall," a square one room building off the green. I sat at the front of the room with Harris, who, it turned out, was the mayor, and he started the Q&A session with "How do you like Athena so far?" Good man.

The atmosphere was friendly, and they didn't ask anything too difficult, except about Cinci. AGNA must have pulled out the stops reporting that.

"It was reported that you killed two hundred people in Cinci. Is that true?" One man asked, his voice quiet.

"There weren't two hundred people there. AGNA exaggerates." I matched my voice to his. "I regret that incident. I walked into a trap and I fought my way out. Bullets were flying everywhere, but I was mostly shooting at the building. People died though, and it was my fault."

They asked about other settlements, about farms and what they produced, and where the nearest Fedguard activity had been in recent months. I answered as best I could, and wound up by offering to work for anyone who needed an extra hand, to which I quickly added, "Lucy has dibs, though, because I'm drinking all her coffee."

I had plenty of takers until Lucy intervened. "Give her a couple of days to rest, my friends. I don't think I've seen anyone so tired since the hay barn burned."

They were kind and civilized people and the whole town ratified my presence.

Sometimes it seems that it was a dream, the two months in Athena. The weather was perfect with warm sunny days, cool nights, and occasional dramatic thunderstorms. I worked in the apple harvest, and the hay fields, and the gardens; learned how to make cider and to preserve vegetables and fruit, stirring, sweating, and laughing with Lucy and other people who came to help. The village worked on a barter system. I traded two days of chipping wood for a wool jacket.

I heard more stories from the early days, inspiring, maddening, frightening, sweet stories, and saw many photographs and vids of the founding mothers and fathers. They were totally different from the horrors I had seen in my women's history class.

Hank and I spent a lot of time together. He was good company. We were teased by everyone about the growing friendship between us. He asked a lot of questions about my life, but didn't get answers. He told me about his life and his dreams. It was the first time anyone had discussed their dreams with me since before First Choosing Day in my quad. I felt cold inside because I didn't think I had any dreams, just ambitions and goals.

I gave my virginity to Hank one Tuesday in the late afternoon. We had worked cleaning farm tools, dirty physical labor, and then I dared him to a swim in the Calumet River. I stripped down to my underwear unthinking, not meaning to entice, and dove in. I came up gasping. The water was so icy cold it took my breath away.

Hank was standing at the water's edge in his blue boxer shorts and red socks, staring at me with his mouth open and his eyes glistening. He looked silly and madly endearing. I stood up. I might as well have been naked. I knew that look — I had seen it in the eyes of the Fedguards at Rehab, but it was different on Hank.

"I'm cold!" I smiled and waded towards him.

"I'll warm you." He opened his arms and I walked into his embrace willingly.

He did warm me. He knew what to do and how, and I think he was in love with me. I loved him, too, but was afraid at first. That didn't matter. We fumbled for a while, and then made love and giggled and got all sandy and laughed about it. We went into the water afterwards to get the dirt off. Hank shivered and quipped that it was a good thing he hadn't gone into the river before we made love. It was, I believe, the first adult joke I ever understood.

Lucy knew — how I don't know — and it made her frown and tilt her head when she encountered us, returning from the fields holding hands. She stood on the back steps with her arms akimbo, hands firmly on her hips.

"You better go home, Hank."

He hugged me briefly and left, smiling. I turned to her, apprehensive because she didn't look happy.

"Flirting is one thing, loving's another, Jemma. You'll break that boy's heart."

"No! No, Lucy. I wouldn't do that!" It hurt me that she thought such a thing of me. I wanted to tell her it was my first time, to share my excitement, my joy. Besides, didn't they believe in free love? I wanted her to know I was a warrior *and* a lover.

"Do you intend to stay in Athena?"

The unexpected question had a bitter edge of criticism. I hadn't thought of that, and I hesitated before I answered truthfully. "Of course not."

She stared at me a moment then went back into the house.

I sat on Lucy's back porch, tears in my eyes, knowing that yet another rite of passage was to be denied me. My euphoria and pleasure seeped from my heart.

She was right. I wouldn't, couldn't, stay. It wasn't just Hank. It was late October; the days were getting short; there was a nip in the air. Snow would follow. I would have to leave Athena soon or risk flying in tricky winter weather.

I knew it was time to go. I didn't want to wear out my welcome, to disappoint Lucy, to hurt Hank, to endanger the town. Knowing that I was right did not make it hurt less.

Lucy was fixing supper when I walked into the kitchen. I began to help her automatically. I had simple chores assigned me: setting the table, cutting the bread, grinding the coffee. She stood at the sink with her back to me, staring out the window at the lowering dusk.

"It's nearly November, Lucy." My voice sounded strange and I cleared my throat. She didn't respond. "It's time for me to go, before I get snowed in."

She didn't turn around. "Yes, that's wise."

I set the table, poured myself a glass of milk, and sliced the bread into hefty pieces. I cranked the old coffee grinder, not even noticing the wonderful aroma, studying the sturdy pine table, the two place settings, and the bright green-striped tablecloth, already overcome with nostalgia.

I had come to think of it as home and it was beautiful to me. But it wasn't home, and never could be. I couldn't help myself. I burst into tears. Lucy turned then, was beside me in a step to take me in her arms.

"Oh, Jemma. It's all right, girl, go ahead and cry. Life isn't fair, we all know that. But you're right, it *is* time for you to go."

I caught my breath and rubbed at my face. "I don't mean to hurt Hank. I wouldn't knowingly harm any of you."

"I know, I know. You're a good person, Jemma. It's been a pleasure to have you here with me. But this isn't your place, your destiny. You have work to do."

She added that nudge about my work with a positive energy, and I knew I must snap out of feeling sorry for myself. No self-indulgence allowed.

Sooner or later, someone would find out that I was here
— a traveler, an unforeseen, roving Fedguard, or one of
the infrequent visitors from another village. I was a danger
to them.

"I'll check the GAV tomorrow and get it ready." I felt
suddenly calmer as I ratified my decision. "It would probably be better if the solars could soak up the sun for a day
or so, to jump-start them."

"Good. That's settled, then. Let's have our supper."

I left three days later, laden with my new clothes, a
basket of food, and Hank's tears on my lips. I had lied to
them about one thing — I had said I would walk away from
Athena and forget that I'd ever been there. That was not
possible.

Chapter 7

I went south, following the sun, avoiding the settlements in general. Labs in Atlanta, Miami, then along the periphery of BosWash went up in green fire and flames behind me. AGNA made an all-out effort to catch me. They were now saying that I was more than one person; that the sabotage was a conspiracy; that the Movers were behind it. Anything to cover their asses.

I stopped in a small village in the Poconos, hoping to get a frying pan. I had left mine somewhere, and its loss made roughing it in the Countryside more primitive than I could bear. They were not welcoming and kept their guns on me. I got the distinct feeling that if I stayed I'd be caught, so I fled.

I flew west and north with a chill in my heart. *If there were good people in AGNA, there were bad people in the Countryside*, I thought.

I figured it was only a matter of time until I got killed or captured. There were 143 labs that I knew about. I had destroyed only fourteen. Well, it was a start. No, it was a statement. I had said it was the idea for which I was willing to die. Maybe I was about to test that resolve.

I wandered around the Northeast for months. I was hungry most of the time, even though it was late summer and the harvests colored the fields again with Impressionist hues I remembered from art class. *Art class*, I thought, *in another life*. At night, watching the stars, I dreamed of making pear jam in Athena. Then one night at an alteration facility near Toledo....

"Don't move."

I froze. I had a piece of demolition dirt in my hand.

"Turn around slowly." The man's voice whispered right behind me.

I turned to face the threat and almost didn't see him. A large black man dressed in black, he was nearly invisible, except for his grin.

He shot me.

# # #

I woke up in a clean bed in a dim room with a pounding headache. The man was leaning against the wall drinking out of a big mug. He smiled: white, even teeth.

"Welcome back. You're not hurt. It was a stun gun. You're Jemma, right?" I said nothing. He chuckled. "Jemma, you're among friends."

"Why did you shoot me?"

"I didn't think I could talk fast enough to get you to come with me. We've been trying to catch up with you for months."

"Are you a Fedguard?" I sat up and dangled my legs over the side of the bed, thinking that if I moved too fast I might vomit. I wasn't wearing my boots, nor my jacket, my clothes were loosened, my pocketknife was gone. Who had done that? Where was I?

He laughed again, a low, throaty laugh. "I'm Nathan. I do pretty much what you do, but I don't do it alone. Want something to eat?"

He pushed himself away from the wall and opened the door beside him. The hall outside was better lit and I could hear voices and laughter from somewhere.

I stood up slowly. Nathan was a big man. A handsome man with an open, friendly face and delicately curved eyebrows. He had a mustache like Daddy wore. He stood beside the door, a slight smile on his lips.

I thought about running, shoving him and running past him, wherever the hall would take me. We both knew that's what was in my mind. His eyes had a twinkle and he shook his head slightly. A warning? If so, it was a gentle one.

"C'mon, Jemma. Everyone wants to meet you."

I thought better of attempting an escape and went ahead of him down the narrow passage and into a big sunny room. I was surprised that it was morning, because that meant I had been unconscious for at least ten hours.

It was a pleasant place: orangy-red curtains on three windows overlooking a barnyard; a long wooden table with a red checkered tablecloth and benches on the sides, chairs at the ends. An open doorway accessed the kitchen. The walls had old-timey pictures on them: landscapes, cows in a meadow, one modern holoprint of kittens curled up in a blue cloisonné bowl, and a spectacular print of a fractal by a famous Canadian artist named Maureen. Against one wall was a sideboard stacked with dishes, none of which matched. I could hear chickens outside. A big yellow cat was sleeping in the sun on a window sill.

Five people were there, eating and talking, joking I guessed, because there was laughter when we walked in. It subsided and they all shut up and turned to us. My stomach growled, prompted by the smell of bacon.

"Here is Jemma," Nathan said.

I didn't smile. Stun guns hurt, contrary to popular belief. They give you a bad headache and flu-like aching in all your joints. If I hadn't been so hungry I would have gone back to bed or tried to walk out the door. But I was hungry, and not just for food. I needed to know why I was there and who they were and what they wanted from me.

"Here, Jemma. Hi. Sit here." An exotic-looking young man with dark, almond-shaped eyes and straight black hair moved his plate over to make room for me between himself and a red-haired woman.

"Welcome," the woman said. She had a lopsided smile and a savage scar on the left side of her face. It had been a pretty face once, with big hazel eyes. She didn't look away when I stared at her.

I moved slowly to sit at the designated place.

"Hungry?" The man handed me an empty plate from a stack at the end of the table. The woman passed me a bowl of scrambled eggs.

I nodded. They set the things down. I wanted to eat, but I suddenly felt trapped, was suddenly afraid.

The two men across the table were smiling nicely at me. One of them passed the toast.

"No one will hurt you, Jemma. Please, have some breakfast."

I turned at the voice. It was the boss voice — a low sultry voice that sounded vaguely familiar. The woman looked familiar, too. Her shoulder-length, wavy hair was white, and where the morning sun caught it, she seemed to glow. Her eyes were intensely blue, with laugh crinkles at the corners and fine lines down her cheeks. I couldn't guess her age. Sixty? Older? I hadn't seen many old women, even in the country towns. I wrinkled my forehead, wondering for the first time why that was. The woman smiled at me and the world bloomed, one of those heart-stopping smiles. She was beautiful. I was sure I knew her, but from where?

I stared, rudely. She chuckled.

"My name is Annie. Welcome." She introduced the others. I dipped my head as I looked at each of them. Then she said, "And, of course, you know Nathan." He grinned.

"He shot me."

They laughed; I didn't. Nathan sat at the foot of the table and began to butter his toast.

Ginger, the woman beside me, reached for a keepswarm on a footed brass trivet. "Coffee?"

Coffee? I couldn't believe it. There had been times in my recent travels when I thought I would kill for a cup of coffee. I'd had none since Athena, in fact. I remembered the village with a twinge of sweet pain.

"Yes, please." I couldn't keep the enthusiasm out of my voice.

Annie chuckled again, and that sounded familiar. "Well, there's one thing we know already. Jemma likes coffee."

I glanced at her and then away. Her eyes were intense, evaluating, asking questions, offering conversation. I stirred sugar and milk into the coffee and took a long sip before I took eggs and toast. The others talked about the weather and about a shipment of tools they were expecting. I didn't have anything to say. I felt guilty to be eating their food. I wanted to leave.

"How old are you, Jemma?" The question came out of the blue and caught me with a fork full of eggs on its way to my mouth. Annie pushed her plate away and leaned back, studying me.

I set the fork on my plate. I drank my coffee. Everyone was waiting for my answer and finally I put the cup down. I didn't trust them. Besides, I had rules for myself that had kept me alive: I didn't talk about my work and I didn't talk about myself, especially not to strangers who had, as far as I could see, captured me. I wondered if the Fedguards were already on their way.

"I don't talk about myself."

"I don't mean to pry, I'm just curious. You look younger than I thought you'd be."

"Am I your prisoner?" I asked as flatly as I could. I had learned it was best to stay neutral in bad situations.

"No, of course not," Annie said, and all the others agreed. They even laughed. "We're on the same side. We're the Movers, Jemma." She sipped her coffee, her friendly eyes shining over the rim of her cup. The veins on the back of her hand were etched blue against fair skin.

"The Movers!" At last. I couldn't suppress my surprise, or my interest. *But they had shot me!* I was confused. I stared at their smiling faces and couldn't think of anything to say.

Ginger poured more coffee in my cup, but I didn't think I could drink it. The caffeine was giving me a jolt, I was aching, and now my stomach was in knots, partly from fear and excitement, and partly because I had eaten too much after a long stretch of near-fasting.

Annie moved her plate to one side so she could fold her hands on the table. "We won't hurt you; we won't keep you here against your will. We need to talk to you. Frankly, we want to recruit you. We admire your work."

She stopped and everyone waited but I didn't say anything. Nathan sighed and scratched his head.

"We admire you, but we fear for you. And, last night—"

I looked at him quickly, and I'm sure with daggers in my eyes. What about last night? They were dangerous to me if they thought I was doing something wrong. I sat up straighter.

Annie started talking again, and this time that velvet voice spiked into an edge.

"About that work, Jemma, and last night. Yes, you're good. But your arrogance or just plain carelessness will betray you."

"Arrogance?" I snapped my head around to glare at her. She didn't know how I planned things, how careful I was! I had blown up fourteen labs! It would have been fifteen, if they hadn't interfered.

"Don't be hostile — we're not. You're getting sloppy and predictable. Nathan was waiting for you. We guessed roughly where you were going to hit next, you see, and we knew it would be in the dark of the moon. If we figured it out, don't you think the Fedguards could, too? If Nathan hadn't picked you up, the feds might have been waiting at the next one."

I didn't know what to say. She could be right, probably was right. I knew I wasn't quite as sharp as I should be. I had lost my cooking things, misread the town where I almost got caught. I sometimes didn't want to work; kept wanting to sleep. I stared at my plate and thought I might be sick.

"Besides, and this is the important thing." I glanced sideways at her. Annie's eyes were narrowed slightly, like Mother used to do when she was about to chastise me for something. "That alteration facility is one of ours."

I blinked, uncomprehending.

"We don't just blow things up, child. It's taken us a long time to infiltrate that lab. We have a lab of our own where we're doing research, slowly to be sure, to see if there's a way to reverse alteration. We get our supplies from that facility. If you had blown it, it would have set us back."

I thought I might die on the spot, but her tone was reasonable. She wasn't angry. "Oh." That's all I could think of to say and I had never felt so stupid in my life.

"So you see, Jemma, we need to coordinate our efforts, at least. You had no way to know about the lab, but we had to stop you." I nodded.

Ginger whispered, "We want to help you, Jemma."

I felt the earth moving under my feet, knowing for a certainty that my life was changing again. I had come so far, had done so much, and knew so little. It made me grumpy. "I don't need any help." It came out as petulant. I was embarrassed and didn't dare look at anyone.

"Well, we'll talk about it," Annie said before she addressed the others. "Now tell me what's on tap for today."

They ignored me while each person spoke of their chores ahead. Simple things, mending a break in the chicken coop, cleaning tools, working on the vehicles, all things that sounded like the work in Athena. Then there was a lull in the conversation. I didn't mean to, but it just popped out.

"I'm sixteen. And a half."

I looked to Annie for a response. Everyone had become silent and still; Nathan's coffee cup was arrested halfway to his mouth. Her eyes were kind, the crinkles in their corners accentuated. "Sixteen... how long is it you've been out of the city?"

"Five years." I was breaking one of my own rules, but somehow it seemed okay to do.

"You're a brave girl, Jemma."

I shrugged. I didn't feel brave, not at that moment. I felt disoriented and edgy. I didn't know what I was doing and this was the first time in months that I'd talked with more than one person at a time.

"You do see that it's important for you to be aware of what we're doing?"

"I guess so." That was dumb! Of course I saw.

"Good."

I was having trouble breathing. Annie exuded a kindness, a power, that was suffocating me.

Nathan pushed his plate away. "There are things we think you can tell us, Jemma."

I couldn't imagine what I could tell them. I took a deep breath and mumbled a "Yes-okay."

Annie stretched and adjusted her chair. Everyone but
Nathan left for their work. I sat still. Another man came
out of the kitchen, smiled at me, and cleared off the plates
and dishes, leaving the keepswarm, my coffee cup, and
the cream and sugar.

When he left, Nathan winked at me. "That's our cook,
Will. Keep on his good side, kid."

"I'm not a kid. Don't patronize me."

He grinned and waggled his eyebrows and made a mock
bow. I looked back to Annie and could not imagine why
I was so uncomfortable and spiky. I was in the presence
of the legendary Movers. Surely it was safe.

We sat for an awkward moment. Annie gave Nathan
a reproving look.

"Jemma, I'm sure you're confused because of the way
we brought you here. Nathan owes you an apology for that!
As we said, it wasn't just to stop you at that particular lab,
but that we need to coordinate our efforts. You need protection, whether you know it or not."

"Protection from what?"

Nathan moved to sit across the table from me, stretching
out long legs, bumping my foot. I recoiled from him but
he didn't adjust.

"From the Fedguards, for starters," he said. "And I *am*
sorry I shot you. I overestimated your size. I gave you a
big zap when a smaller one would have served." He moved
his feet again.

I nodded but kept my mouth shut and moved sideways
a couple of inches, tired of being kicked. What did they
know? I'd been dodging the Fedguards ever since I'd
skipped out of rehab.

Annie put her napkin on the table. Her expression was
pleasant. "You're not exactly what I expected and I don't
mean your age. For such a — vigorous person — you seem
a little.... Are you always this quiet? You must have some
questions for us."

I thought for a moment and played with the coffee
spoon, tracing the interlocking squares on the tablecloth.

"Where am I?"

Annie smiled. "Central Pennsylvania — our headquarters for the moment. We move around."

"Pennsylvania?!" I really had been zapped. I remembered nothing of the trip but was several hundred miles from where I thought I was. I looked at Nathan. "You took my gear."

"It's safe. You can have it back."

"Where's my pocketknife?"

Nathan pulled his feet in. "On the dresser in the room where you woke up."

"Did you bring my GAV?"

"No. We stripped it and destroyed it."

My heart clutched. They had taken away my escape, then. They said I wasn't their prisoner, but I was. Annie seemed to read my mind.

"Jemma, you're *not* a prisoner. We want you to work with us. We need good people like you! You've been all over the country, have seen things we need to know about. Please, forgive this uncomfortable beginning. Trust us. Join us."

I played with my coffee cup but didn't drink it. "What would I do?"

"Well, what you're doing now, but with assistance." She leaned toward me. "We do other things besides blowing up outposts and disrupting AGNA's broadcasting. We help people. We link up communities that want to stay in touch with each other. We get supplies to isolated towns. Many things."

I stared into the flat, oily surface of my cold coffee, seeing my reflection there. "Would I stay here?"

"Yes. You could, of course, leave at any time."

I looked around the pleasant room. My confusion was turning into a warm excitement. They didn't know why I smiled, and Annie's face registered a question that I didn't answer. I was thinking that it was another choosing day.

"I have more questions."

"Good. I'll answer as many as I can. All of us will."

They waited for my answer. She cocked an elbow on the table and propped her chin on her hand, watching me. That made me nervous.

"I could try it. For a day or so. See how it goes."

"Excellent!" Annie stood up and tossed her head to get the hair out of her eyes, and when she did that I nailed her.

"I know you! I knew I did! You're Ann7717 who was AGNA Evening News!" I had watched her throughout my childhood in L. A.

She laughed. "The same. Come along to the staff room, and bring your coffee. We'll get you something to take away your aches and pains, and then we'll talk."

I hadn't moved. "But you're dead." It sounded stupid when I said it and I embarrassed myself again.

"Not yet," she said, and held out a hand to me. From that moment, I think I was a Mover in my heart.

# # #

"In here, Jemma." Annie led me through a door as Nathan continued down the hall.

The staff room was a spacious workplace with three large worktables and chairs arranged for talking. Maps and papers were piled everywhere. Shelves overflowed with printouts and even some hardbound books, real antiques. I wondered where they had got them — I'd only seen them in museums and the rehab library. Comp units and tracking devices glowed and blipped; electronic units were stacked in the corners; sun poured in the big window.

Annie gestured to a map of North America on the wall, drawn in topological detail. "Where have you been? Show me."

I stared at the map. It looked so big. Flat, impersonal. My eyes sought Athena immediately. Nothing was marked to show where the town lived. Did that mean they didn't know about it? How much should I tell them?

Nathan came into the room with a pain patch and handed it to me. "Here, this will take the edge off the aches."

I slapped the patch on my arm, with a nanosecond's doubt about what it really was and a twinge at my paranoia. I had no particular reason to suspect they were not who they said they were, but I was still uncomfortable. Annie sat in front of the map, waiting for my travelogue.

Thus my first afternoon at Mover HQ was spent describing the places I'd been, the things I'd seen, the impressions I'd gathered. I'm good at maps, and they were pleased with the amount of information I could provide. After three hours we had more coffee, Annie and Nathan went off to do other things, and I took a nap, a sound one. Later, Ginger came to show me around the complex.

They gave me clothes and a personal mini-comp unit so I could catch up on what was happening in the world and interface with their database. I had not seen many of the Mover's vids, the ones they scrambled into the AGNA News Network, and those I had seen that included armies fighting I had misunderstood as past history. Not so — AGNA was still at war with organized rebel groups in Mexico and Canada. Well, well.

Other than learning recent history and upgrading myself on their computers, I wasn't allowed to do anything but sleep and eat. That was good for a couple of weeks and then I began to get bored and anxious. Annie had told me they welcomed my expertise with demolition, and my street smarts, but they weren't using it.

"Please, please, Annie, give me something to do." The other Movers, except for two who had gone to pick up medical supplies, were finishing their breakfasts. "All I've done since I got here is look at vids about the wars in Canada and sleep! I need to *do* something!"

She leaned back in her chair. "Well, have you finished the reports I asked for?"

"No, but I'm doing that. That's a huge job I'll have to do over time. I'm thinking of something a little more active. I'm bored."

"What would you like to do?"

"I don't care. Feed the chickens. Go on a mission." I slathered a piece of bread with honey.

"You're not ready for a mission." Nathan's voice was flat, but not a challenge. He was Annie's Second, I had come to realize, so I guessed his observation was shared by all.

"And never will be if I don't start learning what you're doing."

"In good time, Jemma." Annie was smiling her diplomatic smile.

I set my coffee cup down with a clank. "You don't trust me!"

Annie sighed. "You came to us twenty pounds underweight and tired in your bones. There's plenty of time for you to assimilate into our organization. Next week," and the look she shot Nathan made me think she had just thought of this, "we'll start you on the weapons. I don't think you know much about them, do you?"

I sulked. "No. And I don't like them much, either."

Nathan laughed. "Well, you will. If you get yourself into a difficult situation, you'll be happy to have them."

"I've been in difficult situations. And got out without shooting."

Nathan's eyebrows went up. "Like you did in Cinci?"

That defeated me. I shut up then and drank my coffee. I still felt guilty about the raid in Cinci. AGNA said two hundred people were killed. That's a lie, but I know there were some and I was tired of people bringing the damn thing up.

Nathan didn't give it up. "You don't even know what kind of a weapon you were firing in Cinci."

"A big one," I snarled, glaring at him.

The table exploded in laughter, and I finally had to smile myself.

I was abandoned again, as everyone went off to their work. When Will came to clear the table, I helped him and followed him into the kitchen.

Will had been an operative for the Movers until his GAV had been shot down, leaving him with permanent, irreversible brain damage. He was slow, but he did well as the cook and general household aide.

I offered to help him in the kitchen and he was delighted with the companionship. Everyone was nice to him but didn't spend much time in his company.

So that morning I helped wash the dishes and clean the rooms. Then he had me peeling potatoes for whatever he intended to make for lunch.

"We're getting low on potatoes," he said in his slurry drawl.

"Where do they come from, Will?" There was a big kitchen garden that he carefully tended, mostly gone to seed now, but he didn't raise potatoes.

"Annie gets them from farmers somewhere. I don't know. Need onions soon, too."

I checked out our stores, as I had learned to do in Athena. We also were short on flour. I assumed that we would put in extra supplies for the winter. It occurred to me that if I had the equipment, I could be canning things for us. Will didn't know how to do that.

I gave myself a mission. I would go somewhere to get vegetables and fruits, and preserve them for us, and would start by meeting our current needs. That afternoon I studied the maps of the Northeast Region, asked a few questions about farming communities of anyone who would talk to me, checked the supply files in the main database, and made a plan.

I got up in the middle of the night, before anyone was awake, took my carrybag with a change of clothes, and left Annie a message, "Gone for provisions. Back soon. J."

I took one of the GAVs and headed north, my heart quickening as I watched the sunrise from the air. I had been at HQ less than a month, and I'd forgotten how much I liked spinning over the fields. It felt good to be free; it felt good to have something meaningful to do. I disabled the tracking device on my ship with only a tiny stab of guilt.

I had learned we traded with farmers in Upstate New York. I found a farm without much trouble. From the air, the neat furrows, patches of color, and overlapping patterns were easy to spot. The family accepted my offer to work for six bags of onions.

They recognized me from AGNA news, but they said they had "no truck" with the government and were happy for my help. The children, especially the girls, hung around me, asking questions and confiding in me that they always watched me on the news, wondering how many people I had killed. I set them right on that immediately.

After dinner the first night, sitting around their fireplace, I told them about Athena. Not by name or location of course, but what it meant, what I had learned there, and how it fit into history. They listened politely.

The farmer stared at me when I had finished, rubbing a two-day growth of beard. "AGNA really does that to women?"

I nodded. "That. And worse."

No one asked anything more, and I thought they didn't believe me until I was ready to leave two days later.

The farmer's wife helped me load my six sacks of onions into the GAV. The men were still in the fields; the younger children stood in a wiggly, giggly cluster admiring my vehicle. The wife threw in a bushel of corn as well, as a bonus.

"This is to thank you for the story," the woman said. "It's true, isn't it? About that town and the Civil War and the women."

"Yes."

She stared off across the field. "I always figured it was something like that. We watch AGNA News, and Mover News. It's not about us, though, Jemma. We're plain people here." She managed a rare smile. "We hear about those violent things you do and it's like a — a story. Not real." She picked up an ear of corn. "This is real." She nodded towards the gaggle of kids. "They're real. We don't want to be involved with AGNA's wars."

I grinned and hugged her. She stiffened, unaccustomed to a display of emotion from strangers. "You're a poet, ma'am."

She made a scoffing noise, but her eyes were kind and dancing. "You just be real careful, Jemma. Thanks for your help. You come back again."

I said I would try, waved at the children and left, with directions to a potato farmer further north and east.

I worked for two days digging potatoes. Early in the morning of the third day, just as we got into the fields, we heard the whirr of GAVs and all of us — the farmer, his wife and daughter, two sons and a son-in-law — turned our faces to the sky.

They knew who and what I was. The daughter walked towards me, quickly but without running, and handed me her broad-brimmed hat. A paltry disguise, but the only thing we had. It would not do for me to run. Doubtless they had seen us from the air.

"Just stay with me and do what I do," she said, and led me towards her mother. We women stood off to the side, watching, while the farmer and his oldest son walked towards the landing GAVs, three of them.

Three Fedguards spilled out of the first vehicle, guns at the ready. I had a sudden horrid thought. *They know I'm here! These people will suffer for it.* The women thought of that, too, and held their breaths, glancing sideways at me. The men didn't look back.

We were wrong. A sergeant got out of the car and walked towards the farmers. He was a tall, beefy man with graying red hair and a florid complexion. The other guards fell in behind him. He stopped, glanced our way once, dismissed us with a shrug, then looked at the men.

"We need a few pack animals." His voice boomed out, louder than necessary in the still of dawn. He pointed at the farmer. "You stay here, old man. These young men will come with us."

The farmer's lips whitened into a slash. "It's harvest time. They're needed."

His wife's hands involuntarily went to her own mouth to silence her husband. It wasn't smart to argue.

"Well, we need them in Canada. Join the Fedguards and see the world!" The guards behind him laughed. He tilted his head at the corporal beside him, the Fedguards moved forward, guns at their hips. The young men had no choice. They were loaded into the second GAV without so much as a leave-taking from their family.

It was over in a minute. The GAVs took off, heading southeast.

"Sonsabitches!" The farmer spat ferociously. "Their damn wars got nothing to do with us."

"Canada." His wife's face had gone red. She wanted to cry. Instead, they held each other. I backed off a discreet distance.

The old man turned and pointed a bony finger at me. "You just keep doing what you're doing, young woman. You stop those bastards. You hurt those bastards!"

My mind was elsewhere. "The other farms around here should be warned." I knew they had no comp unit. "I'll go now and try to outrun them. If there's any way you can reach other farmers to warn them to get their young men safely away — do it!"

"I'll go, Dad." The young woman was already heading across the field toward the barn where an old chestnut mare stood drowsing in the paddock. We hurried back to the house.

They insisted on loading my GAV with the potatoes I had earned. It was an odd parting. We stood silently staring at each other: the farmer, his wife, the daughter, the horse. Me, with a foot on my GAV. *In two worlds*, I thought.

I lifted off with a wave, saw that they were not going to move until I was out of sight and sped low across the tops of the trees, looking for farms.

I spent the rest of the day going in circles, avoiding the Fedguards, landing at every homestead I saw and telling the story. Not one had a comp unit. I knew I should check in with HQ, but didn't dare transmit from my GAV because the fedcars were still in the area and might trace me. They were doubtless becoming frustrated and I wanted to stay clear of them.

As evening began to fall, I decided I had done as much as I could and headed home, throttle open wide to try to get there quickly.

I made my usual skidding sort of landing in the open meadow behind the barn, clumsier than ever in the dark. The moment the vehicle stopped, I was surrounded by Movers with guns.

I got out waving my arms, but the guns didn't drop. Bright lights came on, dazzling my eyes. Annie and Nathan came stomping around the corner of the barn, hopping mad, I could tell. I held up my arms in surrender.

"I know, I know.... I can see you're angry. Annie, there's a problem."

"There certainly is! Inside, now!"

I gestured towards the GAV. "I brought potatoes and onions and corn. But, AGNA is—"

Nathan took two steps and pulled me up straight, his hand crunching the front of my shirt. "Shut up and get inside."

I should have just blurted my news, of course, but I resented his manhandling. "Let go, Nathan!" I thought he was going to hit me. So did everyone else and they straightened their backs. Most of them probably thought he should. We got through the tense moment, then I shrugged him off and took a step backward. "AGNA is stealing men in New York."

Ah, one of those moments when, as the poets say, time stands still. Then Annie took a step towards me, her eyes snapping.

"Stealing men?"

When I told them about the AGNA conscription, my misdemeanor was forgotten. I learned some colorful words from the group reaction.

Annie's tone to Nathan was urgent. "Get on the comm to Sept Iles. See what they know. I'll get Henri at Lac Manitou!" She turned to me. "Jemma, you're not off the hook for stealing the GAV. We needed it for a mission and had to abort. But we'll get to that later." We all started for the house. "Okay, everyone, the staff room in fifteen minutes."

"Yes, ma'am!" I nearly saluted. I grinned instead and fell in behind her.

A half hour later, Nathan pulled up a fine hologram map of the area from ClevErie to the Atlantic off Newfoundland for us to study. It glowed in the air beside him in the dimly lit room. I was allowed at the briefing and impressed with the sophistication of their tools. They hadn't shown me any of that before.

"Our Canadian friends say they expect an attack coming around Lake Erie, here—" the tronic wand in his hand highlighted the area "—probably meaning to engage them around Trois Rivieres. AGNA will have to bring troops from Chicago and Cinci, and maybe whatever they have at the Albany depot. Henri says most of the Midwest Region Fedguards are engaged in the fighting around Athabasca territory off in the West. They don't have enough air transports so they'll have to use the tunnels."

He pointed to the ClevErie overground and the one nicknamed Buffalley, running from Albany to Buffalo. These were eventually meant to link when construction was finished. It had been held up for years, partly from Mover sabotage, partly from a lack of funds.

"Where the gap is," Nathan continued, highlighting again around Buffalo, "they are most vulnerable."

"And most heavily fortified," someone said.

"Yes, but still easiest to get at. It will help our northern friends if we can delay and harass the Fedguards before they cross over into Canada."

Annie had admonished me not to talk, I was there to listen and learn, but I was thinking about the ClevErie overground and the research I had done on it so many years ago that it felt like someone else's work. I hadn't realized it before, but ClevErie had a weak spot, maybe all the overgrounds did. I couldn't keep my mouth shut.

I stood up. "What if we slowed them down in the ClevErie overground? Shut it down maybe?"

Nathan's jaw clenched. He wanted to yell at me, but he didn't. He pursed his lips and shook his head. The others were willing to be tolerant, too, but that wasn't what I wanted. They shifted in their seats and rolled their eyes.

"Thanks, Jemma. Just sit still and listen."

"But—"

"Ask questions later! Don't interrupt!"

I didn't back down. "I know what I'm talking about, Nathan! There's a weakness in the overground tunnels. I studied that one — ClevErie. We could, I think, close it, at least temporarily."

Nathan and Annie exchanged a glance. They were willing to listen.

"Go ahead. Make it short."

"See that place on the map called Kellogg? It's a ruined town close to the Pennsylvania line." He found it and highlighted it. "There's a mural of a forest painted in that tunnel from beginning to end. Fuel pollutants erode the paints and there's an egress there, at Kellogg. The painters use it to keep those pretty pictures clean and pretty. I'm not sure exactly what it is, but I know it's there. My guess is it's just a door of some sort, big enough for the painters and their equipment. It may not be double plasticrete like the rest of the tunnel."

"How do you know this?" Annie asked.

I laughed. "I had to write a research paper on the tunnels as a penance for being a bad girl in my quad. I hadn't thought of it before, but I'll guess *all* the overgrounds are the same. At least the ones with murals."

A buzz of interest and excitement went through the room.

"You're sure of this?" Nathan took a step toward me.

"Absolutely sure."

"What about Buffalley?"

"I don't know about it. It's not finished. There are no murals yet, but the construction will probably include the same feature."

"All right! Excellent, Jemma! Thanks. What else can you tell us?"

I talked briefly about how I would blast through the door if I were planning the attack, and how the tunnels were sectioned. I was surprised I remembered as much about them as I did. The inside of the tunnels were vulnerable to explosives; the double plasticrete exteriors were not.

We got down to business after that. Their demolition expert was good and they had tronics to set the explosives off, something I'd never had. We used basically the same demolition dirt, except of course that I added barium compounds to mine because it made that gorgeous green explosion that distracted anyone who might be watching. It was considered my trademark. They wouldn't let me use it this time. This was a Mover operation and Annie said she didn't want me linked to them "just yet." I didn't know what that meant and didn't think it was appropriate to ask.

I *was* allowed on the mission, though. I had brought a paint-wand, two in fact: red and black. After we blew the painter's door and got inside, they didn't give me anything to do so I went down the tunnel beyond our demolition site and painted male and female comic figures. I sketched them hiding behind trees, pointing up at the sky, grinning, peeing. They weren't very good — it had been a long time since I'd worked at my skills in that area. Nathan caught me at it.

"It's going to blow. We have to get out of here! What the hell are you doing?"

"Leaving a little message." He didn't look pleased. "Oh Nathan, lighten up. You know what they say — if it ain't fun, don't do it."

His scowl turned into a laugh. He put an arm around me and hustled me back to the hole in the tunnel and onto the waiting GAV.

We stuffed the tunnel full of debris, cracked another section of it, and held up the transport for three days, long enough for the Canadians to disappear into the wilderness with all their equipment and personnel.

The incident was not reported on AGNA Network News. They merely said that the ClevErie tunnel was closed for routine maintenance and they didn't mention my graffiti. I was disappointed.

Chapter 8

After that mission I was a full-fledged Mover and I settled in. Over the next six months they trained me, laughed at me, teased me, and — nice for me — liked me. Nathan was always at my back on any missions that were likely to incur weapons fire, when we hijacked AGNA convoys of supplies, for instance. I was good with the big guns but I still didn't like them. He and I began to work out a friendly relationship. I thought he was sexy. He moved like a cat. A very big cat.

I learned that the Movers did many things, like helping people escape from the cities, then introducing them into settlements where immigrants were welcome. They worked with contacts inside. There were operatives in all the megacities and I guessed the beach boy who had told me how to get out of L. A. was one of them. They didn't come out into the Countryside at all until they were ready to run, to retire; they educated inside the dome and aided anyone who wanted to leave. It was dangerous and few of them lived long enough to get out themselves. They made me ashamed that I thought I was doing hazardous work.

I learned there were more dastardly things the AGNA scientists did. They kept on experimenting, enhancing and retarding children's brains, not like they had mine, through DNA tinkering, but by grafting on the tissue of non-human species; manufacturing viruses that were ethnic specific; and lots of experiments with cloning. The AGNA Constitution specifically set forth strict rules about cloning. People couldn't be cloned, for instance, when they were still alive. Well, hell, that would be confusing.

AGNA was a mess. I was making a list of things I wanted to blow up and change, but Annie wouldn't allow me to freelance, and their priorities superseded mine.

She and I had discovered immediately that we were both early risers. At first I just went into the dining room at the crack of dawn, mumbled at her, got my coffee, and went back to my room. After a couple of weeks of that, Annie set the ritual in motion that would last for the next ten years.

"Good morning, Jemma."

I grabbed a cup and poured with a smile. I've always loved the smell of fresh-brewed coffee. "'Morning, Annie." I hurriedly spooned in the sugar and cream and started for the door.

"If you think you're disturbing me, you're not. It's actually rather pleasant to know there's another morning person."

I stopped in the doorway and turned back. She sat at her place at the head of the long table, a stack of reports on one side of her, a comp unit on the other. Gray light teased the windows but didn't come in.

"I like the morning. It's quiet, private. I like to see the sunrise."

She smiled and nodded agreement. "Sit down, please. Join me. Have your breakfast. I'd like your company."

I did, easing myself onto the bench to her right. I had come to admire Annie. In fact, I think I had a kind of crush on her. She was so self-contained, so even. She was always... appropriate. I was also a little afraid of her. Not that she would harm me, not of what she might say or do about me, but because I felt she had a kind of power over me, an influence, or the possibility of it. I felt she could change me and I wasn't sure I wanted to change.

That first morning, Will asked if I wanted eggs and disappeared into the kitchen. The others would not be down for at least an hour but he was used to taking care of Annie and extended the courtesy to me. She and I sat in silence for a while. I stared out the window while Annie was working on her comp unit.

After Will delivered two sunny-side-up eggs and a plate of cinnamon buns, Annie turned the comp unit off and poured herself another cup of coffee. "Are you comfortable here, Jemma?"

I was still staring out the window, watching as the gray light began to glow pinkly at the edges. "No."

"Why not?"

"I don't know what I'm doing. I miss being my own boss." For the first time I noticed that the big clock over the door ticked loudly.

"Those are serious things." She sipped her coffee. I tore off the corner of a cinnamon bun. It was horribly sweet but I liked the shock on my tongue.

"Yes."

"What you're doing is learning how we operate; finding out if you fit into that operation; and coming, I hope, to appreciate our agenda. I know you have one of your own: to blow up the alteration facilities. That's acceptable sabotage to us, and we'll help you do that, but there are larger issues. We never lose sight of the ultimate goal. We want to take back the country, to overthrow AGNA."

I played with a spoon, stirred my coffee to cool it. "Blow up the megacities."

Annie's voice was mild. "And what would that serve exactly?"

The question seemed stuck in the yokes of my eggs. I stirred them, too. "Then we could start all over."

"Ahhh. Well, you need to think that through. If all you're interested in is violence, then you're not a good match for us."

My head snapped up. It hadn't occurred to me that she would throw me out. Her eyes were neutral; mine weren't. I think my mouth was hanging open. My heart was suddenly pounding with fear. I hadn't known, until that moment, that I *wanted* to stay at the farm, with Annie, with the Movers.

"I mean that, Jemma."

"I don't just want violence." I had a sudden chill. *What did I want?* I hadn't thought about it for years. Annie waited for more. "That's not true. I do mean to do the things I do. I hate what AGNA does. I like blowing up the buildings."

"Yes."

"But, I..." I was embarrassed to say it, "I don't know what else to do."

Annie played with her bottom lip, her elegant finger smoothing out the age lines. "Then let me help you. Believe me, I understand your anguish."

Yes Annie yes Annie yes Annie, help me. I took a deep breath. "I'm listening."

Her eyes narrowed on me, a probing look that made me squirm. "I don't want to waste your background, Jemma. You have social skills, organizational skills, smarts that others don't. I don't see you as just a grunt, a foot soldier."

"I don't know how to do anything else."

She ignored my intervention. "Here's what I can see for you..." She put her cup down and ran her fingers through the tangle of white hair. "Next week Devi is going to Miami. There are two Movers who are ready to come out of the city because they're probably in danger of discovery. We need to meet with their replacements, and get them out and resettle them. While he's there, Devi will be negotiating with some traders in the Everglades. You'll go with him. Observe. Assist. Learn how to do what he does.

"You'll be gone about a month. After that, you'll apprentice on other things. Our major job is to link the settlements, to make life easier for everyone in the Countryside, so that when the time comes — by the sword or the ballot — an infrastructure will be in place for a representative government again. The important work is to organize the Countryside and continue to undermine AGNA's authority in the cities. That's what you'll be doing."

I understood what she said, but I was thinking of settlements that I had visited. I doubted that all of them would appreciate her sentiments. I was slow to respond. Annie waited. "Yes. I understand the overview. I can't see it, but I understand your words. And I guess I'm grateful that you're giving me something real to do."

Annie laughed. "Oh, Jemma! You're a tough one!" She took a cinnamon bun and a big bite of it while I wondered what was so funny. "Okay. You 'guess' you're grateful. Well, that's a start. Pass the coffee."

I moved the keepswarm and the pot closer and searched her face for a clue to her behavior. *Why did I amuse her?* It only occurred to me later that I had been rude.

That breakfast, which spun into breakfasts until I was nearing thirty, was another turning point in my life. It was that morning that I truly committed to Annie, to the Movers, to my destiny. It was another choosing day, and one I never regretted.

I went to Miami with Devi. And wound up sleeping with him, too — a rather pleasant diversion which neither of us mentioned when we got back to HQ. He was exotically handsome, with his almond-shaped eyes and delicate hands. It pleased me to look at him. He was a physician, escaped from the Boston end of BosWash. He was an intellectual, from whom I learned and then debated philosophy and with whom I shared a love of art and music, and occasionally, over the years, my bed.

Next, I spent two months with Ginger training a little strike force in Wisconsin. I fell in love with the deep woods. Ginger of the scarred face was an amusing and steadfast friend under her tough exterior. She was our weapons expert and the most proficient shooter.

Hill, the other important military man at HQ besides Nathan, was a handsome, taciturn, spit-and-polish soldier who always smelled so clean I dubbed him "Soapy." He was Security Chief for the Movers, and taught me martial arts. He rarely smiled, but I think he enjoyed our sessions together and was genuinely anxious when he once dislocated my shoulder. That surprised me, since he seemed to take some pleasure from throwing me around. We risked our lives periodically and, in general, laughed about our hardships.

But the greatest gift to Movers gave to me was Annie, who became my surrogate mother. She took me under her wing, and our relationship grew strong and sweet. I loved her deeply. She was my mentor, my strongest critic, my dearest friend.

More and more I found myself doing different things, and by my fourth anniversary with the Movers, Annie trusted me with increasing responsibility. I was particularly good at negotiating with the settlements, perhaps because I admired them so much. Much as I hated to admit it, the early training to be a woman who marries came in handy.

I was good at picking targets, too. Some sort of odd talent for putting disparate information together made the raids I planned come off sweetly. I liked doing it. Annie sighed and wished I would give it up. I know she was waiting for the day when my rage against AGNA would smolder out.

That was not possible.

# # #

Annie had indeed been Ann7717, the voice of AGNA Network News from L. A., a star from her final choosing day on, and probably before that. Her eyes would get a strange light in them when she spoke of her celebrity days.

"I didn't know, Jemma. The way you didn't know, the way women *don't* know. It seems incredible that such a big lie could be told for so long. But..." and she handed me the keepswarm to refresh my cooling coffee. It had rained in the night and the morning was damp and chilly. "I suppose generations of lies, just the sheer weight of them, makes our ignorance more understandable."

We were alone in the dining room. The sky was beginning to lighten in shades of orange. More rain, I guessed. I poured my coffee and sniffed. I was not as equanimous as she. "Yes, and the fact that many women don't *want* to know. If they did, they might have to do something about it." I was thinking of my mother. I thought so often of my mother.

More than a dozen years before this particular breakfast chat, Annie had found interviews, archival stuff, when she was searching for background for a documentary she was preparing. She heard the voices of the Bad Women, dug deeper, and came to realize the truth of the domed megacity myth. That, coupled with the lies about the battles that still raged in North America, made her begin to question everything, and eventually led her to find a way to escape to the Countryside. She faked her death, and watched with all of North America as she was buried in an elaborate, maudlin ceremony.

She had brought her vid smarts with her, and within a short time had set up the Movers Network News. An organized, charismatic woman, she quickly rose through the ranks of the Movers, and was accepted as the top commander by the clusters of Mover groups all over the continent. She never revealed who she was to the public. Even if AGNA figured it out, and we assumed that they had, it was in their best interests to leave her dead and buried.

"Why are we talking about this again?" I stirred my coffee. "Don't you want to know about the biolab in Chicago? I put a memo on your comp unit yesterday."

"Yes, of course I do. But I'm thinking out loud. There are some changes coming."

"I'd like to hit Chicago, Annie."

She thought a minute. "You're looking at details again, Jemma." She steepled her elbows. "You've been here — what — four years?"

"And a half. But who's counting?" I was. I would be twenty-one in a few months.

"Hmmm." That made her quiet for a minute, so I took a sweet roll Will had prepared for us. Cinnamon buns. He knew I liked them.

"And you've hit how many labs?"

"Nine with the Movers, twenty-three overall." I found that disappointing and cancelled out my chagrin with the sweet roll. It was hot and sticky. I licked my fingers and Annie smiled and handed me a napkin.

She took a deep breath and sat up straighter. "Okay, today we start." But she didn't, so I continued to eat and watch her think.

"Jemma, a third of the women in the Countryside are alters. Almost half of the women in the cities are alters. You're doing a good piece of sabotage on the labs, and eventually it will slow them down, but there are more important things." She held up both hands to stifle my protest.

"You need to think bigger. I don't want you to spend your life, risk losing it, for a set of missions to bring down isolated facilities. We need to do that, of course, but there's much more to it. You have a knack for leadership. I need that from you more than green fire.

"AGNA is struggling at the moment. We've seen it before. It probably won't last, but for now, it's good for us. The wars are draining manpower, goods, and resources. Even some soldiers apparently feel that they're fighting a war they can't win. Morale is low and AGNA can't seem to light a fire under the troops. In the meantime, the infrastructure is breaking down. Sections of cities go without power. The artificial climates don't work properly—"

"Oooh, I want to go after *them*!" I had visions of messing up the grids that controlled the weather. That would make a statement, indeed.

Annie froze my enthusiasm with a look. "Yes, of course. We can do that; we have done that. But that's just harassment."

"You're making me uncomfortable, Annie. Where is this going?"

"Stop thinking about missions and mischief and start thinking about the ultimate goal. What we want is the complete overthrow of AGNA. Peaceably if possible, although that's not likely at the moment. But that time will come."

I couldn't think of anything to say. I sipped my coffee.

"I want you to go to northern New England for a while; work with the settlements there. We need to find a way to connect with them more easily. You'll supply them with comp units; teach them how to use them; fold them into our mix."

"By myself?"

Annie laughed. "You'll be in charge, but you'll take a couple of soldiers and a vid tech."

"I'll be the Regional Director?" That thought startled me. Scared me a little, too.

"Not of the whole region, just the remote part, the north of Vermont, New Hampshire, and Maine, and the adjacent Canadian settlements. We should have all the supplies you'll need in place in a couple of weeks. You're still very young, and there may be some — hesitation, shall we say? — about elevating your status, making you more visible. But I trust my instincts. So until you leave, you can do missions, but no more high risk ones." My head snapped up. We didn't always know which those were. "No rebuttal. I want you alive to see AGNA on its knees in fifty years."

I grinned then. "Fifty years? Omigod, Annie, who thinks that far ahead?"

She didn't smile. "I do. And so will you."

I doubted it. I doubted I would live that long, but I didn't say so. I think she saw that in my eyes, but she let it pass.

"Now, one other thing. We're moving HQ again. We've been here too long. I don't think we're compromised yet, but it would be better to leave."

"Leave?" I loved the farm. It was home. "Where will we go?"

"Hill has picked out another site for us, in the Southeast Region. Tomorrow we'll start packing everything up. We'll leave about the same time you go off to Vermont."

I looked around the friendly kitchen, missing it already. Annie smiled and touched my hand, reassuring.

"The new place is nice, Jemma. Some settlers will take this one over eventually. It won't go to waste." She stood up and looked at her chrono. "Nathan, Hill, and I are meeting at nine. Be there."

She left without a backward glance, but I sat at the table for a long time, doing nothing, not even thinking much. Another irrevocable choice had just been thrust into my life. This time, I wasn't frightened; in fact, I was happy, and, I confess, a bit smug. I was a grunt, not an administrator, but my heart sang that Annie had so much faith in me.

Chapter 9

My life for the next several years became a series of missions to convince the remote settlements to take in new people, and to persuade them that they had like-minded neighbors, not so far away, who would touch them across the miles, and offer comfort, trade, and friendship.

My celebrity helped me, and I never told Annie about the two towns that were hostile and pushed me into corners I had to fight my way out of. I killed some people instead of being killed. I feared that if Annie knew she would have me behind a desk at HQ, something I would not be able to accept. *Thank you, Daddy. You taught me how to lie.*

I did many interviews with those who joined as Movers willing to fight; led training missions; checked back to HQ every six months for orders and updates. From New England I moved to the Northwest Sector, and then to the very center of the country, the place that showed on the map as empty.

I found a few settlements and they were small in this area — four or five families joined together — but the people were eager for news, for company. The work was easy, and everywhere I went I told the stories from Athena, adding the memories and histories of the towns I had encountered.

It was there on the prairie, that my zeal to destroy AGNA was recharged.

I had been working hard. I decided to take some time off, so I camped out in what had been Old Nebraska but was now a wilderness of tall grass and scrubby trees. From the air it looked as flat as a griddle but actually it was undulating terrain, with gullies like pleats on a green sleeve.

It was summer and fragrant on the flowering plains. As the sun was setting, I found a small stream, set my GAV down, and made camp. Out there the stars seemed close enough to touch and I liked to be under them. It reminded me of that night long ago when my father had first shown me the universe.

At morning's first light I saw the horror.

I went to the stream to get water for my morning coffee and noticed rusty parts of machines sticking out from the ground on the opposite side from my camp. The stream was clear and shallow and I waded it, curious about the metal objects half-buried in the grass.

"Oh God!" I whispered and then I think I screamed it at the uncaring sky. I had chanced on what must have been a horrendous battlefield. Acres and acres of twisted and broken machines, guns, old canisters of chemicals and oil and gas, and then of course... bodies. How many I could not say. More than I could count.

Most of the dead were women. I walked slowly among them, seeing a hand, a crushed skull, a crumbled pile of bones. All those dead... unlamented, unmarked, unnamed. A thousand, I guessed, or maybe two. Thousands out of the millions who had perished in the wholesale destruction of small-town America.

They were bones now, fragmented for the most part, bones scrambled by animals and the weather, many with uniforms still covering them in tatters that stirred in the wind snaking across this land. I didn't remember a battle in Nebraska from the ones I had studied in rehab. Lucy had not mentioned it in all the history I had learned at Athena. What was this awesome carnage?

Why were they not buried? Was the area hot?

I hurried back to my gear and checked the water with a toxinchek. It was clean. If there had been nasty stuff, it would have leaked into the water. The toxin patches every GAV carried were a little old, but I hoped still worked well enough to tell me if something were especially dangerous.

They registered nothing. I clipped an airmeter to my jacket, in case there were pockets of poison.

Morbidly, I guess, I spent that day prowling through the waist-high grass and flowers, looking at skulls and bones, chronos, ID tags, occasional pieces of jewelry, military insignia, dead weapons.

The sky was robin's egg blue with puffy clouds; the breeze was fragrant and warm; occasionally, a hawk spiraled overhead, catching thermals. I moved like a ghost across the ghastly field of death.

I wept until I had no tears. The ugliness, the emptiness, the waste....

I discovered a chrono that still worked and took it. A token, a remembrance, as if I needed one. It was gold with Roman numerals on the face. The back was engraved, "Fred to Angela Love Always."

When night finally brought its gentle blessing, I sat at my fire and wept again, full of sadness and rage. That callous, neglected graveyard deepened my resolve to fight against AGNA forever and ever.

I finished my work as quickly as I could and fled back to HQ. To my friends, to Annie. I needed my family. I needed to blow something up, take some action as a protest.

After I had told my story, Annie wanted me to stay around HQ. I think she didn't trust me and she was right. It was better that my missions were regulated. I was ready to firebomb Chicago.

We moved again and that was a diversion.

Hill had found another place that used to be a town called Madrid in southeastern Missouri. The town was gone but some stone structures remained, with their plumbing intact. I liked the new HQ, the big river, and the birds.

The up side, if I could call it that, was that I began to work more closely with Nathan. If anything, he was even more protective of me than Annie, and the night when I questioned that — coming home from a meeting in a settlement when we ran into a group of Fedguards that developed into a running firefight — I saw the light in his eyes as a slow smile lit up his dark face.

"Oh, yeah, baby," he said, "I want to protect you." And he pulled me closer to him in the crowded GAV that was taking us back to HQ. I could feel his heart pounding against my cheek. I loved the smell of him, and the warmth radiating from him, and we didn't say a word about it when we got back to HQ.

I checked in, debriefed, took a shower and showed up later in his bedroom. He was waiting for me with a mischievous grin. I was ready for his strength and his tenderness and, despite our tiredness, we wrapped ourselves in and around each other for a long time. I fell asleep with my head on his hairy chest, his arms around me, feeling well-loved and happy.

That was the beginning of our romance, which only deepened with time and the dangers we shared. Annie was ambivalent about it. She was happy for us, but worried that we would become distracted looking out for each other and careless about our own welfare. So we didn't often go on missions together. Being in love made me mellow.

I wanted to plant a garden, have a child. I wanted Nathan's kid. No DNA matches, just some sweaty love and a desire to prolong that love into a child of our bodies, any sex, any color. Nathan wanted to hold off.

I should have tricked him. My life would have been different if I had, but we were committed to the Movers and the work and I let my chances slip.

I came to regret that choice.

# # #

"Sorry to interrupt, Annie. Turn on the vidscreen!" Parks burst in on our meeting, her brown eyes wide with excitement. She was the newest addition to our family at HQ, lately escaped from Chicago and a computer/vid expert,

Nathan flipped the switch.

"...known to be a headquarters for the outlaws. A patriotic citizen reported that the notorious criminal, Jemma7729, was in the town. Unfortunately, she had fled before the Fedguards arrived, but her rebel band engaged the soldiers in a firefight."

We watched a frontier town in South Carolina go up in smoke and flames, buildings exploding, people running for their lives. Someone was indeed shooting back at the Fedguards, or so it looked on the vid at any rate.

Then my face filled the screen. I shook my head.

"We need to send them a new picture, Annie. That one is at least five years old."

No one laughed. I wasn't laughing, either. The town smoldered on, with the oily, flutey voice of a female commentator rambling on about me, and the Movers, and how we had invaded and enslaved the town. Nonsense, of course, since it was a frontier town. It belonged to AGNA, though why they were blowing it up was anybody's guess. Maybe it got too independent. Maybe some local AGNA yokel needed to destroy something. I understood that feeling.

There was an interview with a handsome but distraught young man who said I had led a band of rebels, cut off their supplies, and threatened to starve them if they didn't allow the Movers to use the town as their base. He identified himself as a farmer, but I thought that unlikely — he didn't look tired enough.

"I've never even been there," I said to no one in particular. All of us watched with revulsion as the town died, taking forty or fifty citizens along with it. AGNA's massacre was the second one in the last five days. The other had been in California.

Annie sighed loudly. "Maybe we should rethink your trip."

"No! Now more than ever I need to go. If nothing else, we need to know how they respond to this; make sure they're safe." I stood up and paced. We had just been discussing my trip. I was to go to L. A. to work with the Movers there. Carlos, our regional leader, needed help. He had requested my presence specifically. It would be my first trip back to L. A. since I'd escaped nearly sixteen years before.

The images continued on the screen then abruptly went to an AGNA Network studio. I started to continue my argument but stopped, arrested by the image. My heart jumped into my mouth and choked me.

Daddy was sitting in the studio. His eyes appeared sad and he looked older than he should have. We had seen him on the AGNA Network News occasionally, talking about the environment and the food supply, but this was different. Those shots had been outside with the wind ruffling his hair. Now he was sitting in a blue studio, in a white chair, in a gray suit, with his jaw clenched. He kept swallowing.

Nathan wasn't paying attention, got up and started to say something but Annie stopped him and turned up the volume.

The announcer said Roger7702, the long-time Regional Administrator for the Environment for the L. A. Basin, was retiring, although he would remain a consultant.

Daddy looked into the camera and my eyes filled with tears. He was pitiful, weak. At the prompting of another tone-conscious announcer, he cleared his throat.

"My resignation has absolutely nothing to do with the recent crimes of Jemma7729. As everyone knows, I disowned her years ago. My wife and I wish to retire, and spend our golden years together. We intend to stay in Santa Monica, as is allowed by the new regulations, instead of moving to a frontier town. I am happy to have been able to be of service to the administration. I thank the many associates who have helped me over the years. I wish my successor good luck."

The image irised out. I sat down. "They fired him. Will they delete him?"

Nathan came to put his arms around me. I had often talked to him about my father. "I doubt it, Jem. They'll probably use your parents as models of retirement couples."

But that wasn't true, I knew it in my bones, and I understood why. "They won't let him move to the frontier. They think he'll go feral. He loves the Countryside." I sprang up and paced. "That's his punishment for my sins! Evil bastards!" I wanted to spit like the farmers.

"Calm down, Jemma. There's nothing you can do about it." Annie was straightening the frown furrows on her forehead with delicate fingers. Thinking.

"Besides," Hill said, "your mother would have to be altered to go with him. You wouldn't want that."

Of course, he was right, but I still felt AGNA was penalizing him.

Parks had stayed with us, leaning against the door jamb. Now she straightened and turned to leave. "Sorry, Jemma. I didn't know your father had disowned you."

"What else could he do?" That pain was long buried.

She shrugged, a bit embarrassed, and left, and we were silent for a long moment.

I stared into space, wondering how Daddy felt; what Mother thought; how they would survive. It hurt that they wouldn't let him see the stars again.

AGNA News had reverted to a cooking show and Nathan turned it off.

"I'm leaving tomorrow, as planned." I walked to look out the big window at the sinuous curve of the Mississippi River that ran past our gray stone HQ. The fog that had hidden the water a few hours earlier had lifted. A great blue heron stood immobile, fishing in the muddy shallows at the edge.

I was ready to go. My body was full of drugs that resisted most of the so-called "tell-truth serums" we knew AGNA used on prisoners. I had a chip implanted behind my left ear that made it possible to track me if I got lost. And in my heart, I wanted to see L. A. again, as much as I feared doing so.

I heard a soft whoosh as a hologram map materialized behind me and turned to them. Annie sat still looking at me, not at North America projected in mid-air. "Let's go over it again, then," she said, her eyes not leaving my face.

I suppressed a sigh of relief. The plans would not change. I traced my route on the map for them, for the umpteenth time.

In the ten years I'd been with the Movers, that map had changed as we had added to it the location of settlements, villages, isolated two- and three-family holdings; as AGNA had built new Fedguard outposts and frontier towns, and destroyed others. I had located the great killing field, styling it a National Monument. The color-coded points of light glowed on the hologram — a universe of stars and planets.

Much of the Countryside was still a blank. The megacities sprawled in lumpy clusters. There were hot spots of radiation and toxic dumps that were to be avoided. The rest was unsettled, but we were mapping it; finding ruined towns that were possible to resurrect; identifying watersheds and fertile soils; mapping fast rivers and streams that would supply power.

There was room for everyone coming out of the cities if they could bear the primitive conditions, if they were brave enough and smart enough, and had the stamina to survive.

I was going to visit half a dozen settlements as I zigzagged my way across the country to L. A.. I would take Ginger and Hill. Ginger would be my bodyguard; Hill our backup, pilot, comm expert, and tough guy. The fact that Annie insisted that these two go with me was a measure of her concern for my life. They were our best. Ginger and I would take the new palm comp units that Parks had devised, which presumably would allow us to stay in touch with HQ no matter where we were.

We went over the plans. When they finished, the hologram whooshed away and we looked at each other. I shrugged. There was nothing more to say.

# # #

Late that night, Annie knocked on my bedroom door. Nathan and I had said our sweet good-byes earlier, and I had opted for my own room, needing uninterrupted sleep.

Annie looked worried when she sat on the side of my bed. I turned the light on but lowered it to a glow.

"We're going to miss your birthday."

"Yes, well, give me a big present when I get back."

She chuckled. "Twenty-seven. When I was twenty-seven I was working for AGNA and thought I was on top of the world. Thought I knew everything, could do anything."

"Yes. Of course. Goes with the territory — that's how I feel."

"How I feel is uneasy, Jemma." Her voice was feathery soft.

"Yes, I do, too. Not because of the mission but because it's L.A.. Not my favorite town." I smiled at her.

She brushed my bangs off my forehead with an elegant hand. "I don't want to lose you, my dear." Her hand lingered on my cheek. I liked that.

"You won't. Too ornery for that, as they say. Besides, Ginger and Hill will be watching my back."

She gave me a grudging smile. Her eyes on me were tender. I knew she loved me, and at that moment I knew how much. I took her hand and held it, feeling the smoothness, the coolness of her skin. I didn't know how to say back how much I loved her.

"I'll be careful, I promise." I kissed her hand and leaned into her embrace.

We sat not talking for a moment, holding each other. Then Annie swallowed hard and pulled away from me. She took my face in her hands and kissed me on the forehead.

"I know you will. Please: no tricks, no chances. We need you. *I* need you. I love you, Jemma." She stood up with a groan. "Old bones." Then I got Annie's star smile. "I'll see you at breakfast."

The door closed softly and I felt a twinge of anxiety, the melancholy of love. I turned out the light. I fully intended to be careful. I wanted to live.

# # #

The Mexican town was a tangle of ten or twelve tarpaper and corrugated steel shacks, straggling down a single dirt road in the middle of nowhere. Hill landed the GAV and the whole village disappeared in a cloud of dust. When it cleared, there were guns poking out from behind every structure — big, good guns, like the ones the Fedguards use — but no people showed themselves.

Ginger pushed me down on the floor of the GAV and set her foot on my back to hold me there. Hill kept his hands on the T-bar and the vehicle on standby as he reached for his demolishing sidearm.

"Shit. What is this?" Ginger had her big gun at the ready. She could flatten every building there if she wanted to.

"Wait. They're probably saying the same thing!" I squirmed to get her foot off me. "Only in Spanish, we hope."

Hill pulled the window of the GAV back, picked up his gun, and leaned his head out. "Compadres! Amigos!"

Ginger reached behind the seat and got another gun. She was deadly with either hand. I coughed on the dust. No one moved for what seemed like forever but was really a second or two, then I heard the crunch of boots.

"Hola!"

I started to sit up but Ginger wasn't buying. "Ginger? What's going on?"

"Men coming from behind the buildings. A lot of guns, Jemma. Keep your head down until we're sure."

"We can't expect them to—"

"There's a guy coming over now." I could see her face. She squinted into the bright sunlight. Devi had removed the terrible scar that had so disfigured her, but her cells remembered the trauma, so it was still there, ghosting now because of the tension in her face.

"Buenos dias, senor," Hill said in his flat voice with a slight nasal twang.

"Buenos dias! We're expecting a shipment of dragon's eggs."

I recognized the voice and grinned. That password was my idea. Ginger nodded and took her heavy boot off my back. The GAV door opened, and Ginger released me to sit up. When I did, I was face to face with Carlos, our regional director.

His smile was broad and welcoming in his ruddy face. He'd grown a mustache since I'd seen him three years before at HQ, but the high cheekbones, the elegant long nose, the laughing eyes under a straw hat, and, above all, the panache of the man, were unmistakable.

I scrambled to my feet and took his offered hand to jump down. He grabbed me in a bear hug that nearly knocked the wind out of me.

"Jemma! You beautiful outlaw! I'm so happy to see you. To see you *here*!"

I returned the hug. I liked this guy. "Carlos! You old coyote! Good to see you, too."

He put an arm around my shoulders and we turned to his renegade bunch, all now coming forward out of the still-swirling dust, guns lowered. I glanced back at Ginger. She was slower to relinquish her advantage, but she finally put the safeties on and climbed out of the GAV. Hill shut the engine down and joined us.

Carlos turned to his group. "Here is the famous Jemma. Now we'll get something done."

I had to meet each of them formally, seven men and two women, shake their hands as they stepped forward, their heads bobbing. They greeted me with such a show of chivalry that I was embarrassed.

"Thank you, amigos! I'm happy to be here, but hot and thirsty." I glanced around at the seedy village.

Carlos laughed. "Come along, then. We don't stay here." He turned to Hill. "Stay on the ground and follow us." Obviously, I was to go with him.

Ginger stepped forward, a hand on his arm. "Carlos, I go with her."

He grinned. "Ah, Ginger, we won't kidnap her." She didn't move. He nodded. "Of course, of course." He waved to his companions. "Don't mess with this woman. She's the finest shot in North America!" Applause and yells of approval greeted his remark. Ginger saluted them grimly, but her eyes were sparkling.

Carlos stared at her. "Good. Good you took care of that scar. You're a beautiful woman." Ginger grunted an acknowledgement and sinuously moved to stand on my left. The adulation was good for her.

Carlos hadn't relinquished his hug around my shoulders and he nearly carried me as he moved forward, even though I was taller than he, going past the flimsy shacks and into a grove of scrubby trees. Three spanking new GAVs waited there. I wondered where he had got them.

"Impressive, Carlos!"

He grinned. "We have good friends in Adelaide."

I couldn't begin to speculate how the GAVs got from Australia to this Mexican sand trap, and I knew from his grin that he was not about to tell me. Maybe later I could wheedle it out of him.

Hill caught up and we loaded, with a lot of pushing and scrambling and laughing. I liked that, their camaraderie. Carlos, Ginger, a driver, and I went in one car; everyone else piled in the others and we drove off across an un-marked tract of sand and jojoba bushes, mesquite and rocks and arroyos, hovering just over the landscape to make the ride smoother in the uneven desert.

Carlos had finally let me go, but kept one of my hands in his. "Thank you for coming, my darling. I need you to pound some sense into the Movers out here."

"What's the problem?" I hadn't thought we would get at it so quickly. His intensity concerned me.

"Impatience! These puppies want to start blowing everything up before they've learned how to tie their shoelaces." I grinned. He laughed and ruffled my hair. "Like you, my favorite bandita. But you learned. And so must they." He stared out the window a moment. "Not these, not the ones with me here. It's the L. A. groups. The city is in a lot of trouble."

"What kind of trouble?" I moved to get more comfortable and he finally let go of me.

"The climate doesn't work in areas of the southern part, under the Redlands Dome. The dome itself is crumbling along the edge and they can't seem to fix it."

I laughed at this news. "That would be spectacular, Carlos! If the dome crumbled then they would all have to learn that the Countryside isn't toxic. We might be able to help it along, in fact." My mind was jumping ahead.

He didn't laugh with me. "In theory, yes. In practice, Jemma, the Fedguards deleted anyone who was near the break, said they were contaminated. The area is patrolled. Even we haven't been able to get into it."

Ginger tensed. "You don't expect Jemma to go there?"
My protection in full bloom.

He studied her face. "No. I want Jemma to meet with
the group leaders. Help us to come up with a plan to deal
with the people who want out of L. A. We're overwhelmed," and he turned back to me. He touched my face
gently. "You, we want you just to talk and then get the hell
out."

Ginger nodded. I shrugged. He'd brought me all this
way to talk to a few group leaders?

"That's all, Carlos? That's all you want from me?" In
the corner of my eye I could see Ginger thinking about that
and probably growing suspicious.

His driver spoke to him and they talked briefly in
Spanish. Ginger cleared her throat to catch my attention.
She was sending a silent message that she was uncomfort-
able. I smiled and shook my head. I didn't doubt Carlos.
I was sure there was something more he wanted from me.

Carlos swiveled in his seat with his sunny smile. "Five
minutes and we're there. At my house. We'll let you bathe
and eat, then you and I must talk. I saved a fine vino to
loosen our tongues."

"That's a deal!" I was sticky, dusty, and hungry, and
tired of traveling. Nothing sounded better than a soak and
food, and I knew from experience I could count on a good
vintage from Carlos.

The convoy set down in a flat area beside a long, low
hacienda snuggled up against a knoll. It was pleasantly
shaded by cottonwoods and big cactus plants. The double
roof of the house was covered by desert shrubs. I guessed
that made it nearly invisible from the air.

We bathed and ate a good supper. Most people disappeared afterwards and I took a swim, enticed by the roofed,
azure pool.

Later, Carlos and I sat at a small glass table on the patio
under the spectacle of desert stars. The air was fragrant.
I was relaxed, content. We watched Hill leave the hacienda
at a trot for his evening run.

"He's a cold fish, that Hill."

Of course, I thought, *Carlos would not be attracted to a man who didn't smile*. "He's good at what he does, amigo."

"Si. So I've heard."

I sighed and leaned back in the chair, stretching out my legs, staring at the night sky. "I will never tire of seeing stars, Carlos. And I will never forgive AGNA for denying them to the cities."

Carlos poured the wine and my glass glowed crimson. We were in a friendly, alone space. The wind was still but the night air was chilly on my head, still wet from my swim.

"AGNA has much for which it must atone." He raised his glass to me. "Thank you, Jemma. I know what you risk coming here. I wouldn't have asked if it weren't important."

"How can I help you?" I sipped and made a guttural sound of pleasure. The wine was crisp and full-bodied and fruity with a lovely aroma and no bite. "Lovely! Better than the last bottle I had with you."

He smiled and leaned back, taking two cigars from his pocket, offering me one.

I laughed. "They make me choke." He registered his disappointment and started to put them away. "No, no. Please yourself. Out here it doesn't matter. I appreciate that some enjoy those things."

He fussed with the cigar, lit it, took a drag, and sent a long column of blue smoke into the night. Then he leaned forward, elbows on the table. "You can help, my friend, just as I said. Talk to them. Oh, yes," and he shrugged, "my demolition people would like a quick refresher course, especially if you have anything new to tell us about. But—" He stared at me a moment.

"You must understand, Jemma. Some people, especially the younger ones, think you don't really exist. They think you're a hologram or some damn thing. The fact that you're here represents—" he looked across the desert as a family of coyotes began their evening concert, "—*is* continuity, history, organization, and power. They only half believe that the Movers are spread out across the continent."

"There are so many lies, Carlos, all their lives. It's difficult to know what's real."

"Yes. But you are not a lie. They need to see you, talk to you, hear you speak, watch you laugh." He chuckled. "One of my men said, after you had left the dinner table, 'She's a real person. She makes jokes.' You see, you're something special to them."

I had grown used to this argument; I even understood its worth. Annie had made it clear that the Movers needed something more tangible than a vague organization with a leader who was never seen. That "something" was me. Part heroine, part stalking horse, part decoy, part idiot.

"I'll do whatever I can, Carlos."

He spread his big sunburned hand over mine and squeezed gently. "I know you will. Ah! I almost forgot!" He pulled his hand away and reached into the pocket of his jacket. "My friends wanted me to give you this gift. One of them made it for you but is too shy to present it himself." He put a paper-wrapped, oblong package on the table.

I opened it carefully. A beautifully wrought leather sheath and in it a knife. A strange-looking, black knife. I held it close to the light bar, smiling and curious, watched it glisten darkly.

"Careful." He grinned.

I tried the edge. "Ouch! What is it?" It was the sharpest knife I'd ever handled. I sucked the blood oozing from my thumb at the slight touch I'd made on the blade.

"Obsidian. Here in Sonora there is an ancient lava bed. We find good obsidian there. The original people made their weapons from them. It passes metal detectors, which is often useful."

"Obsidian? That's a kind of glass, right?"

"Yes. The heat of a volcano melting the very earth we walk upon."

"That's thoughtful of him. Please, convey my thanks." Obsidian. I began immediately to think of projectiles that could not be turned away by defense systems seeking metal.

"It's actually fragile, Jemma. If you drop it, it will chip. But it gives you one helluva sharp weapon until you've used it up."

He smoked and we drank the wine, letting the evening unfold slowly. He asked after Annie with obvious fondness. I got a summary of the six separate Mover groups in L. A., and an update on AGNA's latest attacks on our organization. But our conversation was lazy from the wine and the beauty of the night and our affection for each other.

At last he carefully meted out the last of the bottle in equal parts. "Now, my pretty outlaw, tomorrow we go to San Diego and thence into L. A.. You will go as an alter. A fisherman's wife. It's all arranged."

"Fisherman's wife?" I laughed.

"Yes. We go overland to Rosario, then you will sail up the coast on one of our vessels. You'll land in San Clemente and I'll meet you there." He shook his head. "You, and Ginger, of course. I'm not sure how we can disguise her arsenal."

We stood up. I was a bit unsteady from the wine and my tiredness. Carlos came to put his arms around me. He kissed my hand and looked out across the rocky landscape in the starshine.

"Hill has met with my security people. You're guarded, protected at every turn. This once, we need to smother you. You're going into the capital, where every fifth person is a spy, every fourth person a Fedguard. We expect you to be a good girl."

I hugged him. "Absolutely. I am yours to command."

He chuckled and held me at arm's length. "Ah, pretty lady, would that it were so!" He suddenly tensed, looking past me.

"What?" I squeezed my eyes shut, expecting a shot, a knife, something bad.

He smiled and spoke softly. "Turn around slowly and look at the table."

I did so, holding my breath. It was as we had left it: the empty bottle, the discarded paper that had wrapped my knife, our glasses glinting in the glow from the lightbar. "What?"

"The moth... beside the light."

Then I saw it. A tiny olive green and red flutter of soft-
ness clinging to the side of the bar. "It's beautiful!" I went
closer to look at it.

"It's a terloo. We see them sometimes, not often. They
were once thought extinct. When AGNA domed the cities,
it forgot the Countryside. Things survived in that neglect.
Good! This means we will have good luck!"

I really loved this guy. I took his hand. "Do you think,
Carlos, that when we have won, and people are back in
the Countryside, we'll treat it better? We'll let the terloos
live? Have we learned something during our captivity?"

"I believe that with all my heart. Why else would we
bother?"

We went back inside the hacienda to our beds. I thought
of Nathan and missed him and wished he were there. I
trusted Carlos and his handpicked crew. I staked my life
on Ginger and Hill, but L. A. was a bad place and I was
uneasy, despite their assurances.

Chapter 10

"There are quicker ways to kill someone, Carlos." I leaned against Ginger for support, happy to be standing on solid ground again, but the dock was heaving, or so I thought. She was as ghastly pale and grim as I was. I put an arm around her. "You're a good woman, Ginger! You're as sick as I am and you're still standing." She couldn't answer.

Carlos chuckled as he reached for my carrybag. "A little seasick, eh?"

"What does 'a little' mean, amigo? You can shoot me now. Put me out of my misery."

He put a finger over my mouth, his eyes suddenly bright and slitty. "Not even as a joke, Jemma! Don't say such things."

I was too queasy to care that I had annoyed him. We trailed after him to an empty, nondescript waterfront utility building, hulking over the dock in the growing twilight. He handed Ginger and me black armorweave pants and shirts, and we gratefully shed our soggy, smelly skirts and jackets. I smiled as I fastened the shirt. It had a green and red design meant to be a terloo moth painted in primitive splendor on the left breast pocket. A gift from a romantic soul.

We got into the waiting GAV and slumped into our seats. At least the ride was smooth. The driver put the air conditioner on full to give us cold air to breathe. Carlos handed me a bottle and I almost vomited at the thought.

He laughed. "Aqua! Water! Drink it — it will make you feel better. Take these." He handed us small white pills, which we gratefully downed with big draughts of aqua.

I settled back and watched the houses, the people, the public buildings flash by. All vaguely familiar, but smaller and narrower than I remembered, probably because I was five inches taller than I'd been the last time I was here. That got me thinking that cities are a measure of ourselves, or should be, and AGNA had made them prisons. *That's why I am here*, I reminded myself, *to work for the change*.

Carlos passed me a small palm comp unit. "Something we developed. Comes in handy."

It was a mini motion detector, and quite sensitive, with a broad range for its size. "Handy gadget," I said. I didn't dare look at the moving blips. I held it out to him but he shook his head.

"Keep it. Extra insurance." Carlos leaned toward me. "Also, my black-eyed friend, this car handles like any other, except that it will take off nearly vertical, at about seventy degrees. At ninety degrees it flips over backwards, so don't try that.... It has special features. There's a small blue panel on the right of the console. Inside it is a switch which will activate two .980 Blazers forward and one aft, each carrying fifty rounds. If you need it, press the yellow button to your extreme left and you lay down a smokescreen."

I stared at him. "More insurance?" He shrugged. I put the detector in my carrybag with my obsidian knife, my special HQ comm unit, my extra clothes, and boots. "Good. Thank you."

We rode for twenty minutes, sometimes pausing and waiting in the dark shadows of buildings, for what I didn't know. Patrolling Fedguards, perhaps. Carlos and the driver were relaxed, talking softly in Spanish.

By the time we stopped and the GAV shut down, Ginger and I felt better. The pills, water, and cold air had done their work. Carlos jumped out and handed us down from the car and led us through an alley and into a warehouse where we met Hill.

We threaded our way through a cavernous, gloomy room full of immense derelict machines with the remnants of cranes and turbines. I couldn't imagine what they had been used for. We arrived at a narrow door; Carlos flung it open to a brightly lit room.

When we stepped inside, Carlos and Ginger ahead of me, Hill and the driver behind, all the people in the room, about twenty of them, stopped talking and stared at us. One by one, they stood up. My heart stuttered. It reminded me of my entrance into rehab. I shook that off — this was certainly different. I had traveled many miles since then.

Carlos stood in the front of the room, smiling broadly, flapping his arms like a terloo in his excitement. "Amigos, my friends. We have an honored guest. Here is Jemma, come from Mover HQ to work with us."

I looked out at the audience. They were mostly young, mostly men, and all of them staring at me as if they were seeing a ghost. Carlos had been right. Clearly, some of them hadn't thought I existed.

I gave them my best heroine smile. "Good evening! I'm Jemma. Please sit down." Their fixation was unnerving.

"I told you I had a surprise," Carlos said, his eyes dancing, "and now you will believe that the Movers care about what we're doing here." Carlos brought a chair for me and I sat. There was a scuffling while the Movers arranged themselves.

"You're not a myth," said a blond man in the front row, as if he still weren't sure.

"Only on my bad days." I looked to Carlos but he was talking to Ginger off to the side. I turned back to the group. "I have a question for you.... You all know AGNA has recently raided some frontier towns and a lot of people have been killed. In case you *didn't* know, we don't hang around those towns much, although there are some friendly ones. The Movers had nothing at all to do with the raids. The massacre was reported on AGNA Network News so I assume there's a reaction. What are they saying in the city about that?"

I waited while they thought about my question, then a dark-haired young woman stood up. "Hello. Uh, thank you for coming. I'm Sara7714—"

"No numbers. No classes. You're Movers. Go ahead, Sara."

She smiled, embarrassed. "Sorry. I'd say people, mostly women, are frightened. AGNA has been ordering more alterations lately, too. We're all frustrated because there doesn't seem to be anything we can do."

"Blow up the dome!" The young man beside her sent me a challenging look. I didn't take the bait, glanced at him with what I hoped was a pleasant expression, and turned my attention back to Sara.

"The people are frustrated? Or you?"

"Both." Her gaze at me was level, but her face was flushed with excitement. "People believe you, Jemma. Many believe *in* you and what you represent. You got out, you're alive, and you're free. They believe, in general, what the Movers show us, but they want something done. Some action. Many feel what AGNA does is wrong and they probably would like to see it go, but until something real and big happens, they don't think the Movers can do anything to change their lives."

"Except hold out promises?" I asked in my carefully neutral voice.

"Yes!"

I understood the feeling in my guts. But it was too soon, and I knew that, too. "But Carlos tells me you're overwhelmed with people wanting to leave the city. So they must see that as a first step, a change, a hope. There's room in the Countryside for them. It's a hard life, but a free one."

"Well, I wouldn't say 'overwhelmed' exactly, although it's more than it was last year. Leaving the city is the only thing they know to do. Many are afraid, so it isn't a — a pleasant choice." The woman shrugged. "I'm sorry, but that's the truth."

"Thanks, Sara. I need to hear these things. That's why I'm here."

The blond in the first row sat up straighter. "Give us the word, Jemma, and we'll demolish this town."

There were grunts and mumbled agreements around the room. I looked to Carlos, but he was leaning against the wall, his arms folded on his chest, his mustache twitching.

"And accomplish what?"

"Save this child for one thing!" A woman's voice called out from the back of the room, and a tall blond person pushed through the Movers, dragging a small child with carrot-red hair.

"What do you mean?"

The woman thrust the child forward at me. "She's like you, Jemma. You're her idol. She's seven and won't choose and the master of her quad has recommended that she be altered."

I looked at the pretty little girl. She met my gaze but had caught her bottom lip in her teeth, holding her fear in check. "Is this true?"

"Yes." She glanced at the floor, at her mother, then back at me. "I got into trouble."

I guessed it, looking at her. "The boys teased you about your hair and you fought back."

Her eyes widened in surprise and then she smiled self-consciously. "Yes, ma'am. Now they say I'll be altered."

"They used to tease me about my eyes. I know how you feel."

She looked at me and shook her head violently, almost like a spasm. I knelt down and grasped her shoulders, my face close to hers. "What's your name?"

"Tara." She was trembling.

"What's wrong, Tara? Why are you so frightened?"

Carlos suddenly pushed himself off the wall, as if he were just waking up, his hand at his side going for his gun. "Who is this woman?"

Hill took a step towards me.

Tara grabbed my hand, her face wild, tears welling in her eyes. "It's a trap, Jemma! She's not my mother! They made me!"

An explosion. Two. Three. Shots. Debris rained down from the ceiling; lights in the room pulsed and dimmed. Shouts from outside the room. I was grabbed from behind and lifted to my feet by Hill and shoved away from the crowd, towards the door. Tara was right beside me.

"Is it true about you?" I had to yell to her above the noise.

"Yes. They made me do it!"

She disappeared as I was hauled off by my bodyguards. "Get that kid, Hill, or she's dead meat! Get her!"

More shots and the lintel of the old wooden door and its overhead light fixture exploded above our heads, throwing me and Hill to the ground. I felt a sudden stinging on my face. The armorweave held, but the splinters found my skin.

"Get Tara! Someone get her!"

There was nothing I could do. I was smothered, as Carlos had promised, and taken out a different door than the way we'd entered. Outside there were flares, explosions, fires, people running, and a lot of shooting.

Suddenly the GAV was there and I was inside it, on the floor with boots on my back again.

"Go! Go!" That was Carlos.

Also as promised, the car lifted almost straight up. and we were speeding off.

"Uno-tres," Carlos said and the GAV started a turn.

My ears popped. We were high, higher than normal in a GAV, almost at the top of the dome.

"Ginger, let me up!" I was tired of being stepped on.

"Sorry, Jemma, it's me." Hill's voice was tense as he moved his feet, releasing me.

We were crowded into the car: Carlos, the driver, Ginger, Hill. I looked around. "Where's the kid?"

Ginger had her stony stare in place. "We couldn't bring her. We told the others. Someone will take her."

Hill shrugged. "She risked her life; we'll save hers. She may know things we'd like to know."

My face was tingling. I reached for it and felt wetness. Oh hell, blood. "Why are you here, Carlos? You should be—"

"We should go back to Mexico." I couldn't see his face as he said it.

"No, dammit!" He turned away at my outburst, didn't reply. He should have stayed with his people. "Where are we going?"

"Someplace safe." Carlos spoke so softly I had to strain to hear.

"What the hell *was* that?"

"I don't know." He was breathing heavily, his face stricken with anxiety. "They're trusted. I handpicked them.

I would have sworn on my life, Jemma, that you were safe."
His voice trailed off and he turned away from me again.

We all sat in silence for a moment, then slowly I realized what had just happened. A spy. A traitor in the group, a disappointment for Carlos. A set-up, which meant AGNA knew I was in the city.

Carlos got on a comm unit, speaking softly and slowly in Spanish. The GAV eased on a slow slope to the west and landed.

I was pushed down on the floor again until the coast was clear then hurried into a dark house, bundled down a pitch-black hallway, and half-carried down narrow steps.

"Enough! I can walk." My protests were in vain. It was Ginger with her arm around me.

A door opened at the bottom of the stairs to reveal a large, pleasant room. After the darkness and the flares, the warm browns and reds of the walls and the carpeting were a relief. A black-haired woman sauntered across the room to us.

"My sister, Rosa." Carlos slumped into a chair.

"You're bleeding," the woman said. Her voice, her face had no expression. Was she an alter?

There was a sudden flurry as the driver got a medkit from a cabinet in the corner, Ginger stared into my face, pushing me into a chair. Rosa stood back, arms akimbo on her waist, waiting.

"I'm not shot. It's just splinters." I twisted in my chair. "Hill? Did it get you, too?"

He was squinting at Carlos. "No."

Ministering to me postponed what must be said. Ginger mopped the blood off my face. "Just scratches, Jemma. I've seen you with worse."

Her eyes caught mine as she leaned towards me. Her jaw was tight, the tiny lines around her vanished scar showing. It was a bad situation, and as always, there was no fear in her face, just concern and determination.

Rosa had disappeared, now she returned with bread, cheese, wine, and water.

"Rosa, could I trouble you—" she turned to me with the same blank look.

Carlos spoke softly. "What do you wish, Jemma?"

"Coffee. Milk and sugar."

"Of course." He turned to speak to her, but Rosa was already returning to the other room, which I assumed was a kitchen.

"Is she an alter?" Something made me think not.

"No. They merely experimented with her brain when she was a girl. She's fifty-two years old now. They were trying some new serum and tested it on my people. She's like a zombie. She feels little emotion. I don't think she suffers."

He sat at the table in the middle of the room and poured himself a glass of wine, then stared into space. The driver took a glass as well. Ginger drank water. Hill wanted nothing. I waited for coffee. The tense silence permeated the room like smoke.

"I'm sorry, Jemma." Carlos waggled his head and sipped his wine. "I don't know what happened. I can't believe..."

"AGNA knows she's here." Ginger rubbed her eyes and stretched, working out tension kinks.

"We'll have to leave now; it's too risky for her," Hill said.

"Yes, I agree. We'll have to get her back into the Countryside." Carlos whispered. He had already downed a glass of vino and was pouring more. His shoulders were hunched.

I stood up, impatient with them. "Please stop talking about me as if I weren't in the room. And the response to you all is no. Absolutely not. That sends the wrong message. I'm here. I'll stay until I'm ready to leave, until I'm satisfied with what's happening. I don't like it much, either, and I know the risk. Carlos, you will protect me; your groups will protect me. I'm not going to run. What would your friends think?"

"I don't give a damn what they think," Ginger said mildly. She played with one of her guns, ignoring me.

I spun on her. "Well, you should give a damn! They're the ones who will take over from us eventually."

Carlos answered a beeping tone on his comm unit. He listened, then stood up slowly, his mouth hanging open.

We waited. He mumbled a thank you and placed the unit carefully on the table.

"Let's hear it." I stepped over to confront him.

"Two of the Mover groups have blown up AGNA buildings: the justice facility in Brentwood Sector and a Fedguard barracks in Hollywood."

My blood seemed to turn to ice water. Wrong. That was wrong and stupid and was going to complicate our work. I wanted to smash something. Instead, I held Carlos's eyes steady in mine.

"Fix it! Call them off. Now." He nodded slowly. His spirit was failing him; I could see it in his eyes, like a candle guttering out. "Carlos! Pull yourself together. Do what must be done!" I turned to my crew. "We need to help here."

I picked the up comm unit from the table and thrust it at Carlos. "Talk to your groups. Get in touch with the leaders. I want to meet with them."

Rosa ambled into the room bearing a tray with my coffee. She set it on the table and stood back, arms folded, watching me pour a cup, add cream and sugar. Getting it gave me a moment to break my concentration on Carlos and think. And I needed the caffeine fix.

Carlos took the comm unit and sat on the sofa, staring at it. I turned to Ginger and Hill.

"We need to know what's happening out there." I turned to the driver. "Where are we?"

"Fullerton." The young driver, Ruiz, was staring at Carlos but he spoke to me, his voice low. "He will be all right, Jemma. This will pass."

"Help him, get him back on track. Tell me how to reach the Brentwood leader."

He reached in his jacket pocket and handed me his comm unit. "Use the first seven digits to connect you to the leaders. Brentwood is three. We're one."

I picked up my coffee cup and headed for the door. "Let's go."

"Senorita!" I turned back. Ruiz was holding out a .870 Winner. I took it awkwardly under my arm, not willing to forgo the coffee. "The GAV code is one one one seven four. I will do what I can here. Carlos, he — he does not let each group know much about the others. For protection, you see."

I ground my teeth and nodded. No wonder he had wanted help from HQ — he was in over his head.

We piled into the GAV, I punched in the number sequence and steadied the T-bar. It was super-responsive and Ginger laughed as we took off steeply and climbed. I took us high. I could see Fedguard GAVs under us. They obviously didn't know we were there. *This was one helluva fine vehicle*, I thought as I brought it around and went north. We could see the fires in the city. I handed the comm unit to Hill.

"Punch in three. See if we can get the Brentwood leader." I concentrated on flying, circling so that we could observe the Hollywood Sector.

"He's on, Jemma." Hill passed the comm unit forward.

"This is Jemma. What's going on?"

There was a silence for a moment on the other end. "Jemma? Is this a trick?"

"Not a trick. You must have heard I'm in town by now. What are you doing? Call your people back in!"

"Yes. I heard you were in Anaheim. I can't call them in. After the explosion, it escalated. There's rioting, and looting. It's a spontaneous insurrection. People are fighting the Fedguards. It's not just us."

"Control your group in the sector. What's your name?"

"Finn. God — you're really here!"

"I'm really here and I'm mad as hell! This is not a good idea, Finn. Do your best to stop it." I clicked him off.

"Jemma..." Ginger's voice was a cautionary whisper. "Look below."

I did and saw a new, violent explosion to the west. "Where would that be?"

Hill frowned at the locator. "Redondo Beach Sector, I'd say. Something else just blew up." He made a guttural, disapproving sound. "They're using green fire. They're copying you."

I groaned. I would face the fallout from that later. For their benefit, I laughed. "Guess I'll have to start using purple." They didn't respond.

The comm unit beeped. I punched the speaker button so we all could hear. "Yes?"

"This is Ruiz. Carlos says to tell you that he has arranged a meeting with leaders of groups five and six on San Miguel Island in twenty minutes. Take the Simi Sector gate. It's not well guarded."

"Okay. Tell him to keep working on the others."

"Yes." I could hear Carlos say something in the background. "And he says he's sorry."

"Right. Tell him we'll talk about that later. Help him, amigo. Muchas gracias, Ruiz." I hung up and touched the locator to find Simi Sector. "We're going down. I want to see what's happening."

I had my hands full falling out of the sky into L. A. We were over Pasadena Sector. There were no fedcars in the air, so I went all the way to the ground and used the excellent locator to take me through the broad streets toward the Simi gate.

Hill and Ginger got their guns ready. I could hear them breathing and my own heart pounding. Why? We had all done this before. Why was this different? I didn't know, but it was.

In the business sections and the market areas, the streets were full of people breaking into stores. Glass shards littered the streets, glittering eerily in the light from fires; citizens ran with their arms full of goods; fedcars raced along the streets. We could hear gunfire and see people shooting at each other. Movers? No way to tell. I flew low above them with the landing lights on, trying to understand who they were. A few random shots bounced off the belly of the car without hurting us, but I turned my brights off.

The locator led me over a small hill with no houses. When we crested the hill, there was a straight road and two fedcars directly in front of us, coming at us fast. I didn't think. I popped the blue panel and fired.

The fedcars went up like rockets in a blaze of flame. I tilted slightly and flew over them. The Simi gate was dead ahead. I fired again and blew it away, crumbling a piece of the dome as it did.

"Some guns!" Ginger breathed in my ear in obvious satisfaction.

We were through the hole that had been the gate and I climbed steeply again. "Hill, see if you can get HQ. My special unit is in my carrybag."

Hill rummaged around behind me. "Where's your carrybag?"

"Oh hell! I don't know. Maybe they took it into the house."

"I have mine, Jemma." Ginger searched her gear and came up with the unit and punched in numbers as I looked below me.

"Hill, try to reach groups two and four. See if they can meet us." I tuned them out as they began to search for contact.

I went back to the locator. A map came up; San Miguel was not far. It was marked "contaminated." I trusted that was not the case, but at this moment, who knew? It was the only thing we could do.

"Can't get through, Jemma. Maybe it got wet on the boat." Ginger shook the unit as if that would help.

"Ruiz will bring mine." I hoped.

"No response, Jemma," Hill said.

The GAV nosed higher into the quiet of the night. The stars held their silences, and I felt better, calmer, just being out of L. A. and under their radiance. I flew over Santa Cruz Island and saw the smaller San Miguel beyond it, its surf glowing on white sand under a three-quarter moon. The land mass was pitch black. I would have to be low, and lucky, to find a landing place.

I circled the island and my heart squeezed my breath away. "My God!"

"What?" Hill leaned forward over my shoulder.

Beyond us to the east, the whole coast was aglow. We were, I guessed, at least 150 kilometers from LA and the blaze was lighting the sensuous, breast-like domes of the great megacity like a gigantic red lightbar.

A feeling of profound sadness came over me. There had been a time when I had wanted to see such a sight, but no longer. That was not the way, could not be the way.

Ginger touched my shoulder. "Below us, Jemma."

A beacon light flashed on San Miguel; I flipped on my landing lights. Other beacons suddenly lit as I neared the ground, and I set the GAV down in a flat sandy area. Ginger and Hill got out, guns ready, as two men with a light hurried across the field.

I sat at the controls, unable to move for a moment, envisioning the chaos inside the twenty L. A. domes. Oddly, I didn't think of my Daddy, but of Tara, and then Reesie. I wondered if our old cook was still alive, if she would survive.

Ginger leaned into the GAV and touched my arm lightly. "Jemma? Are you all right?"

I shook off my morbid thoughts and clambered down, my boots sinking into the soft sand. "Yes, just thinking." I followed her across the field to the waiting L. A. Movers, wondering what I could possibly say to the people who had allowed this to happen.

We gathered in a one room utility building with no furniture and no lights. One of the group leaders had brought a lightbar and he held it up so we could see each other — Carlos, Ruiz, a tall brown-haired older man, a short blond guy.

The tall man grinned at me, his beautiful teeth showing in the odd blue glow of the lightbar. "The pictures on AGNA News don't do you justice. You're beautiful."

I nearly smacked him in the mouth. "I'm also angry, and worried. Are you Finn?"

"No, I'm Finn," the blond guy said, holding out his hand. I ignored it. He withdrew it and stopped smiling. "He's Waren."

"Okay. We're not going to talk now about how this happened, just what we can do to stop it."

"It's out of control in my sector," Waren said. "I'm East L. A. God, there were people dying in the streets." He wiped his face with a handkerchief pulled from the breast pocket of his very nice suit. "Never saw anything like it."

I turned to Ruiz. "Where's my carrybag?"

"Here, Commander." He retrieved it from a corner of the room.

I didn't correct him for calling me that, nor did those who knew who the real commander was. It wasn't important. I got the special unit out and tossed it to Ginger. "Get HQ. Fill them in. Tell them we're going to stay to coordinate efforts and we need help." Ginger nodded, punched in numbers in the light, then went outside to talk.

I turned back to the group. "Go back to your sectors. Get as many of your members together as you can and *help people*! Try to stop the looting. Don't fire unless absolutely necessary. Keep your eyes and ears open and relay info to me. You contact—" I hesitated for a moment, but it had to be done, "—Ruiz. He'll be in touch with me."

Ruiz was suddenly beside me, his eyes shining in the dim light. Carlos didn't move and didn't change expression. He looked like a whipped dog.

Finn nodded. "Where will you be?"

"I'll be a moving target. Reach me through Ruiz. Go. Go do your work and be sure you contact Ruiz every hour, more often if something important happens." The light went out as Finn and Waren left the room. Hill followed them outside. I turned to the defeated leader.

"Carlos, you wait, my friend. I'm not angry with you, I just don't want you involved right now. Do you understand?" I wished I could see his face and it felt odd to be talking in the dark.

"I understand, Jemma. But we must take you to the hacienda." His voice seemed even enough, but he wasn't making sense.

Ruiz touched my arm and whispered. "May we speak? Outside?"

"Yes."

It was lighter outside, with the moon reflecting off the building and the light sandy soil. Ruiz had brought my carrybag and he set it at my feet.

"Can I trust you, Ruiz?"

His head snapped up. "Yes, Jemma, you can trust me." He rubbed his face. "You — uh, even when I was a boy, you were my idol." And he smiled, the first time I had seen that. He suddenly looked like a boy.

"How old are you?"

"Twenty-three."

We held each other's eyes. I felt connected to him; my gut said it was right to trust him. "Old enough."

"Yes." He didn't break our stare, but his face became wary and sad, and he lowered his voice. "Carlos is... unsafe. Especially with something like this. He has often failed for a moment, like now, lost heart, become unstable. He does strange things. Drinks. Shoots at fedcars. Or just disappears into the desert for a day or a month. He makes bad decisions, or no decisions at all. He's done it before and people have been hurt." He sighed, running his fingers through his curly hair. "I'm sorry, but I must say this. I think he wanted you here to fix what he can't. He's lost control of the groups. He's a great motivator, sensitive, and ro- mantic. A beautiful man..." he took a step closer, his face close to mine, "but dangerous. I fear for us. I fear for you."

I knew what he was asking. God, I hated this part! My mouth was suddenly full of spit and I swallowed.

"Would he retire to the hacienda?" I knew the answer as I asked. For a nanosecond I wondered if Carlos could be like Will the cook, someone we could keep around HQ just for his company. No, we couldn't. He was too vola- tile.

Ruiz shook his head. "He always comes back, as if nothing had happened. The Movers find him hard to understand, to follow."

"Yes, he's a beautiful man. He's my friend. But, as you say, dangerous to us." I heard the cold finality of decision in my voice; knew Ruiz heard it and read it correctly; knew that I would never see Carlos again.

He nodded. "Adios, Jemma. I'll be in touch." He turned to go back into the house, I collected Ginger and Hill and got us out of there, flying us high against the stars where we could talk. I did not have time to grieve.

#

"Annie's on." Ginger touched the speaker pad.

"Is everyone listening?" The welcome, familiar voice made me smile despite the circumstances.

"Yes. It's a mess here."

"Are you all right, Jemma?"

"Yes. I'm fine. We've more or less taken control of the Mover organization, such as it is. Carlos is out; Ruiz is in. It appears to be an insurrection of sorts."

There was a slight pause. I could imagine Annie touching her forehead, thinking. "Nathan is already on the way." That made me smile. "And Teddy is coming down from SeatVan."

"Good. We need help. We still can't coordinate all the Mover groups."

"When they get there, I want you to come home, Jemma."

My turn to pause. "I understand the impulse. AGNA knows I'm here, so yes, there's a risk. But I think my being here helps."

"Hill? Ginger? Do you agree with that?"

They exchanged a glance. Hill leaned towards the unit. "Yes, I do. I think they'll rally around Jemma more than they would anyone else. Carlos isn't able to take control. We'll get her out as quickly as we can."

Ginger added, "Control is what we need right now. I agree she should stay at least until we're closer to that."

My comm unit was buzzing. "I'm going to give you to Ginger and take this call. See you soon." I handed over the unit and picked up the local Movers.

Ruiz's voice was steady but urgent. "The group in West LA Sector — that runs from West Hollywood to the beach — they're pinned down in a warehouse on the wharf."

"Got it. Any other group that can help?"

"No. Can't find anyone who isn't busy."

"We'll take care of it." I hung up and activated the locator.

Ginger handed the HQ unit back to me. "Annie says Nathan will be here in a couple of hours, unless he hits bad weather. He'll key in on your locator chip and find us. Teddy will arrive in an hour or so, too. She'll tell him to meet us on San Miguel. That seemed easiest."

I nodded while I was making a visual on the coastline. "Help me out. Look for a group of Movers besieged in a warehouse here. They need us."

There were fires all along the coastline, which at least defined it. I wondered why AGNA didn't bring the lights up. Maybe they couldn't; maybe the whole climate control grid was blown.

Hill spotted it. "There! To starboard."

Off to my right I could see a derelict building, half of it engulfed in flames, three tanks ringing it; a fedcar in the air and several on the ground.

"Let's see just how good these guns are." I said it jauntily enough, and came down at the scene at a steep angle, guns blazing. I hit the airborne fedcar with a lucky shot and it fell like a comet and exploded in another warehouse.

"Hill — have you done air combat?"

"Yes."

"Good — I haven't. Prompt me."

"Make a pass at them. Come in at an angle, shooting, then pull up steep and to the left once you pass them. You aim for the tanks. We'll go after the rest."

The dive was bringing us close to the ground quickly. Ginger shoved a window open. "Get lower!" She had to shout over the sound of air rushing into the car. Hill pushed his window open, too.

My big guns shattered everything they hit. I made two runs at the circle of vehicles around the building; Ginger and Hill leaned out and fired incessantly. My ears were ringing and I felt dizzy, but it worked.

I climbed steeply and made a turn to come back in a third time. One tank was dead and smoking; another was limping away; the third was firing at us and I squeezed off more rounds at it. By the time we'd passed over it, it was running, too, trailing flames.

Suddenly, the area around the building was deserted except for the dead and dying.

"I'm going in," I yelled, turning again and decelerating.

Hill touched my shoulder. I couldn't hear him but he was shaking his head in an emphatic "no." I went down anyway.

I landed, deafened by the sudden lack of noise. Ginger and Hill jumped out, I grabbed the gun Ruiz had given me and got out, too. They crowded around me, but I pushed past them to the door of the building and blasted the frame, kicked it in.

"Don't shoot! I'm a Mover!" No answer. "The Fedguards are gone. Get out of there!" Still no answer. "I need to talk to your leader. I'm Jemma. Talk to me!"

We waited. Ginger whispered in my ear. "They'll be back, with reinforcements."

"Maybe. In the meantime, we need these people." I stepped into the interior of the building before Hill could grab me. It was murky, smoky. Fire blazed along one wall.

"Dammit, Jemma!" Hill stepped in front of me.

"Jemma?" A woman's voice.

"Yes. Come out. You've got to get out of here. They'll be back."

The Movers showed themselves slowly, guns ready. There were ten of them, four with wounds. A short, dark woman separated herself from the others and came forward warily.

I stepped out from behind Hill and held my left arm out, pointing the gun in my right hand at the floor. "Are you the group leader?"

"He's dead. I'm his Second. I'm Alis." She turned to the others. "It's all right. It *is* Jemma." Then she strode forward. "Are we glad to see you!"

We conferred briefly, set them up with contacts, missions, and sent them off to try to link up with the Hollywood group, then they were to head for the Countryside and help anyone leaving the city.

I got on the unit to Ruiz and told him we were going back to San Miguel to await more Mover leaders coming in. He seemed relieved.

There were sirens wailing all over the city, but far away, not in this sector. Here the streets were empty. Across from the warehouse was a commodities store. We raided it, taking food, water, first aid supplies, and a bundle of lightbars. I surreptitiously grabbed a bottle of California red. For later. For Nathan.

When we were loaded, I turned to Hill. "Keypad one one one seven four. You fly."

I crawled in and leaned back, hugging the wine bottle under my jacket. I was hungry and thirsty and needed sleep.

"Fedcars in the air, Jemma. We need to go down."

"Do it." I didn't open my eyes. They were gritty and wanted to stay closed. I heard the strange breathy noises Hill and Ginger were making. "What is it?"

"You should see this," she said, her voice a whisper.

I forced my eyes open and for a moment didn't register what I was seeing. Wilshire Boulevard, Millennium City, the justice facility — all rubble, or on fire. Firefighters waved us around them, too busy to care that we were an inappropriate GAV.

"What is it?" Hill drove cautiously but slowly as we took in the damage.

"It used to be the financial and legal center of L. A." Was that my steady voice?

Ginger blew out a breath. "The people must be very angry, Jemma. This is not Mover work."

"Yes."

Gunfire erupted, some of it directed at the firefighters. Fedguards shot back; GAVs were coming in low.

I tapped Hill on the shoulder. "Go north. Actually, north-northwest." He nodded and I leaned back in my seat and closed my eyes again briefly, this time because I didn't want to look.

"How far should I go?"

An idea was in my head, a vague idea. A stupid idea. I looked around us. "Just about five more minutes. Can you go up? If you can, fly low and slow. I want to see something."

He did so and I watched the smoldering buildings give way to green patches here and there, more gutted buildings but fewer, and then none. This area looked untouched.

Things looked different, so I had to be careful. Then I saw the long row of Jacaranda trees in a straight line down the middle of San Vicente Boulevard, their deep fuchsia blossoms like another kind of fire.

"They're still there." It pleased me greatly. I had looked forward to their flowering every year. I touched Hill again. "Go down. Follow the pink trees."

I was going home.

# # #

Trees were taller. Houses looked different. The rising sun was the same, though. I opened the window and the fragrance of this section of Santa Monica wafted in the window.

Ginger smiled, enjoying the view and the scent of flowers. "Where are we?"

"Santa Monica. Hill, see that turn on the right? Make it and then stop."

He did so. We sat a moment. Ginger took the safety off her gun. I felt a kind of paralysis. Could I really do this? It was crazy. It was imperative.

I popped my door and my bodyguards stiffened. Maybe they guessed, but they said nothing.

"That house with the avocado tree and the flagstone entry is my house. I'm going there. You stay here, please. Don't try to stop me. I know it's crazy but I'm going to do it anyway. It's very important to me."

Hill was squinting; Ginger moved restlessly, but I was already out of the GAV and walking. *Thank you thank you*, I thought. *Thank you for Movers who are not just killers.*

I felt old and young and tired and excited. All of it, all at once, walking down the street and up the driveway. No hovercar in front. Possibly no one was home, but then, my father didn't go to work anymore, so the vehicle was probably in the garage. If they had still let him have one.

I went around the side of the house and tried the French doors. One of them was unlocked. That meant someone was inside. I slid it open quietly and stepped inside.

My living room. Gracious as ever, the sense of it was an avalanche of good, expensive taste washing over me. But it was quiet. I could hear a vid from upstairs, tuned low and I couldn't understand the words.

I went further in, tears welling in my eyes, my chest constricting with love and remembrance and fear.

A noise in the kitchen. The only weapon I had was the obsidian knife, but I didn't touch it. I stood still and waited.

Daddy came out of the kitchen door with a coffee mug in his hand. He saw me and stopped. Eyes widening. Jaw dropping. Straightening to his full height.

We didn't breathe. He was beautiful. He looked older, sadder, and tired, but beautiful. I wanted to cry.

"Daddy."

He set the coffee cup on the sideboard and stared at me. Then he laughed softly and we crossed the ten feet separating us in two steps and he had me in his arms.

"Jemma!" He held me close and I hugged him back hard.

"I didn't do this, Daddy. I'm trying to stop it."

He pulled away from me, arms still encircling me. Tears were rolling down his cheeks but his eyes were merry. "I didn't think so — not your style."

Then we didn't say anything. Just looked. Trying to say with our hearts all that needed saying. He pushed the hair off my face gently, the way he had done in the mountains when he gave me the stars.

"I needed to see you again. Mother? Is she all right?"

He nodded. "She's a good woman, Jemma. I hope you know that."

I thought of her naked body in the pool in the phony moonlight and nodded. "Yes, I do know that."

"She's upstairs."

I shook my head. "I won't compromise her."

He nodded, his eyes bubbling. "You're... tall." We laughed and I realized I had his smile. We were awkward with each other, like young lovers.

I suddenly wondered what I must look like to him, standing there in my black armorweave suit with the silly moth drawn on the pocket. There was too much to say and no time at all. We quieted our breathing.

"You can't stay."

"I know. I'm sorry they won't let you go into the Countryside."

He nodded, his mouth tightening. "I'll be fine. You must go."

"I have a GAV outside, Daddy. There's room for—"

"Don't! Don't go there, Jemma. You know we couldn't do that. But it's a beautiful thought." There was a catch in his voice that broke my heart.

"I love you, Daddy."

He smiled. "I love you too, Baby. I always have. Go now. Be careful."

"I will."

I backed away from him and fled to the GAV, flung myself into it and Hill took off quickly. Neither of them said a word, for which I was grateful.

I closed my eyes, replaying in my head the moments with my father and trying not to cry. No, he couldn't come with me. He could have gone feral long ago. He belonged to AGNA.

Ruiz had brought supplies to San Miguel: a cooking unit, pillows, blankets, two air mattresses already inflated, electronic maps, sensors, and more guns. Our purloined goods added to our comfort. Importantly, he had installed a vidscreen. AGNA Network News was running a gardening show at the moment, but eventually they would have to admit to the riot and we needed to know how they were handling it.

"Just like home," I said, heading for the nearest mattress. Ruiz smiled at me again. "Thanks, Ruiz. Good thinking. Is there something incredibly pressing I must do in the next half hour?"

"No, Commander. I've set up a meeting with all the leaders, or what's left of them, at 0900. L. A. is out of control, but the Movers aren't. We're pulling it together."

"That's what I wanted to hear! Then, I'm going to rest. Wake me if you must." I didn't want to play commander. I wanted to sleep and think about my father and look forward to Nathan.

#

I was smiling before I opened my eyes. I could hear Nathan's rumbling voice, speaking softly to be sure, but my ears loved his music, were tuned to it. I pretended sleep and listened.

"Bad weather over the Rockies." Hill mumbled something. "Anything on AGNA News yet?" Ginger responded negatively. "Is she all right?" And the voice was closer and the she was me, so I opened my eyes.

Nathan hunkered down beside the mattress and leaned over to kiss me.

"I'm fine. I missed you." I got up and leaned into him. He smelled good. He put an arm around me, but he wasn't smiling. "I don't like it that we're all in the same place. Where's Teddy? He should be here by now."

Ginger was frowning. "You're right, Nathan. And we haven't heard from Teddy."

"Of course! We should split up. This is dangerous," Hill said tensely. He should have, I should have, thought of the foolishness of clustering. We all should have.

Nathan smiled. "No harm done. Jemma and I will go off now. I want her debrief. Ginger, you stick with Ruiz; Hill, team up with Teddy when he gets here. We'll be in touch as to where each of us will meet. We'll be in motion at all times. Hill, if it's not in place, think about teams to facilitate transport through the Countryside"

Hill clenched his jaw. "We're working on that. Ginger has been sticking with Jemma, Nathan. She could—"

I stepped forward and poked Hill in the chest. "Soapy, if you get in our way, I swear I'll whack you!"

Nathan laughed and Hill even managed a rueful sort of smile. I grabbed my carrybag, including its cargo of wine, and headed for the door.

"Wait a minute, Jem." Nathan turned to Ruiz. "We need to get Jemma on the news. Can you set it up? With a vid relay?"

"Yes. It may take a little time. I don't know which facilities are still operating."

"Do it as quickly as you can. Call me when you have it. Thanks, Ruiz! We'll be in touch in half an hour. Ginger, let HQ know I'm here. I'll call in as soon as I'm debriefed."

I was already out the door, wasting none of that half hour, and into the GAV with Nathan right behind me. We didn't look back.

I opened the throttle going up the coastline. Nathan was impressed with the new GAV. I told him everything as clearly as I could, and he listened with his arm around me, nodding now and then, asking an occasional question. He kissed my ear when I told him about my father. He was silent on the issue of Carlos.

"It was my call. And I feel guilty and sad and I don't have time to feel those things. Ruiz took care of it."

Nathan shook his head slowly. "I'm sorry, Baby. I trust your instincts. And you like Ruiz?"

"Yes. The West L. A.'s Second is named Alis. She seems okay, too."

I looked below me, searching for a place to land. A small cove appeared, with a beach wide enough for the GAV and I brought us down. Beyond the beach was a thick stand of shrubs and dark, wind-sculpted trees. We got out, pushed the GAV closer to the tree line, and found ourselves a place to sit.

I wanted him. Wanted the sex and shelter and the strength, the warmth he had for me. I needed to give love, to prove that I was not just a killer. We made love in a kind of frenzy, and wound up giggling.

"Darling," I snuggled, "we're at war. L. A. is crumbling, the organization is a mess, I'm too visible; our movement will be blamed and that will set us back, and we're behaving like a couple of randy teenagers."

Nathan smiled when I brought out the wine. We opened it badly with my obsidian knife and we drank a couple of swigs from the bottle, cork bits and all. We made love again, slower, and had just relaxed when the comm unit bleeped at us. Nathan picked it up.

"Yes." I leaned my head on his to hear.

"Ginger here. Ruiz says he's found a vid set-up, but the window of opportunity is small. AGNA will be able to trace it, so Jemma will have to get in, speak her piece, and get out fast."

"Okay, thanks," I said.

"We're leaving now." Nathan raised his eyebrows at me. I got the message and got back into my armorweave suit. "Give us the coordinates when we're in the air."

"Will do."

Twenty minutes later we were on the ground, making our way through the still-smoking streets of what had once been Burbank Sector. We pulled up at a building with a blue glass front. Most of that was missing, but the guts of the structure were still intact. Ruiz came out of the entrance flailing his arms at us to hurry.

I didn't have time to think. I was shoved in front of a vidcam, technicians — who came from I knew not where, but they were Movers and grinning at me — gave me a go-ahead and I was broadcasting. I was disheveled and self-conscious. I wasn't even sure that I had fastened my shirt properly.

"This is Jemma." I looked into the vidcam but couldn't flash my famous smile for them. "You know that I'm a Mover. What's happening here in L. A. is *not* our work. We do not condone this violence. Please — stay in your homes, get off the streets, stop the shooting! Destroying L. A. will not make things better for you, it will make them worse. We call upon AGNA to use restraint and common sense, to have compassion. We Movers want to see the government change, but not this way. Get off the streets! Take care of each other! Let order be restored."

"Jemma, that's it. You're off. Get out of here!"

"Did I say anything?" It had all happened too fast.

Nathan smiled in encouragement. "You've been more poetic, but it was fine. Now leave."

Teddy spoke up. "I need to talk to Jemma."

Nathan nodded. "We'll split another way. You go with Teddy and fold him into the mix. Ginger, you come with me and give me your debrief. Hill, go with Ruiz. Everyone checks back in half an hour."

We sped from the place. Nathan took my GAV, I climbed into Teddy's. It was an older one, sitting high on struts.

"Where are we going?" I hadn't seen him for a year and he'd put on weight. He was tall and sandy-haired, still a good looking man in his thirties, despite the extra pounds. He was beginning to have jowls.

"I'm heading up towards Pasadena Sector. Ruiz gave me a safe place where we can hole up for a while." I nodded. "We really didn't start this?"

I sighed and leaned back in the seat. "I dunno, Teddy. The first incidents may have been ours. I was told they were, but I'm not sure of that. I do know there was a leak. AGNA knew I was coming, knew where I was."

He shook his head. "Well, we'll do the best we can. Tell me what you need from me."

We talked about where we might transport immigrants from the city, how many settlements he knew of in the beautiful mountains a suitable distance from SeatVan, and how dangerous that might be. People leaving now in panic might not want to stay, might compromise our Countryside network.

Teddy set us down in a park. It was untouched and empty and lovely. Beds of flowers glowed red and white and yellow; eucalyptus trees hummed slightly in a breeze and perfumed it; birds were singing. He got out and reached back to help me.

I took his hand to steady myself as I jumped out of the GAV. He didn't help. Instead, he pulled my arm hard, so that I was sent sprawling into the dust. Then he hit me with his gun before I could get up.

I yelled and scrambled to my feet, dizzy and angry.

"Dammit, Jemma! Go down!" and he hit me again.

I did go down. It felt as if I went slowly, falling horizontally into a spiral that swung me around and around, deeper and deeper into the darkness at the bottom.

Chapter 11

I couldn't process what was happening. Someone was right in my face making weird noises, and there was pain and I couldn't move. Then I realized it was a man's face next to mine and that he was *in* me, raping me, and my arms were pinioned above me and my feet were on the floor. He shuddered and thrust and clawed at my back. I realized I was naked.

Oh, yes. Teddy. He hit me. Fell into this trap.

I opened my eyes but the Fedguard's face was too close to see. I grit my teeth and tried to move. He laughed and pulled out of me. When he came into focus, I kicked. Mistake. His big boots stomped and ground my foot into the floor. Then the other one. He smashed my feet and I screamed and snarled at him.

Focus, I thought. *Keep breathing*. Teddy was across the room, arms hugged against himself, leaning against the wall. The Fedguard backed away, fastening his fly and turned to Teddy.

"Want some?"

Teddy cleared his throat. He wouldn't meet my eyes. It wouldn't have mattered. I couldn't really see him, but I pretended, glowering in his direction. "Naw I've already had it," he mumbled, body language telegraphing the untruth.

"You wish, you liar."

That got me a backhand across the mouth. But it was worth it — Teddy wasn't good at deception, and he immediately lost points when the Fedguard believed me, not him.

There were others in the room. The Fedguard turned to them. "Anyone else up for this?" And they all laughed that low, slow, actually rather sexy laugh that men do.

Teddy pushed himself away from the wall and hunched his shoulders. "We need to turn her in, Marsh."

Marsh, the Fedguard, made a mocking laugh. "Oh yes? And who would we turn her in to? There's nobody at Central Command. We can't even reach our sergeant." He turned back to me with a leer. "It will all settle down in a day or two. In the meantime, we get to play with Jemma."

I stared at Teddy. His discomfort was clear — he hadn't meant this part. He had betrayed me, but did not want me hurt. He was having second thoughts. Too late. It didn't excuse him, but I actually felt sorry for him, for his stupidity. I couldn't imagine what AGNA could offer him that would make him give up his freedom.

I knew I should keep my mouth shut. I had been through Hill's grueling torture training, and he had stressed, especially with me, that saying or doing anything provocative was a bad idea.

Marsh pinched my nipple and I yelled and tried to kick at him. My feet hurt abominably. He stepped on one again and I screamed and the tears flowed.

"Look at that. Why are you crying little girl?"

"Because it hurts, you ugly bastard!"

That earned me another backhand. I was trapped, already dead, really. *Quicker the better*, I thought.

Teddy started to leave the room and I yelled at him, "Teddy! You're a dead man. They'll kill you, if I don't do it first!"

General laughter. I squinted, expecting another crack on the head, but the Fedguard was grinning at me.

"Well said," he acknowledged.

Another Fedguard approached and pushed Marsh to the side with a smirk. He went behind me and grabbed me, hugging me to him, his hands hard and painful on my breasts.

Then I saw it: my death was a matter of time. I was too visible, too busy, too everywhere in the country to survive. The Movers all knew it; Annie knew it; Nathan knew it.

Their elaborate protection of me — the bodyguards, the locator chip behind my ear, the constant accompaniment on the simplest of missions — was just to hold off the inevitable. I had joked about it, but now I knew absolutely that there was no escaping my martyrdom.

And it made me furious that they were raping me, victimizing me. I would not end my life this way! They weren't just raping Jemma, the public leader of the Movers, they were killing Women, as they had been taught.

Despite my sore feet, I kicked out. Fruitlessly. But as if it had caused the explosion, the end of the building blew up. Fire and smoke were everywhere. The man behind me yelled, ran a couple of steps and fell on the floor. Dead. Shots. The door blew in.

Marsh turned to me, gun blazing and I knew he had shot me but didn't really feel it. I watched him fall with half his head gone. Beyond him was Nathan, a dark, beautiful, avenging angel, a gun in each hand, shooting. Other Movers crowded into the room.

Then Nathan was cutting the ropes that held me and kissing me and taking off his jacket and wrapping me in it.

"Teddy!"

"We know."

Of course, of course. We were overdue checking in. Nathan had followed the chip in my head! Thanks for modern technology.

"Can you walk?"

"No. They killed my feet."

He swept me up in his arms and we were outside and running for the GAVs. Shooting everywhere, as our tribe of Movers blazed away, the building on fire, chaos. I clung to Nathan and snuggled into his neck, talking to him, breathing him. He was mumbling, "You're safe, baby. I gotcha,." at me as he ran. Then he staggered and fell heavily, spilling me beside him, and blood was everywhere.

We were down. I was wearing his armor. His chest had a hole in it and he was dead. I screamed, grabbed his gun. There was Teddy, running for his GAV. I got to my knees and sent his name like a voice from hell and he hesitated. I don't know how many times I shot him. A lot. So many that as he fell he kept jerking upwards.

Then I was pinned again, a strong hand holding my gun arm down.

"Stop it! It's Ginger. Stop it, Jemma. You got him. Come on."

She hauled me to my feet. But they didn't work. I couldn't stand on them. When I slumped she yelled and Hill was there and I was over his shoulder and he was running.

"Don't leave him!" I screamed it back at Ginger. "Don't leave him. Bring him!"

"Get her out of here! Take her home!" Ginger took command.

Hill dumped me into the GAV, the fancy fast one, and was airborne in seconds. I lay on the floor, panting, hurting. Screaming, I think. Minutes passed while I agonized and the GAV blasted through a gate and climbed.

Sudden silence. Hill had leveled off and kicked in the automatic. He was beside me, cool and professional. He took off the bloodied armorjacket Nathan had wrapped around me, and studied, with no change of expression, the surface wound Marsh's shot had made in my thigh. He checked the split lip and the bruises from my beating and Teddy's clouting me. I thought I heard a kind of low growly sound as he sorted through the medkit to find the right pain killer. He mopped me up and carefully covered my nakedness with a thermal blanket. His hands were sure and gentle.

Then he leaned close, ready to put the patch on my arm that would ease the pain and probably knock me out. He looked unreal, handsome but inhuman in the dim green light from the control strip.

He stuck the patch on my arm and tucked the blanket under my chin, smoothed it over my shoulders. "It will ease the pain, Jemma.... I'm taking you home. I'm sorry about Nathan."

# # #

I remember things: Annie's stricken face; Devi's dark almond-eyes glowing as he leaned over me; questions.

"What hurts most?" Devi ran a scan over my body.

"My feet." Was that true? Was that really what hurt most? Or was it Nathan's chest with the hole in it because I was wearing his armor?

Hill was standing at the foot of the bed. "Sorry, Jemma, and I already know the answer, but I have to ask. Did you tell them anything?"

I think I managed a kind of laugh, because it made my ribs hurt. "No. They didn't ask me anything."

His eyes went dead for a moment and then glittered, like a predator, and his teeth showed. *He's baring his fangs,* I thought. But then I wasn't thinking clearly. Hill stalked out of the room.

I tried to focus, but couldn't see out of one eye. "Annie—" she took my hand. "The next time I'm captured—" She made a face and a disparaging sound, but I shook my head and it silenced her. She pursed her lips. They had known my destiny all along and now they knew that I knew it. "The next time, don't try to rescue me."

Annie leaned close to me, "We keep you as safe as we can, Darling."

"I know."

She wiped the blood out of my hair. "Did they rape you?"

"Yes."

A cool voice from Devi. "We'll take care of it."

I closed my eyes and then it struck me! "No! No, don't take care of it!" I tried to sit up. "It could be Nathan's — Nathan and I.... If — maybe there's a chance. I want his child, Annie!"

My caretakers exchanged a look I couldn't decipher, but I was panicked. This was too awful. "What if — don't do it!"

Annie shushed me, Devi peeled the old patch off my arm and had another one ready to go on.

"Annie, promise me!"

"Are you sure, Jemma?"

"Yes. No. I don't know! Just leave it, for now at least."

The patch was on and I watched Annie's face dissolve into gray and then darkness.

# # #

There was a lot of that — darkness — for the next couple of months. I wasn't badly injured — my feet were the worst — it was nothing that Devi couldn't fix physically, but I was slowed down, exhausted emotionally. I was not pregnant.

It wasn't enough that Nathan had died in my rescue, AGNA Network News also had to explain in gruesome detail how I had hacked Daddy and Mother to pieces with a machete.

I healed from those deaths slowly, thinking I was a damn poor soldier, thinking I didn't want to continue, thinking I wanted revenge, and finally, not thinking at all.

I went for R&R to a settlement where I was safe, where I worked in the fields and around the farm. That healed my spirit more than any listener's therapy. The farm couple had three children, two girls and a boy. I loved them dearly, loved to play with them and sing with them. After a month, though, I knew it was time to go back to work. It had been half a year since L. A.

When I left the farm, the youngest girl presented me with a tiger kitten. It had been born just before I'd arrived at their house. I dubbed him Fred, in memory of the unknown lover of Angela, immortalized on my chrono from the killing fields. His name made the kids laugh. I stuck him under my jacket and he slept all the way back to HQ.

We concentrated on Chicago for the next six months. Their new Regional Administrator was a tyrant, given to wholesale alterations and frequent raids into the Countryside. We went after every lab and outpost we could find.

Annie allowed me a couple of missions but mostly I was pulled off the line. We had new ideas. We still actively fought AGNA's military, and targeted facilities that harmed the populace, but we began to report on the normal things in the Countryside along with our criticisms of AGNA. We were saying that our world under the stars was superior, despite the hardships, to AGNA's world under the domes.

My first documentary was on what immigrants could expect when they moved into the country, pulling no punches about the difficulties. It led to an increase in immigration, which AGNA quickly closed down, especially around Chicago.

An odd and maybe significant breakthrough occurred in California, where renegades who had escaped during the L. A. Terror, as it was now being called, had taken over some of the frontier towns. They were banditti, bad guys, pillaging their way through the Countryside, quick to kill. For once, the Movers and Fedguards cooperated, although we never talked, in shutting down the most notorious of these outlaw bands.

Annie set me up with a news show on the Mover Net. Fred the cat and I were the stars, and I adopted an animated terloo moth as our logo, in remembrance of an old friend. Good things were happening that we could report. A theatre company had been formed and was touring settlements, doing old and new plays and musicals and encouraging the other arts; a baseball league was forming; the harvest was good; there was a tremendously exciting thunderstorm I caught on vid which showed the power and the danger and the beauty of Countryside weather. Every night I could, I showed them the moonrise.

Just when we felt that there was some hope, that we might be headed toward a peaceful coexistence with AGNA, the Fedguards would descend on villages and destroy them. And they still took every girl child they could find back to the cities. Annie was never discouraged; I can't say the same.

I enjoyed being a sort of vidstar, though, Fred and I. The new Mover, Parks, was a splendid vidcam operator and a crackerjack communications innovator, and taught me well. Of course, everywhere I went, at least two bodyguards went with me as my vulnerability had been increased by my vid celebrity. And the locator chip stayed in, a tiny flat lump behind my ear. I even found comfort in Devi's bed occasionally. He was sweet and passionate and I think in love with me, but he never mentioned it. Nathan was still first in my heart.

Four days after my twenty-eighth birthday in August, I went into the hills of southern Wisconsin to do a vidstory about a woodworker whose cabinets and tables and chairs were works of art. My two bodyguards, Danno and Mike, went with me.

I had one of the older GAV's and had elected to pilot myself. I was tired of being hauled around by others. I set the ship down in the barnyard of a tidy homestead. The clearing was quite small and beyond it the hardwood forest stretched for miles, an ocean of green. Chet, the woodworker, had his raw materials in his back yard.

I shut down and popped the doors. Danno and Mike got out. I crawled over the seat to get the small vidcam, then joined them. I was surprised that Chet wasn't coming from his house to meet us. He must have heard the whirr of our landing.

I had taken three steps when a shot exploded behind me. I whirled around. Mike was on the ground, screaming. Danno shot him again and then leveled the gun at me. I hadn't carried a gun since my frenzied kill of Teddy had cured me of shooting.

Fedguards boiled from around the house and the barn, fifteen or twenty of them at least, heavily armed. A lieutenant was in charge. He strode towards me, flanked by his sergeants. Déjà vu of potato digging in New York when AGNA stole the farm boys for its relentless war in Canada. But this was now and there was not a chance in hell of escaping, so no point in resisting. It crossed my mind to bolt, but I didn't think they'd shoot to kill.

The lieutenant was a good-looking officer, reminding me of Hill with his button-down appearance. He held out a piece of paper. "Jemma7729," he began. It had been years since I'd heard that. "This is an arrest warrant. Read it, please."

So, they were doing this by the books. I opened the paper, one page, folded in half, and read: "JE2MDRA-77290FF400RT913, greetings. You are remanded to the Admin Justice Facility 247 in Chicago."

It was dated 14 August 2214, and this was the 16th, so Danno had planned it all along. I handed it back to the officer. "What's the charge?"

His lips quirked. Not quite a smile. "I think, Jemma, you can pretty much take your pick." He turned away from me and nodded to his cohorts.

They cuffed my hands behind me, put shackles on my ankles. It was all quite civilized. The barn door swung open and a GAV was brought out. Danno was standing off to one side.

"Mike was a good guy. You shouldn't have killed him, Danno. It would have been more valuable to send him back, or interrogate him."

"Shut up!" He growled. Guess he hadn't thought of that.

"Why? What does AGNA offer you?"

"I joined the Movers to get some action. All I've done is to babysit you."

"Ah, so you'll join the Fedguards?"

"Damn straight."

"If I were a Fedguard, I wouldn't trust you to babysit a fish, after this disloyalty." That made the guards smile.

Danno started to lunge at me but was stopped by the lieutenant. "Enough! Fall in with the other men."

Danno grumbled and went slinking away. The guards made a place for him but didn't seem friendly. Good. I hope he got what he deserved. I wondered momentarily why we had taken him in. I even made a mental note to check on that. Reality wasn't quite sinking in.

Chet came out on his rustic, sagging porch. He stared at me, his eyes sad. I'd enjoyed talking to him when we set up the vid shoot ten days before. He was an old, gangling man, with longish white hair and scarred, knobby hands. The tension in his face made him look years older than I remembered.

"I'm sorry, Jemma."

I smiled at him. "Not your fault."

"They're taking me into the city. Chicago." He obviously was unhappy about that, and spoke the name of the town as if it were garbage.

I glanced at the lieutenant, but his expression was neutral. "I'm sure they'll let you do your work. You're an artist. You'll just have a different clientele."

He wasn't fooled. "And a different kind of freedom, eh? I hope they treat you well, Jemma."

I nodded. The lieutenant was getting restless. "Let's go. Bring her."

He loped off on his long legs towards the waiting fedcar. I had an escort on either side. The shackles made walking difficult, so they half-dragged me and boosted me into the vehicle. We took off immediately, heading south.

I looked out the window at the miles of treetops, at a stream or a lake sparkling through them here and there, at the beautiful Countryside, saying goodbye. I hadn't said a proper farewell to Annie and my friends that morning. I trusted that Annie would take care of Fred.

Chapter 12

There was vid coverage of my incarceration since I arrived at Justice Facility 247. It's a new plasticrete monolith of bad municipal architecture, squatting in the middle of Chicago. I was escorted into the building by a company of Fedguards in dress uniforms. I didn't resist; kept my head up; didn't smile but didn't frown, either.

Strange what we remember. I thought of my mother's advice to me when I had to apologize in quad for hitting Thom. Be gracious, simple, keep your dignity, be smart. I could almost hear her voice in my ear, so softly that night, "We're women, we endure." I swallowed a sudden clutch in my throat. AGNA had hacked her to pieces in my name.

I tried to do those things, revealing nothing of what I thought, being cooperative. I was stripped and examined; blood tests were done; vids and freeze photos were made. They removed my locator chip and I wondered if anyone at HQ saw it disappear from their screen. Probably.

After they had thoroughly explored my nakedness — I think it was supposed to demean me but didn't — they dressed me in white. They're big on symbols in AGNA and think white is the color of innocence. The law says, but doesn't trust its own myth of "innocent until proven guilty," of course, so really really bad guys wear white. The obverse of sympathetic magic.

I sat in a small room with four guards for a while, then a major came in and directed that I be cuffed again. This time a neck cuff went on as well, and the leg shackles were even closer together so that the guards had to carry me into another room, where I was pushed into a chair, fastened with additional restraints, and waited some more.

The door opened to admit a very tall, very handsome guy with brilliant blue eyes, a deep tan, impeccably dressed and coifed. He stood in front of me and examined me shamelessly. Then he smiled. It was a smile like Annie's — it lit up the room. I recognized him from the vids.

"So this is the notorious Jemma7729." Voice well-modulated and deep, sexy to me, like Nathan's had been.

I smiled back, my heroine grin. "And you are Marlin9910, the Butcher of Chicago." Aha! That's why they had fastened me so I couldn't move. It was protection for the Regional Administrator. If I hadn't been smiling already, I would have grinned just then, thinking that they were afraid of me even in this impossible situation.

His expression didn't change, but his jaw tensed. He looked to the major and a chair was brought for him. He was so tall it was awkward for him to talk to me standing up. He had gained prominence as a basketball player, I remembered. Yes, sports hero, one of the main trails that lead to public office in AGNA. Guess it has something to do with hormones.

"We've caught you, Jemma."

"I noticed."

His smile faded. "I guess you'll refuse to talk to us."

"Why should I? We talk all the time on Mover News. You see it. What else is there to say? Unlike you, we have nothing to hide."

"You have a long history of crime. I've read your dossier."

I smiled again and shrugged. "No, you haven't. You've read a one-page summary."

His hairline moved. If he were an animal, it would be pulling his ears back. I was right, of course, and that annoyed him. The room suddenly prickled with his hostility.

The major moved uncomfortably. "Watch your mouth, bitch!"

Marlin held up a restraining hand. "No, no, Major, it's all right." He relaxed and smiled again. "Legally, Jemma7729. I'm going to take you legally. We've got you for rebellion, inappropriate behavior, female aggression and failure to make choices. Any one of those puts a noose around your neck. You're a dead woman."

I put on a studiously serious face. "I hope that doesn't mean I won't get any coffee while I'm here."

He laughed. "You've got balls, girl!"

"Actually, I don't." I said it mildly and it made him laugh again.

He stood up. "You're a nice-looking female. Too bad you wasted your life."

"I could say the same about you."

He went to the door, conferred quietly with the Major and a security chief and left, with an amused glance back at me. Interesting. He had just wanted to meet me. And he hadn't even taken pictures.

They needed to punish me. I spent the next two days confined in a box, unable to move. Obviously, *someone* had read my file. I suppose that was Marlin's pay back for making him uncomfortable.

The isolation box bothered me more this time than it had those many years ago at rehab.

#

That part is over. Now I'm here.

I'm considered extremely dangerous so I'm in isolation in a white cell and have been for at least a week, maybe more. I'm losing track of time because the lights are always on. I sit on a white bench in a white tunic and trousers, barefoot, in a dazzling windowless room. The pupils of my eyes must be pin pricks. They ache. I'm wearing electronic bracelets to keep me away from the one door. I haven't tried it; I know how they work. The surveillance cameras are the old horizontal strip kind.

They expect me to attempt an escape, to antagonize them, to moon them, masturbate, or pee on the floor. I haven't done any of that. I'm going to bore the guards to death. I'm a model prisoner.

It's not too bad. Not like L. A. But women like me are considered feral, so they can treat me as if I were a dangerous, wild animal if they feel like it. So far, no one has come in the night to whack me around; the food is good, and they allow me coffee; no sounds of chortling or snuffling when I use the toilet or take a shower, although I'm sure the vidcams are on all the time. I can't rule out their staging an escape attempt, for the thrill of the chase and the kill.

They have just informed me that my lawyer is here. They'll take me to him shortly. If they're going to stage an attempted escape, it will be now. I don't expect anyone to rescue me, don't want them to try. Annie promised, and I hope she damn well keeps her word. Chicago 247 is, I believe, escape-proof. People would be hurt, arrested, killed. It's not worth it.

Four guards with stun guns come through the door. My, my, they do think I'm dangerous. Two strapping female monitors, with forearms like hams. What kind of a workout does that? They shackle my hands behind my back, put a silver gringostrip around my forehead. We call them that because the Fedsquads used them first in Mexico, in the final phase of the Consolidation War. One press of a button from a remote somewhere and I'll be flat on my butt with the biggest headache of my life.

I stand still and don't smile. I don't wiggle. I say nothing. They're looking at each other sideways, which makes me suspicious but there's not much I can do.

The hallway is painted vomit green and I can't see for a moment. I blink and shake my head and everyone comes to alert.

"The change of scenery hurts my eyes." I smile. That's a waste of effort — what a grim-looking bunch.

The hallway is full of people — guards, officials, press reps, dunnos — lined up, backs pressed against the wall to allow our passage. The media people are mumbling into their headsets, vidcams hum. I can hear safeties clicking on the guns as we walk forward. The end of the hall is blocked by guards standing elbow-to-elbow, stun guns cradled in their arms, to channel me into a room.

My lawyer sits at the table in front of his console. I am secured into the chair across from him. I have a console, too, but no keypad. It may be a voice console but I doubt it. Justice facility equipment is notoriously, inexplicably, obsolete. He stands up. He's about my height, short for a man, although by AGNA's "Perfect Sizes for the Female," he would probably say that I'm too tall.

"You may call me Frank."

I suppress my impulse to pun on his name and nod. He wears a serious but sympathetic look. He wears a proper, dark gray suit, is impeccably groomed, his buffed finger-nails shining pinkly in the bright lights in the room. He looks like my father, but fatter, his jaw line drooping like a bulldog.

He walks up and down a moment, hands behind his back as if he, too, were fettered. Well, he's stuck with me, so I guess he is. He comes closer and leans in, friendly-like.

"I've tried to get them to reduce the charges, Jemma7729. I wasn't successful. I'll try again."

I clear my throat. I haven't said much in a long time. "Thank you. Could we skip the number? At least when we're alone." He nods. "Will we get to answer them one by one? I'd like that."

"I doubt it." He sighs, pulls out a white monogrammed hankie and mops at his face. It's a bit warm in the room. "That would take longer than they want to spend on you. They say they're preparing an elaborate performance for the trial, but they won't want it to run too long. Marlin wants a public affair, of course, to prove your guilt, and to serve justice." I snort at that, and he sighs again and sits on the edge of the table looking at me, shaking his head slowly. "I can't save your life, Jemma. The best I can do is to get them to let you choose your death."

That makes me smile. "I think one of the charges is failure to make choices, isn't it?"

The humor of it eludes him. Pity.

I decide to be the good professional criminal. I straighten in the chair as far as the cuffs and restraints allow, tuck my chin down and look up at him, pinning him with my eyes, the way I was taught so long ago. It always works, makes me look serious and sincere, but vulnerable. "Frank, I've been accused in the past of a lot of things I didn't do.

I'd like to set the record straight. I did not—" I surprise myself with the emphatic tone, but have had a sudden anguish and an adrenaline rush, thinking of my murdered family, "—did *not* instigate the L. A. Terror." He rises and walks away a couple of steps. I say more softly, "That was not my work."

"Well," and he drawls it and I notice for the first time that he has a slight accent. Maybe the Southeast Region? He says, "Wahll... today we'll go over the charges one by one and you tell me — and tell the truth, mind you — on each and every one of them. Guilty or no." I nod. He sits at the console and taps out something and my screen fills with words and pictures.

"Illustrated," I mutter.

"Just look at the charges, Jemma. They have given us this afternoon, no more."

There is a color snapshot of me with a .620 Winner slung on my back, wearing a camouflage jumpsuit and black boots. I wonder who took it. It makes me happy. The sun is shining; I am smiling; behind me is a lean-to and a pile of carrybags; and beyond that, off at the horizon, a Vermont mountain — Ascutney I think it was — soaring upward. I was about twenty-four then. On that caper we took out a couple of relay stations and messed up the weather in BosWash. It rained for days before they could put the connections back. Probably not nice for the people.

Underneath the picture is a copy of the handbill we had plastered everywhere and posted all over the Mover News:

RAIN ON THEIR PARADE
TAKE BACK THE COUNTRY
THERE IS A WORLD OUTSIDE YOUR WALLS
IT IS SAFE FOR ALL LIVING THINGS
COME AND VISIT US
    — THE VERMONT DIGGERS

Pretty crude, I guess. I had thought up that name. We never got caught; but obviously, someone connected me with it.

"Is this what they mean by "'inappropriate behavior?'"

"Yes, we'll look at those charges first. Quite a long list. Guilty or no?"

"Guilty. Who took that picture?"

He taps the keypad again without answering.

A series of pictures begins to scroll slowly. Various installations, all of them a mess, burning, wrecked, trashed, leveled.

"They've lumped all these together. It is inappropriate behavior to destroy scientific buildings. Guilty?"

"Guilty. I did those by myself. See the green fire? My trademark. Except in L. A. They were alteration labs, where they manufacture the drugs to kill women's brains." He nods, goes back to his console. "What do you think about that, Frank?"

"About what?"

"About killing women's brains?"

His eyes widen suddenly and shift around. I'd seen animals do that when I'd startled them in the woods. That was an unfair question. It could compromise him because doubtless we were being recorded, but I need a measure of the man.

He stares at me, absolutely expressionless. "I don't think about it at all." He presses a key and more pictures pop up on my screen.

I don't blink. "What's happening outside? In Chicago? In the Countryside?"

He doesn't look up. "I don't know. I'm too busy to watch the vid."

"Are you locked in here with me?"

"Yes."

"The bastards. What kind of fairness is this?"

He is sweating. "Please, Jemma! Please. We only have this afternoon. The trial is in two days. Help me out."

He looks at me then, fear in his eyes. There is something soft about him, and appealing. A little like Carlos, maybe.

I sigh and turn back to the console. I might as well enjoy the pictures.

We work through the afternoon, then the guards come for me and I run the gauntlet back to my cell. At its door, the major steps forward and stops our progress.

"Jemma7729, you are now in isolation. You will see no one until the trial."

"Not even my lawyer?"

"No one."

The vids are going. Maybe even going live. Time to make a statement. "That's unfair. That's not due process."

Vid operators in the hallway press forward, squeezing among the guards, smelling the scent of drama. There's a mix-up here somewhere, and I seize my chance to grandstand. My feet aren't shackled, I forget about the gringostrip, I push a guard out of my way and put my back against the wall, clearing out a space in front of me so the vidcams can see me.

"This is illegal! I'm being denied appropriate counsel!"

"Get her!" The major snarls at the stunned guards, and of course they lay hands on me.

I look straight into the vidcams and smile my Daddy's smile. It's a message to my friends — a kiss to Annie and the others at HQ. It says I'm alive and there's more to come.

The major shouts and I am shoved unceremoniously into the white room. They forget to bring my dinner, but I don't care. It was worth it.

# # #

So now I wait some more. I'd like to go outside. The air conditioner is on, perfectly healthy air blowing zephyrs at the ceiling, but I have been too long under the real sun to enjoy it. I want the taste of a Minnesota pine woods in my mouth. I want to watch big clouds scuttling over meadows of grass and buttercups. I want to laugh with my friends around the dining table at HQ with Fred on my lap. Most of all, I want to see the stars again.

God, I hate white! My eyes are hungry for color. I told a guard the sterility was cruel and unnatural punishment and he looked at me as if I were crazy. Guess he doesn't notice.

I've had a shower. They gave me new clothes. Right after I dressed, a male medical person came in and handed me a small gelatin capsule. I held it up to see inside it. A tiny computer chip.

"Swallow it."

"Something new?" Interesting. To blow up my guts, obviously.

I swallow it. A guard holds a stun gun against my temple as the med feels around in my mouth to be sure I have actually done so. At that range even stun guns kill, so I resist the obvious opportunity to taste his stupid blood. It was tempting. It would be quick, but I keep feeling there is something more I need to do.

The med snaps out a wad of tissues from his pocket. "You will have a haircut." He heads for the door, wiping my saliva off his fingers with obvious distaste.

"I'm not toxic!" He doesn't react.

A young woman comes in. An alter? She's lovely. Skin the color of dark coffee, close-cropped hair glistening. Her eyes are only slightly lighter than my own. She has a hair cutting outfit on a tripod stand and sets it up quickly. Just as quickly, two guards step between us.

One of them puts a headset with a microphone on me. Of course they're afraid we will whisper. Oh hell — it will make the cutting of hair more difficult.

The hair person waits placidly, gracefully, her weight on her back foot. Smiling. When the guards finish, she begins to trim my mop.

"Not too short. I have big ears." She chuckles.

She leans close, so close I can smell her body and feel its heat, and deftly shoves the tip of my headset mike into my mouth. I close my lips and lick the head of it to cause static, and she whispers, "We will see the stars. If not me, then my children."

I spit the mike out. I don't dare say anything, but I look into her eyes. There's a light in hers, a double dot, one of them my reflected face. I can't suppress a tiny smile. No movement of recognition from her. Is it a trap?

She finishes trimming my hair, brushes me off, and picks up the dark threads around us with a cordless vacuum.

I stare straight ahead, but I think I see her pluck one lock of my hair and put it into the pocket of her smock. A souvenir? She dares that much? Did I really see that? Look at my black eyes and ask me and you will see nothing but blackness.

#

We're in the largest hall available. The place is packed and noisy. I was brought in, cuffed, then released to stand on a silver metal square. A spiral cage descended over me, the top of it attached to the ceiling. I am surrounded by coils of metal. I can see everything, and be seen. I assume that if I touch a coil something rotten happens. I also assume that someone is in front of a console somewhere on which are buttons that control the electronics outside and inside my body.

The five justices will sit on an elevated dais to my right. My cage is at one end of the large open area, with the audience seated on three sides, like a stadium. The holograms and live actors dramatizing my sins and misdemeanors will be performed on my level. I'm actually eager to see the trial. I've always loved the theatre.

"Frank?" My lawyer turns from the white table they have provided for him beside my cage, eyebrows raised. "They didn't give me a chair."

"I'm afraid you'll have to stand, Jemma."

"That's unfriendly." There is a fuzzy white sound in the room. I still have the headset on. It pops.

"Jemma? Uh... Jemma7729?" An unfamiliar voice speaks in my earplug. "We're going to check the electronics." I nod. There is a bonging sound, meant to quiet the audience, which it almost does. The syrupy, baritone voice of an announcer booms out too loudly and is instantly filtered and tweaked.

"We're now testing the electronics, Jemma7729. This is only a test."

Instant pain inside and out that makes me straighten up with a jerk. "Test?" I whoosh out a breath and the audience gets quieter. I grin at them. "If that's the test, I

think I missed the question. But please don't repeat it."
Laughter.

More bonging, quieter audience, and a phalanx of
Fedguards enters, stepping smartly, wearing dress uniforms but carrying weapons. They surround the room,
enclosing the audience and me, some of them on the stage
floor. The audience settles back still whispering, the noise
in the big hall subsides to a seaside sibilance.

Music begins. Muted brass with a flugel horn flourish,
and the five justices enter, wearing black robes. They take
their seats, rather grimly, I think. I wonder who composed
the theme music.

"Whose music is that?" I ask Frank, and my voice
booms out in the hall. Whoops. On my headset I can hear
breathing and something like keys clicking. The audience,
released from watching the solemnity of the Entrance of
Justice, laughs and applauds. I throw a quick glance at
the dais.

"Sorry, Your Honors," I grin, "I wasn't being disrespect-
ful. I didn't get a program. Who's the composer? The
music is wonderful." The audience applauds.

"Jemma, please." Frank whispers, but his mike is too
high, as well, and the audience hears.

I whisper back, "Sorry." But this is troubling. "Are they
going to hear everything I say to you? Doesn't seem fair."

Booming of a gavel. Bonging of the chimes for quiet.

The Chief Justice stands like a great black bird stretching in the sun on a dead tree. I smile, remembering a crow
do just that one late fall day in Massachusetts. A tall bald-
ing man, deeply sun-tanned. Where does he go in the
Countryside and what does he do there that he looks so
healthy? His hands are long fingered. His canine teeth
are outsized, appropriate if odd, giving him a predatory
look. I wonder why they weren't fixed when he was a
boy and why he has allowed himself to lose his hair. Some
kind of reverse snobbism?

The gavel bangs. Silence comes quickly. "Jemma7729,
you are charged with inappropriate behavior, rebellion,
female aggression, and failure to make choices. The
charges are, sadly, so many it would waste the court's

time, and your own, to read them all. This court, and indeed
this great nation, is well aware of your activities over the
past years. Will you accept that we declare you guilty of
rebellion, and try you for inappropriate behavior, female
aggression and failure to make choices only?"

Frank bobs a bow to the blackbird, throws a glance at
me. I shrug. "Yes, Your Honor. We accept. We do request,
however, that the charge of female aggression be collapsed
into the rebellion charge, since they are, in truth, one and
the same."

The justice thinks a moment, glancing at his colleagues,
then bangs the gavel. "So ordered. Thank you. That will
save more time."

Frank nods. "We thank the court for considering our
welfare."

I laugh and try to turn it into a cough. The gavel bangs
again but it is too late. The audience laughs with me.

"I remind you, Jemma7729, that you are in a court of
law. Inappropriate behavior here will not be tolerated."
He leans towards the tabletop, picking up a black, wand-
like tronic stick and points it at me. It looks small in that
big hand. "This tiny device operates your electronics." He
holds it high for everyone in the hall to see, and they lean
forward and a buzz goes through them.

I smile sweetly. "I understand, Your Honor." Hmmm.
Is that all that operates them? Can't be. I didn't see anyone
touch that when they tested the damn thing. But maybe...

He sits, carefully placing the wand on the tabletop. He
bangs the gavel once. Music begins, strings, 'cello, viola,
violin. It is lovely but ominous. Bassoons, too. Wow. A
special Jemma theme. I smile. I wish I could sit down and
listen. The composer is really good.

The hologram is me. The scene is Final Choosing Day.
It's all wrong. My hair is too long. I wasn't wearing blue,
I had that beautiful mouse-gray suit. There's Daddy and
Mother. They look too old, but the holograms are pretty
good. Hologram Jemma flings herself on the ground and
screams, froths at the mouth, kicks arms and legs. The other
figures try to soothe her but she is hysterical.

The dulcet tones of the announcer come in over the music, which is now *agitato*. "Jemma7729, you refused to choose."

Then it's gone. I am speechless and then I burst out laughing. The audience has been whispering. Some of them laugh with me.

Chief Justice turns a beady eye on me. "You failed to choose."

"Yes, I'm guilty. It wasn't quite like that, Your Honor. I wanted to raise puppies and they wouldn't let me." Laughter. "Actually, I wanted to make something of my life! To use my mind and my body. I wanted to go into the Countryside and see the stars."

Frank takes a worried step towards me. The Chief Justice puts his big hand on the wand but doesn't rise to the bait. The audience loves it. They applaud. I am thinking, *I will say "Countryside" until they get it. Until they cannot deny that I live outside and I am not sick, not dying.* Well, at least I wasn't.

The justices to the crow's left and right hand him tiny scraps of paper, which he reads. He bangs the gavel.

The audience inhales. "Guilty of failure to make choices," he says. Exhale. Applause.

I applaud, too. I smile at the audience, and then at the justices. Frank is pale and trembling. I turn to him. "It's okay, Frank. You can't do anything but just be with me. Thank you for that." My voice is heard over the speakers, so I grab the moment. "They didn't give you adequate time to prepare, nor me."

A rumble of discontent from the audience, which the Chief Justice quickly silences.

I won't describe all the rest, except the ones that really matter. Inappropriate behavior includes my blowing up labs with pretty good special effects and again, nice music.

But, now you must know this. The scene is the Countryside, a slice of green valley with great soaring mountains behind it. The visuals are lovely. They make me homesick and the audience is preternaturally quiet with the beauty of them. I keep thinking, *why can't they see that it's real? That this gorgeous place is there and is theirs?*

An actress enters, playing me. *Oh, good*, I think, *the
live theatre part*. Then my mouth falls open. I shoot a quick
glance at Frank, but he is staring at her, too. She doesn't
just look like me, she could *be* me. She is maybe ten years
younger, and the hair isn't quite right, and she isn't missing half of her little finger, but the resemblance is so star-
tling that people in the audience are on their feet applaud-
ing.

There is a hologram of a shack. Player Jemma hides
beside it, a pistol in her hand. An actor comes out of the
shack, looking for all the world like Teddy who betrayed
me and got Nathan killed.

Player Jemma steps out and I start shaking my head.
This is wrong. Player Teddy stops.

> Jemma: Teddy... you betrayed us. You betrayed
>   me. (*What???*)
> Teddy: I'm sorry, Jemma. I had to. What we're
>   doing is wrong. (*He didn't say that.*)
> Jemma: You must die. (*I didn't say that.*)

Player Jemma shoots him, twice. Loud explosions in
the hall, and Player Teddy falls over, blood exploding
from his head and his chest. It's a really good effect and
the audience applauds. The actress laughs, pockets the
gun, and moves to the side of the playing area to wait
for her next scene. Fedguards pull Teddy's body out,
leaving a smear of blood on the floor. Alters come in and
clean it up while the audience settles down and I try to
catch my breath.

I look at the Chief Justice. "Yes, I killed Teddy. He
handed me over to AGNA, and I was tortured and raped
by your Fedguards."

Quick as a wink the wand is pointing at me and I stag-
ger back when the pain hits.

"But this was not right. I shot him with my dead
lover's gun when the Movers rescued me. And you left
out the part where I couldn't walk after the beating the
Fedguards gave me."

I'm panting. The zap the Chief Justice gave me hurts, but is not insurmountable. It's the chip in my gut that really pinches.

The audience stirs and mumbles, and then I hear, softly at first, my name chanted almost as a whisper, "Jem-ma. Jem-ma. Jem-ma." I don't know what that means, but I think it's good.

The gavel is banged repeatedly and Fedguards start patrolling the aisles, jerking people out of their seats and hustling them outside. After a few moments, a relative but crackling silence settles in.

The crow raises an arm and the performance continues, an interior takes form: my house in Santa Monica, the living room. The actors enter. Mother looks beautiful. Daddy is — well, so like Daddy my heart hurts. He sits in a chair and opens a newspaper. He is not wearing a tie. That's wrong. Mother is watering house plants. Where did they get *that* idea?

Then Player Jemma enters again carrying a machete.

"No! Not the L.A. Terror! THAT WAS NOT MY WORK!" My voice sails over the courtroom.

Frank turns quickly. "Hush, Jemma! Please!" I look at him and am surprised to see compassion. Well, well — he believes me.

I look back at the scene, still astonished by the incredible likeness of the players. Then it hits me! And I shout, "They're clones!"

Under the AGNA Constitution it is illegal to clone anyone who is still alive, and I am still alive. My voice comes booming out and the wand comes up and I fall against the cage.

"This is all a lie! They're clones and one of them was killed in front of us! It's murder. It's Unconstitutional! Mistrial! Mistrial!" I am screaming, and the justice points the wand again.

The audience is on its feet yelling, many of them echoing me. The guards are not sure where to point their guns.

Then I hear it. A woman's voice I do not know, but as loud as mine, "Let us see the stars!" Other women's voices pick it up as a chant.

Another voice, a man's, "The Countryside is free." Then there are lots of voices, shouting, "Mistrial! No more alters! Let her go!"

Clearly, I hear one voice above the rest, "I love you, Jemma!" I recognize it and search, but cannot find the friendly face. I'm sure it's Devi.

The Chief Justice is banging for order. The chimes are bonging and my guts are on fire. The audience continues to shout and to scramble from their seats. I sink to my knees, and turn back to the scene, where Player Jemma is hesitating, looking fearfully at the audience, and then approaching my Mother clone with a machete. She doesn't seem to know what to do.

"No. No, Jemma!"

Player Jemma stops, her arm in midair and turns towards me. I grab the bars of my cage. It's death now anyway, but they're not wired. "Jemma! No! This is a lie! Don't do it!"

The hall is in turmoil. The words "mistrial" and "unconstitutional!" are screamed from many mouths. People spill into the playing space and fight the Fedguards. An insurrection! A damned spontaneous insurrection! Whoopee! This one I want! The guards are confused; the justices are running for cover.

I can taste my salty blood. On my knees, I reach through the cage — reaching out to the other Jemma, who is wheeling about, confused by the shouting.

Then guns start blasting. Sirens. A fire breaks out in a corner. Player Jemma sees me and moves toward me as if in a dream.

Then she is here. Close enough to touch. She kneels, too. My nose is bleeding and blood dribbles from my mouth. I suck my lip. My eyes are caught by her eyes. Is she an alter? A clone alter?

No, there's a spark. "Jemma..."

I reach for her. She is smiling, excited, looking at my face as if she would devour it. Looking at my face with love.

It's as if a cone of silence, of isolation, descends over us. I smile and cough.

"Who are you?" I love her face. It's mine, of course, but something more. Did I ever look that innocent?

She hesitates. She smiles, my heroine smile, her black eyes bubbling, just like my — our — father. She reaches through the cage and touches my face, sweetly, wipes the blood off my lip.

"Hello, Mother."

"Mother?"

She giggles and says, "That's what I call you! I'm J2. That's my name, Jemma2. J2."

Mother! Of course! I laugh and she does and we cling to each other. "Yes, my darling girl! Yes! You're me and I'm you. J2, listen, we don't have much time. You can do what I did, learn what I learned. But go now. Be free. Get out of the city. Go find the stars. And don't be afraid."

She shakes her head vehemently. "Mother, you're hurt. You need me."

"No, no, J2. Get out of here. You'll be all right. Find my friends, the Movers. Tell Annie I love her."

"I don't want to leave you."

I want to hold her. I feel like she is my child. But this is crazy and there's no time. I bring her hand to my lips. Her eyes are shining. She holds on to me tightly. "Leave now. AGNA tells lies. It's safe outside. It's beautiful. Go!"

She gets up and backs away, smiling, her eyes glowing. Then she dives into the milling crowd. Barely breathing I watch her bully her way through the fight. She turns back and I want to run to her, run with her. I want to know her, teach her. The tears in my eyes are not from the pain, they're because I will not, cannot, have this rite of passage, either. Will not talk to my daughter, live and laugh with her, watch her grow.

We hold each other a sweet moment with our eyes. Then I see her reach the door on the far side of the hall. She's free. She's me. Now I'm free, too.

I drag myself up. "Yes!" I am crying. I have never been happier.

I turn and there is the great black crow. Blood oozes through his left hand clutching his chest, his mouth is an open bloody smear. He is pointing the wand at me. There will be a sudden explosion of red and an overwhelming paaaaaiii

"Mother! No! I don't know what to do!"

I watch her die, my hand on the door jamb, feeling the silky wood, I watch my mother die, crumpling into a heap inside that cage. Inside me is our last look — her eyes dancing with love, with life. How can this be that I hurt so much? That I *know* her in my guts?

I have to get out. Mother said to get out! Running, slamming my shoulder into a big uniform blocking the way. Past him into the corridor. I try the handle of the first door. It's unlocked. I step into the room and lean against the wall. It's empty. It's the prep room, where we actors waited for our entrance. I was here before the trial, before I met her.

I feel as if the world has stopped turning. I look in the mirror and see her staring back. I reach out to touch her face. "Help me! I'm an actress! I don't know what to do."

My hands have blood on them. I lick it off. My mother's blood. Blood of my blood. My heart hurts and it's hard to breathe.

I peel off my armorweave and grab Teddy's street clothes. and I think I will die on the spot. "My God, I killed him. That was real blood, not the phony stuff we've been rehearsing with. And they will kill me, too. They'll have to."

I can't stay here. I pull on Teddy's trousers and belt them tightly. The jacket is too big, and his shoes won't fit. I'll have to wear these boots. What else? I toss my makeup, and Teddy's, into my carrybag. Then I remember that the cute techie was going to make a vid for me.

The vidcam is up high, at the ceiling, focussed on the courtroom through the horizontal window there. I crawl up and get it. I was going to use it to get another acting job. What was I thinking? How could I be so naïve?

Suddenly I have no bones in my legs and I slump into a chair. "Mother's dead. And I'm a murderer. Who is Annie? And why am I talking to myself? " I want to scream. I want to weep. I can't do the things that Mother did. She said to go into the Countryside. How will I live? But I have to do *something*!

I see her face again. So alive! So strong. So full of love. She called me her "darling girl."

I take a deep breath. All right, Mother, I'll go down fighting. Just like you.

I stash the vidchip in the carrybag, stuff Teddy's cap on my head, and have to push hard to get the door open because the corridor is jammed with people rushing for the exit. I plow into them and am carried along, into the entrance hall and through the main door.

Sirens, shots, and Fedguards everywhere.

Outside, I join the throng of people on the street rushing away from the scene, hidden by their panic.

I'm free. Now what?

How do I find the stars?

Our titles are available at major book stores and local independent resellers who support Science Fiction and Fantasy readers like you.

EDGE Science Fiction
and Fantasy Publishing

Tesseract Books

Dragon Moon Press

www.edgewebsite.com
www.dragonmoonpress.com

Our titles are available at major book stores and local independent resellers who support Science Fiction and Fantasy readers like you.

Alien Deception by Tony Ruggiero -(tp) - ISBN-13: 978-1-896944-34-0
Alien Revelation by Tony Ruggiero (tp) - ISBN-13: 978-1-896944-34-8
Alphanauts by J. Brian Clarke (tp) - ISBN-13: 978-1-894063-14-2
Apparition Trail, The by Lisa Smedman (tp) - ISBN-13: 978-1-894063-22-7
As Fate Decrees by Denysé Bridger (tp) - ISBN-13: 978-1-894063-41-8

Billibub Baddings and The Case of the Singing Sword by Tee Morris (tp)
    - ISBN-13: 978-1-896944-18-0
Black Chalice, The by Marie Jakober (hb) - ISBN-13: 978-1-894063-00-5
Blue Apes by Phyllis Gotlieb (pb) - ISBN-13: 978-1-895836-13-4
Blue Apes by Phyllis Gotlieb (hb) - ISBN-13: 978-1-895836-14-1

Chalice of Life, The by Anne Webb (tp) - ISBN-13: 978-1-896944-33-3
Chasing The Bard by Philippa Ballantine (tp) - ISBN-13: 978-1-896944-08-1
Children of Atwar, The by Heather Spears (pb) - ISBN-13: 978-0-88878-335-6
Clan of the Dung-Sniffers by Lee Danielle Hubbard (pb) - ISBN-13: 978-1-895836-05-0
Claus Effect, The by David Nickle & Karl Schroeder (pb) - ISBN-13: 978-1-895836-34-9
Claus Effect, The by David Nickle & Karl Schroeder (hb) - ISBN-13: 978-1-895836-35-6
Complete Guide to Writing Fantasy, The - Volume 1: Alchemy with Words
    - edited by Darin Park and Tom Dullemond (tp)
    - ISBN-13: 978-1-896944-09-8
Complete Guide to Writing Fantasy, The - Volume 2: Opus Magus
    - edited by Tee Morris and Valerie Griswold-Ford (tp)
    - ISBN-13: 978-1-896944-15-9
Complete Guide to Writing Fantasy, The - Volume 3: The Author's Grimoire
    - edited by Valerie Griswold-Ford & Lai Zhao (tp)
    - ISBN-13: 978-1-896944-38-8
Complete Guide to Writing Science Fiction, The - Volume 1: First Contact
    - edited by Dave A. Law & Darin Park (tp)
    - ISBN-13: 978-1-896944-39-5
Courtesan Prince, The by Lynda Williams (tp) - ISBN-13: 978-1-894063-28-9

Dark Earth Dreams by Candas Dorsey & Roger Deegan (comes with a CD)
    - ISBN-13: 978-1-895836-05-9
Darkling Band, The by Jason Henderson (tp) - ISBN-13: 978-1-896944-36-4
Darkness of the God by Amber Hayward (tp) - ISBN-13: 978-1-894063-44-9
Darwin's Paradox by Nina Munteanu (tp) - ISBN-13: 978-1-896944-68-5
Daughter of Dragons by Kathleen Nelson - (tp) - ISBN-13: 978-1-896944-00-5
Distant Signals by Andrew Weiner (tp) - ISBN-13: 978-0-88878-284-7
Dominion by J. Y. T. Kennedy (tp) - ISBN-13: 978-1-896944-28-9
Dragon Reborn, The by Kathleen H. Nelson - (tp) - ISBN-13: 978-1-896944-05-0
Dragon's Fire, Wizard's Flame by Michael R. Mennenga (tp)
    - ISBN-13: 978-1-896944-13-5
Dreams of an Unseen Planet by Teresa Plowright (tp) - ISBN-13: 978-0-88878-282-3
Dreams of the Sea by Élisabeth Vonarburg (tp) - ISBN-13: 978-1-895836-96-7
Dreams of the Sea by Élisabeth Vonarburg (hb) - ISBN-13: 978-1-895836-98-1

Eclipse by K. A. Bedford (tp) - ISBN-13: 978-1-894063-30-2
Even The Stones by Marie Jakober (tp) - ISBN-13: 978-1-894063-18-0

Fires of the Kindred by Robin Skelton (tp) - ISBN-13: 978-0-88878-271-7
Firestorm of Dragons edited by Michele Acker & Kirk Dougal (tp)
   - ISBN-13: 978-1-896944-80-7
Forbidden Cargo by Rebecca Rowe (tp) - ISBN-13: 978-1-894063-16-6

Game of Perfection, A by Élisabeth Vonarburg (tp)
   - ISBN-13: 978-1-894063-32-6
Green Music by Ursula Pflug (tp) - ISBN-13: 978-1-895836-75-2
Green Music by Ursula Pflug (hb) - ISBN-13: 978-1-895836-77-6
Gryphon Highlord, The by Connie Ward (tp) - ISBN-13: 978-1-896944-38-8

Healer, The by Amber Hayward (tp) - ISBN-13: 978-1-895836-89-9
Healer, The by Amber Hayward (hb) - ISBN-13: 978-1-895836-91-2
Hounds of Ash and other Tales of Fool Wolf, The by Greg Keyes (pb)
   - ISBN-13: 978-1-895836-09-8
Human Thing, The by Kathleen H. Nelson - (hb) - ISBN-13: 978-1-896944-03-6
Hydrogen Steel by K. A. Bedford (tp) - ISBN-13: 978-1-894063-20-3

i-ROBOT Poetry by Jason Christie (tp) - ISBN-13: 978-1-894063-24-1

Jackal Bird by Michael Barley (pb) - ISBN-13: 978-1-895836-07-3
Jackal Bird by Michael Barley (hb) - ISBN-13: 978-1-895836-11-0
JEMMA7729 by Phoebe Wray (tp) - ISBN-13: 978-1-894063-40-1

Keaen by Till Noever (tp) - ISBN-13: 978-1-894063-08-1
Keeper's Child by Leslie Davis (tp) - ISBN-13: 978-1-894063-01-2

Lachli by M. H. Bonham (tp) - ISBN-13: 978-1-896944-69-2
Land/Space edited by Candas Jane Dorsey and Judy McCrosky (tp)
   - ISBN-13: 978-1-895836-90-5
Land/Space edited by Candas Jane Dorsey and Judy McCrosky (hb)
   - ISBN-13: 978-1-895836-92-9
Legacy of Morevi by Tee Morris (tp) - ISBN-13: 978-1-896944-29-6
Legends of the Serai by J.C. Hall - (tp) - ISBN-13: 978-1-896944-04-3
Longevity Thesis by Jennifer Tahn (tp) - ISBN-13: 978-1-896944-37-1
Lyskarion: The Song of the Wind by J.A. Cullum (tp)
   - ISBN-13: 978-1-894063-02-9

Machine Sex and other stories by Candas Jane Dorsey (tp)
   - ISBN-13: 978-0-88878-278-6
Maërlande Chronicles, The by Élisabeth Vonarburg (pb)
   - ISBN-13: 978-0-88878-294-6
Magister's Mask, The by Deby Fredericks (tp) - ISBN-13: 978-1-896944-16-6
Moonfall by Heather Spears (pb) - ISBN-13: 978-0-88878-306-6
Morevi: The Chronicles of Rafe and Askana by Lisa Lee & Tee Morris
   - (tp) - ISBN-13: 978-1-896944-07-4

Not Your Father's Horseman by Valorie Griswold-Ford (tp)
   - ISBN-13: 978-1-896944-27-2

Tesseracts 7 edited by Paula Johanson & Jean-Louis Trudel (tp)
- ISBN-13: 978-1-895836-58-5
Tesseracts 7 edited by Paula Johanson & Jean-Louis Trudel (hb)
- ISBN-13: 978-1-895836-59-2
Tesseracts 8 edited by John Clute & Candas Jane Dorsey (tp)
- ISBN-13: 978-1-895836-61-5
Tesseracts 8 edited by John Clute & Candas Jane Dorsey (hb)
- ISBN-13: 978-1-895836-62-2
Tesseracts Nine edited by Nalo Hopkinson and Geoff Ryman (tp)
- ISBN-13: 978-1-894063-26-5
Tesseracts Ten edited by Robert Charles Wilson and Edo van Belkom (tp)
- ISBN-13: 978-1-894063-36-4
Tesseracts Eleven edited by Cory Doctorow and Holly Phillips (tp)
- ISBN-13: 978-1-894063-03-6
Tesseracts Q edited by Élisabeth Vonarburg & Jane Brierley (pb)
- ISBN-13: 978-1-895836-21-9
Tesseracts Q edited by Élisabeth Vonarburg & Jane Brierley (hb)
- ISBN-13: 978-1-895836-22-6
Throne Price by Lynda Williams and Alison Sinclair (tp)
- ISBN-13: 978-1-894063-06-7
Too Many Princes by Deby Fredricks (tp) - ISBN-13: 978-1-896944-36-4
Twilight of the Fifth Sun by David Sakmyster - (tp)
- ISBN-13: 978-1-896944-01-02

Virtual Evil by Jana Oliver (tp) - ISBN-13: 978-1-896944-76-0

Phoebe Wray

I started making up stories before I could actually write, encouraged by my family, especially my Dad, who was a great story-teller. My nick-name was "Phoebe the Fibber," not because I told lies, but because I would make up a story on demand. Adults indulged me shamelessly, I'm afraid, but it only made me eager to learn to write and read. My first poem was published in the local weekly newspaper of my small hometown when I was nine. It was dreadful doggerel but had perfect rhymes. I was the editor of our class newspaper in the 5th grade.

My ambition was to be a journalist, especially a foreign correspondent. That had a romantic, exciting allure, and I went slinking around in a trench coat. I majored in journalism at Santa Rosa (California) High School, was editor of the school newspaper in 11th and 12th grades, and worked as a reporter and music critic for the daily Santa Rosa Press Democrat. I also served briefly as Assistant Editor of The Montgomery Village News.

Then I ran away with the circus, so to speak, and became a stand-up comic in the avant-garde cabaret clubs of San Francisco. I had always harbored a secret desire to be an actress — well, what else is a story-teller? — and finally wrote my own comic material and started a long career in the theatre. I quickly moved from clubs to the stage, settled down to serious study of the art, and eventually made it to New York City. I had a nice career for a dozen years, mostly Off-Off-Broadway (the avant-garde, again!), Off-Broadway, cabaret revues, summer stock, and regional theatre.

But I never gave up writing. I supported my theatre habit by writing travel brochures for travel agencies and airlines, promotional copy, song lyrics, an occasional scholarly essay for journals such as Modern Drama, poetry (in Cat's Magazine, Quartet), and, of course, plays, some of which were done in NYC, Boston, London and, I think, elsewhere.

I switched gears again, left New York for Boston, and founded a non-profit international environmental education group and started writing teaching materials and public information on endangered species (especially the neglected ones like bats, manatees, and the unarmored three-spine stickleback), and marine mammals. I was an advocate as well, and three times served on the official United States delegation to the International Whaling Commission, the treaty organization that meets annually to divvy up what's left of the whales, not always a happy time. I wrote white papers, teaching kits, articles, fact sheets.

I'm still writing for the environment, most recently an essay on people's involvement with dolphins for The Encyclopedia of Nature and Religion, but spend my "other" time teaching in the Theatre Division of The Boston Conservatory. I had always promised myself that "some day" I would get around to writing fiction. And so I have.

The other stuff: I was born in Franklin, Pennsylvania and raised in near-by Cochranton (a "Brigadoon" kind of village of a 1000 souls), then went to Santa Rosa, California, with my parents for high school. I lived in San Francisco, Los Angeles, and New York City before settling in the Boston area. I live in Ayer, Massachusetts, in an 1860 farmhouse with my three cats, Max, Mouse and Jenny.